BUYING BETH

DISCIPLES 3

IZZY SWEET
SEAN MORIARTY

Copyright © 2017 by Izzy Sweet and Sean Moriarty

All rights reserved. This book or any portion thereof may not be reproduced or used in any manner whatsoever without the express written permission of the publisher except for the use of brief quotations in a book review.

Published by Izzy Sweet and Sean Moriarty

This is a work of fiction. Names, characters, businesses, places, events, and incidents are either the products of the author's imagination or used in a fictitious manner. Any resemblance to actual persons, living or dead, or actual events is purely coincidental.

Copyright © 2017 Izzy Sweet & Sean Moriarty

❀ Created with Vellum

NEWSLETTER

Sign up for our newsletter - no spam- and download an Izzy Sweet book for **free**

http://bookhip.com/CKHPSJ

ABOUT THIS BOOK

I thought he bought me to save me... but he's keeping me for himself.

It was a girl's night out gone wrong. Like some awful horror movie, my friends and I were grabbed in a dark parking lot and shoved into the back of a van.

Coming from powerful families, we thought we were untouchable.

We thought wrong.

Our captors trapped us, violated us, and put us up for sale on the black market.

Johnathan was sent to buy me so his boss, Lucifer, could have leverage over my father.

He was supposed to save me, protect me, and return me.

Not claim me and keep me for himself...

1
JOHNATHAN

September

It's already in the fucking twenties right now in Neryungri, Russia. Back home in Garden City, it's in the eighties to nineties. Not fucking here, though. No, right fucking here it's cold and fucking wintery.

Fuck this country and these cold-ass fucking snow flurries.

I don't like seeing snow in September, it's just not right. The sky doesn't look like it's going to ease the fuck up, so it's probably only going to get worse.

That's my fucking luck so far on this little job. I've been in Russia for almost three weeks now. Trailing a sack of shit from one city to the next, then chasing him from town to town.

Little fucker has a sixth sense when it comes to trouble. I'm fucking certain he doesn't know I'm after him, but he hasn't stayed in one place long enough for me to get to his ass.

He knows he fucked up in Garden City by trying to help Ivan, the man who tried to take Andrew's daughter, Abigail, and hurt Lucifer's daughter, Evelyn. It's been a madhouse full of rage for those two over the past few months. It's been kill this man, and find this guy, for just about any Russian our guys could get a lead on.

Then the little evil prick that he is, Simon, gets a lead on Yuri Popov.

Yuri Popov is a shitstain of a human being. Just like Ivan, he never got his hands dirty. He just pushed money into the hands of the people who would. He's a bit nastier than Ivan was, though. Ivan got all his money from his ruthless determination and his wife's deep pockets.

Yuri got it peddling child porn.

When he had enough money over in Russia, he bought his disgusting way to America. Leaving his business behind, he started running drugs and slaves out of small border crossing towns down in Texas. He still has operations down there too, but he had to hightail it out of America when he got word of Ivan getting toasted.

That's when our shitboy, Yuri, decided to head back home to the motherland.

Not that they are especially happy to have a child pornographer back. Still, he has the money and connections to run and hide for a good long while… except Simon and Lucifer aren't going to allow it.

Looking back up to the sky one last time, I growl at it. This fucking cold weather.

Standing on top of the building ledge in this shitty little town, I can't fathom why every building looks so uniform and block style. It must be the former communist way of building things, I guess.

There's a roof access hatch beside me, and with the one piece of luck I've had this whole shitty trip, I was able to jimmy it open.

Two-thirty in the morning should be a good time to sneak in, but for the last twenty minutes, I've been listening to a man and his woman screaming at each other drunkenly over some shit I can't figure out.

They've got five more minutes before I go in regardless.

The small camera I have inside of Yuri's father's apartment shows he passed out on the couch about two hours ago. Shithead took some pills and drank some cheapass vodka. He should be sufficiently out of it while I break in.

Five minutes later, I've finally figured out the couple fighting below me are screaming something about him stealing her cigarettes and her fucking his brother.

I'm pretty sure the fight isn't going to end any time soon.

The live feed from Yuri's apartment shows him still passed out. Pulling the black ski mask over my face, I then snap and check once more that the leather gloves on my hands are tight.

It's go time.

Moving to the roof access, I lift it up as silently as possible. The woman wailing like a banshee as she protests her innocence helps a lot with covering the sound.

Moving down the ladder quickly, I have two doors to choose from, left or right. I avoid the door where all the screaming is come from and kneel before Yuri's door.

Pulling out a small set of picks, I quickly unlatch the first lock then move up to the second one.

It's a deadbolt, but there are ways to bypass these fuckers.

I push the door open just barely to test if the chain has been set. Pulling a pair of bolt cutters form my backpack, I snip the chain during an extended wail from the lady across the hall.

Opening the door quickly, I enter the living room and shut the door as quickly and quietly as I can.

Looking left, I spot Yuri still passed out on the couch, his chest rising and falling steadily. I watch for a moment to make sure I haven't disturbed him before I take quick, quiet steps back to his father's bedroom.

The door is open, and splayed out on the bed is an elderly old man.

I feel bad that such a shitty son is going to be the end of his old man, but then again I don't have a clue what type of fucker he is either.

Slapping my hand across the old man's mouth, he lurches up, towards the ceiling, but I don't allow him to go far.

Pressing the barrel of my pistol to his temple, I murmur, "Don't make a fucking sound."

He says something in Russian behind the hand I have placed over his mouth, but the moment I push the pistol in hard against his head he shuts up. He may not know what the fuck I said, but I'm pretty sure he gets my meaning.

I quickly wrap his arms up in tape then stuff an old sock in his mouth. I tape the sock in place to keep him quiet.

Securing his feet, I stand up to assess my work.

He's pissed as fuck, and I can see in his eyes how much disdain he must have for me, and probably some for himself for getting old and feeble. I bet he would have put up a lot more of a fight in his younger days.

Walking past him, I move back out into the living room where Yuri is still passed out on the couch. The couple across the hall from us have gone from wails and screaming to thumps and vocal yells of pain. He's probably thumping her around pretty good over there.

Fucking drunk assholes.

I hear shouting now from other apartments.

That should help with all the shit that's going to happen to Yuri.

The first thing that must go through Yuri's mind as he wakes with a start is half of the fucking teeth I smash in with my hand.

He bellows in pain, but with all the shouting going on around us, it goes unchecked.

I slap him a couple of times with my fists in his ribs to get him to shut up enough to look at me.

He's a pitiful little fucking pile of shit, and I feel no remorse at all that he's on the very bottom of the food chain.

He's the fucking mouse and I'm the fucking lion.

"You may not know me, Yuri…" I snarl at him as I push him into a rickety old wooden chair.

"I no Yuri! I Gregov!" he whines at me.

Slapping him with an open hand, I treat him like the little bitch he is. "No, I know who you are, Yuri. Lucifer doesn't make mistakes when he sends me after someone."

Just the mention of Lucifer causes the man to begin shaking mightily. His eyes begin to dart all over the place as he looks for a possible escape.

Slapping him again, I say, "Pay attention, asshole. I know you speak English. I know you're Yuri."

He tries to stand up but I push him back down hard in the chair. "Quit fucking moving, asshole. You behave and I just kill you tonight. If not, your dad gets to go a couple of rounds with me too."

His eyes widen for a moment and his mouth opens, but then he shuts it.

"Good, I see you understand."

I pull a phone from my jacket pocket and then start recording.

"Ready to talk?"

Nodding his head, he says through his bloody mouth, "Da."

Pulling my fist back, I slam it into his gut. All the air in him explodes out as his eyes bulge. Coughing and sputtering, he looks up to me with tears streaming down his cheeks.

"I need to know names, Yuri. I need to know who else had a hand in the attack."

"I don't... I don't know... Ivan and me... we set up..."

Lifting my fist in the air, I threaten to hit him again. "We know him, Yuri. I need to know who else wanted this set up."

"I don't know anyone else. Ivan came to me, asked me if I wanted to look good for Gre..." His eyes widen and I can see he was about to say something he shouldn't.

He tries to look away.

"Don't clam up, asshole. I need the information, and I can always go back to causing pain if you don't talk."

He looks back at me and I think he finds some type of hope in my words.

Whatever gets him through this, I guess.

Grabbing another chair, I sit it down in front of him. "You were going to say someone, who was it?"

"Gregory Vasiliev. Ivan was trying to move up in his good graces, and if I helped out with getting some weapons or guys in... I would look good to the Bratva. He said I could start getting in..."

"In?"

"In with them... They would help my business back in states. I could..."

"Could what? Have a bigger slave market? Sell more coke?"

"Yes... I could take sliver of pie for me."

"Was it Gregory who called for the attack?"

"I don't know. I never met big head guys..."

He goes quiet then.

"Yuri, did I say to stop talking, you shitstain?" I ask as I tap my gun against his knee.

"No... No... I just... I don't know. He wouldn't let me in."

"He, who?"

"Ivan. He kept giving me reasons to not meet big guys." He shrugs his shoulders. "He made promises to me but it was lots of talk."

His mouth still oozes blood and the gash over his right eye has dried a bit. I guess he's feeling safe now. Pain must have dulled.

"What else, Yuri? Give me information for my boss. Make me look good."

"They wanted to make my business bigger!" he says, smiling. His nasty bloody mouth gaping open.

"Which business?"

"My slaves... They wanted to take more from your schools and campuses."

That's fucking interesting. That's real fucking interesting. Looking at the phone I sat on the table near us, I make sure it's still recording. Good.

"Were they planning on any more hits?"

Yuri pauses a moment while he tries to think. I can see the gears slowly grinding in his head. He wants to please me. He wants to give me the right information. I don't need that shit; I need all the information.

"No..." he says slowly. "I never heard. They knew that Lucifer was on warpath. They knew they riled beast. I don't know anything else, though... Like I say, they didn't let me in on things. They just wanted to use my businesses."

We discuss a couple of other things, and by the time we're done, it's close to dawn. He really hasn't given me any more information beyond a couple of contacts he has near Garden City, and I need to get moving.

The one thing he gives me that stirs the bile in my stomach is the name of a child pornographer and where he lives.

It's smack dab in the heart of Garden City. That, above all else, sentences him to death. I couldn't give two shits if Lucifer wanted this man alive. Thankfully, he doesn't.

Standing up from the chair, I stretch out my back and hear the pops from where I've been hunched over, interrogating this asshole. "Good job, Yuri."

The smile on his face couldn't be more hopeful, like he thinks he has a chance. Grabbing some tape from my bag, I also grab a rag from their kitchen sink. "Can't have you interrupting my getaway."

Stupid child molesting *fuck*. Doesn't even understand

the pain that's getting ready to come. He probably thinks I mean to let him go.

I gag him up then pick up the phone from the table. I stop the recording and dial Simon.

"Johnathan, what's going on?" he asks immediately.

"I'm wrapping up here. I wanted to make sure you didn't need anything else from him?"

"No, he's useless now. See if you can find any other information in the apartment, but from the broadcast you were sending me, I'd say we're good."

"Good. I'll put this to bed then and head home."

"Call me when you get out of the apartment. We need to talk."

"Will do," I say, disconnecting.

Reaching into my pocket, I pull out a pair of brass knuckles, and the asshole realizes the truth.

He's going to die.

He tries to stand up from the chair but my fist shatters his jaw. The scream from behind the gag isn't too loud since I stuffed some good insulation in there, but I need to make this quick.

I want to drag this out for hours, to torture him for days, to vent my rage of someone hurting kids... but I just don't have that kind of time.

The punches to the face and body have rendered him a bloody broken mess. He no longer screams loudly. He just blubbers little bubbles of spit and blood, his lungs filled with liquid.

He's going to die soon, so I make the best of it.

Grabbing his cock and balls, I cut them both off with a steak knife. Ripping the gag off, I shove them both into his mouth.

Let him choke to death on those.

Going to his ear, I whisper, "Now I get to torture your father."

His body jerks at my words but it doesn't last. He's bleeding out fast. Moving to his wrists, I slit each one with a long, straight line down the center.

There will be no second chances for this guy.

Walking past his bloody corpse, I head to the father.

He's where I left him, still wide awake. His eyes are wide with rage as he feebly struggles to break his bonds.

Shaking my head, I screw the silencer on my gun.

Lifting the gun and aiming it at his chest, I say, "He was a child molesting sack of shit and he's headed straight for hell."

He stills then, staring at me long and hard. Does he recognize my words? Does he understand?

Fuck him if he doesn't.

I pull the trigger three times, two to the chest and one to the head.

Yanking my mask back on, I head out of the apartment.

It's quiet in the building now. So much so, that I'm alone with my thoughts. Thoughts that are much lighter in mood than when I first entered the building.

Even the snow that's lacing the streets doesn't change my good mood.

2

BETH

October

"This place is a dump," my friend, Amanda, declares loudly as we stumble into the bar located on the very fringes of Garden City.

"Shush," I hiss at her and shoot a glance towards the bartender. Seriously, she's going to get us tossed out before we even order our first drink.

The woman standing behind the counter gives us the stink eye and crosses her thin arms over her ginormous fake breasts. She's got that awful bright red hair that's so unnatural you just know it came out of a box. She probably does it in an attempt to look younger, but it only ages her. If I had to guess at her age, I'd put her in her mid to late thirties. Give or take a decade, depending on if she smokes or not.

Amanda's not wrong. The place is indeed a dump, but

it's also the perfect hidey-hole for drinking and having a good time without it ending up in the gossip rags. As a group of girls that are always in the spotlight because of our famous fathers, we want to drink and have a good time without worrying about who could be watching.

Amanda just shrugs her shoulders, completely unapologetic. I sigh and drag our little group over to one of the few open tables that actually has stools.

"Seriously, who names their bar *The River Waters*?" Amanda goes on with a wrinkle in her nose as we each take a stool. "It's almost like they don't want anyone drinking here…"

Looking around the place, I don't think the bar's unfortunate name is what keeps most people from coming in. The lighting is dim and the air is thick and hazy with cigarette smoke. Apparently the no-smoking ban in public spaces the city passed a couple of years ago doesn't apply here.

Heavy metal blasts from the back where a few unsavory looking fellows with long, dingy hair and bushy beards play pool and drink beer. If I'm not mistaken, the leather vests they wear declare they belong to some type of motorcycle club or biker gang. Hanging on the wood paneled walls are posters of half-naked women with enormous fake breasts that are so old they're covered in dust and a film of brown.

This place is in a desperate need of a good scrubbing from top to bottom.

Setting my purse down, it seems to stick to the table

and I change my mind. This place is definitely in need of a fire. They should just probably burn it down and start all over again.

"I don't want to be drinking here," Lindsey whines unhappily and flips her blonde hair over her shoulder before shooting me a glare.

You'd think after all the pre-partying we did back at Sophia's condo that she'd loosen up enough to pull the stick out of her ass. But then again, her father is one of the richest real estate investors in Garden City, and she's used to all the glitz and glamor money can buy.

I sigh again and start to wonder if maybe this wasn't such a good idea after all...

But then Sophia seems to bristle, taking Lindsey's glare personally. "Oh shut up, Lindsey. You're such a fucking snob."

Lindsey sniffs and begins to shrink under Sophia's hard look like someone just sucked the air out of her.

"I don't see why we couldn't just drink back at our place," she whines softer now. Looking down at the table, she makes a face of disgust as she watches me try to free my now stuck purse. "At least there we won't catch any incurable diseases."

Sophia rolls her eyes hard and shakes her head, her blonde curls bouncing around her heart-shaped face. "We always party at our place. It's boring."

Amanda's green eyes light up. "I know a few guys—"

She doesn't get to finish before Sophia cuts her off. "No, dammit. We already talked about this." She shoots me a can-you-believe-these-idiots look before going on. "You know we can't have anything showing up on social media. If Beth's father finds out she was out partying, he'll lock her up and throw away the key."

Ugh. Just hearing that said out loud is enough to kill the buzz I had going on. Both Amanda and Lindsey look at me sympathetically, and I couldn't feel more like a loser if I tried.

Yeah, I'm sheltered and my father is way overbearing. It's his way or *his* way, there's no arguing.

You see my father is Senator Richard Norton, and to him appearances are *everything*. His career and his connections depend upon it. He's planned every aspect of my life, from the schools I've attended, to the hobbies I enjoy, to the friends I keep, and even the guys I date.

And God help me if I try to defy him.

In the past, he hasn't been above locking me in my room and withholding food until I give in.

"Look around, ladies," Sophia goes on. She's the sober one of the group, acting tonight as our designated driver. "No one here knows who we are. No one gives a *shit*."

"I think that guy over there gives a shit." Lindsey shudders, and we all follow her line of sight to the man sitting at the bar.

He's huge and intimidating, his large body looking as if it needs two stools rather than the one he's sitting on. With his head of dirty blonde hair, bushy beard, tattoos, worn jeans, and black t-shirt, he looks exactly like the type of guy you'd find in a place like this.

My eyes meet his for the briefest of moments and I feel this strange jolt before looking away.

Lindsey shudders dramatically. "He's probably casing us. Sizing us up for how much we're worth."

"Don't be such a drama queen," Sophia groans and then glances at the guy. She looks thoughtful for a moment then says, "Just hold on to your purse."

Speaking of purses, I give mine one last hard tug and it peels away from the table, leaving a swath of designer logo covered fabric behind.

"Great," I mutter, and inspect the damage done to the purse my father gifted me for my birthday. The entire middle of the bottom has been ripped off.

"Oh, that sucks," Lindsey says, sounding just a little too cheerful to my ears.

I shoot her a dirty look, but before I can say anything nasty, Sophia jumps in. "Drinks. We need drinks."

She jumps up from her stool and grabs me by the arm, dragging me off of my own stool before I know what's happening. "What does a girl gotta do to get a drink around here?"

Dragging me up to the bar with her, she mutters, "Just ignore them. They'll loosen up once we get a few drinks in them."

Maybe, or maybe not, I think to myself. Lindsey has always been the stick-in-the-mud of our little group. I don't think I can remember a single time we've gone somewhere and she didn't complain about something. It's almost like she just has to find something wrong.

Amanda, on the other hand, tends to loosen up a little too much when she gets a couple of drinks in her. I wouldn't be surprised if we have to pull her off a table before the night is over.

Sophia flashes a bright smile at Mr. Tall, Dark, and Intimidating, before turning that smile on the bartender.

"I'd like four cosmos please," she orders sweetly, turning on her charm.

"We don't serve those kind of drinks here, *honey*," the bartender responds with a contemptuous smirk.

Mr. Intimidating snorts and takes a big drink from his beer.

Sophia's eyes flick towards him then back to the bartender and her smile tightens. "Alright, then we'll have four vodka cranberries."

The bartender shakes her head and I can't help but be amazed that her hair barely moves. "We don't serve those either."

Sophia scowls. "Rum and cokes?"

The bartender's burgundy lips peel back in a sneer. "Nope."

"What do you serve then?" Sophia groans.

The bartender opens her mouth, probably to brush us off again in hopes of getting us to leave, but then Mr. Intimidating speaks up. "Whiskey, beer, and tequila. Take your pick."

He looks directly at me then and I feel that jolt again. Butterflies take flight in my stomach, and as if he can see it, his lips slowly curl into a smirk.

"That's it?" Sophia asks with disbelief.

"That's it," Mr. Intimidating grunts, tearing his gaze away from me to look to her then back down at his beer and plate.

My face flushes with heat and finally I feel like I can breathe again.

I must be really drunk if I'm starting to feel a connection with a guy like him. He might as well have *bad news* tattooed right on his forehead.

Sophia looks over at me and I'm so ready to go. I'm ready to bolt like a startled rabbit.

"Sophia..." I say, but she turns back to the bartender, ignoring me. "Tequila it is!"

Oh god, I groan inwardly. I just know this isn't going to end well. I know Sophia wants to have a girl's night out because we haven't had one in over a year, but I've got a bad feeling about all of this, and it's not just because of the crummy place we're in.

There's just this dark cloud hanging over my head. A sense of dread and foreboding floating around in the back of my brain.

It could be because we haven't been here for more than two minutes, and Amanda and Lindsey are already complaining. Or it could be because the last time my father caught me out by having his goon hack into my Snapchat, he withdrew me from college and forced me to move back home.

His reasoning was that if I'm going to act like a whore with no care for the wholesome image he's built, then I don't deserve the money he's worked so hard for.

Now I'm trapped at home, under pretty much 24-hour surveillance, and I have a weekly allowance that he completely controls.

The only reason I'm even out tonight is because he had a trip to DC suddenly sprung on him at the last minute and he didn't have enough time to tell his goons to keep me locked in.

The bartender shoots Mr. Intimidating a look as if she needs his approval before she pours the shots. He looks up from his plate of food long enough to nod his head at her.

With a sigh and a mutter, the bartender turns around and grabs a dusty bottle of tequila off the bottom shelf.

"Not that one, Missy," Mr. Intimidating growls, his head popping up. "Grab the one off the top shelf."

The bartender shoots him a startled look, but he just stares at her as if there will be no arguments. With a curse, she turns back around and slams the bottle back down on the shelf causing a small cloud of dust to puff up.

Sophia smirks triumphantly as the bartender grabs a bottle of silver tequila off the top shelf and turns back, pouring our shots.

"That will be forty dollars," Missy says expectantly and cocks her hip.

Sophia just rolls her eyes and digs around in her

purse. After a moment, she pulls out three bills and slaps them down on the table.

The bartender quickly grabs up the cash, counts it, and proceeds to stuff it down her bra.

"Hey…" Sophia says to Mr. Intimidating just as I reach for two of the shots.

"Yeah?" he grunts, glancing up.

"I didn't catch your name? I'm Sophia and my friend here is Beth." She sticks out her hand and he looks at it as if it will bite him or something.

"Johnathan," he says and looks towards me. Once again, there's that little jolt and I feel a little breathless.

Now that we're closer, and I can get a really good look at him, he seems even bigger than he did from afar.

With a start, I realize his face is actually quite handsome.

With his beard and ruffled hair, there's a rough, untamed gruffness to him that I'm not used to seeing on a daily basis. Most of the men in my life are clean-shaven, sharply dressed, and polished to the point that they're almost girlish.

This guy, though, there's nothing polished about him. He's rough and gruff all over.

My father would *hate* him. He'd probably have me committed if he found out I was even near a guy like him.

"Nice to meet you, Johnathan," Sophia says and drops her hand once she realizes he isn't going to shake it.

Johnathan nods his head and starts to turn away from us.

"Hey, Johnathan," Sophia says, pulling his attention back.

Johnathan arches a brow at her.

Sophia smiles and says sweetly, "May we borrow your salt?"

"Sure," Johnathan says and slides the shaker of salt that was next to his plate over to us.

"Thank you, Johnathan," Sophia says, her smile growing even wider.

He grunts and his eyes slide back to mine, lingering. I swear it's a force of will for me to turn away.

Picking up our shots and newly acquired salt shaker, we start to carry it all back to Lindsey and Amanda.

"He's totally into you," Sophia giggles as we walk.

I cast a glance over my shoulder and sure enough Johnathan's eyes are locked on me. I can feel his eyes on my ass, searing me with heat.

I shake my head. "My father would have an aneurism if I hooked up with a guy like that."

"That's why you should totally do it!" Sophia says, her eyes lighting up.

"I can't," I protest with a laugh. "I'm still in deep shit from the last time we went out."

Sophia's face sobers and she comes to a sudden stop. "You know I worry about you. It's not... healthy for your father to keep you locked up."

The dark cloud over my head seems to swell and grow bigger, and I force a smile in an attempt to block it out. "It's only temporary. He'll get over it eventually..."

Sophia looks me in the eye and says, "You know you can move in with me. You're a grown woman, you don't have to put up with this shit."

I know she means well, and I know she is being completely sincere. She is worried. She's always worried about me. She's my best friend and she's been looking out for me since we were in Kindergarten. But even she doesn't know the full extent of my father's control.

Over the years, since my mother passed, it's only grown worse.

I shake my head. "You know I can't."

I can't because my father wouldn't let me get away that easily, and helping me would only cause trouble for her. Her father might be the Chief of Police in Garden City, but even he isn't untouchable.

Sophia continues to look me long and hard in the eyes, but I stand my ground. I'd never do anything to put her in jeopardy. She means too much to me. And this shit with my father is *my* problem. I'll figure a different way out. Even if I have to marry the sleazy son of one of his political allies, I'll find a way to get myself out from under his thumb.

"Fine," she finally gives in with a sigh. "Have it your way, but tonight I'm going to make sure you have some fun."

"Fun sounds good," I smile at her and we start walking again.

"Took you long enough," Lindsey says with pout.

Sophia rolls her eyes as she sets two shots and the

shaker down on the table. "We were getting friendly with the locals."

Amanda shoots a look over her shoulder at the bar. "They don't look very friendly…"

Sophia pushes the two shots she carried over towards Amanda and Lindsey. "Have a drink and loosen up. We're here to have fun, ladies!"

Amanda and Lindsey pick up their little glasses, throw back their shots, and immediately start to grumble about how harsh the tequila is.

Picking up the salt shaker, I can't help but glance towards the bar. There's like some invisible cord that keeps tugging me in that direction.

Johnathan is still there, turned towards me now with his beer gripped in his big hand. I lick my hand between my thumb and forefinger and see his eyes flash with heat as he watches my tongue come out of my mouth.

Fun, yeah, we're here for fun. I throw my shot back and feel the tequila burn its way down my throat.

I should probably take Sophia's advice and loosen up a little, I think as I lower my now empty shot glass.

Sophia pushes the fourth shot towards me with a twinkle in her eye and a smirk.

Yeah, she's totally trying to get me drunk.

3

JOHNATHAN

It's fucking hot as balls in this fucking sweatbox of a city. I could use a good nap, a bottle of cold tequila, and a hot pussy snuggled right up against my leg just humping it in anticipation.

But that's not how shit works now.

Maybe in the bygone days of being in the family, but with the ever-present war going on, it's work, work, and death.

I've taken on a lot of shit jobs over the last year. Ever since Lucifer, my boss, took Lilith to be his lovely bride, it's been one fire after the other we either have to put out or start. Shit, the Yakuza getting kicked the fuck out of Garden city was a monumental fucking task. That the Russians are now trying to claim their territory as their own is making things quite explosive.

I often question if Lucifer would have taken the

woman if he had known the shit path it would lead us down.

When I think of war, though, I imagine trenches dug out, lines drawn on some arbitrary map, bullets and grenades flying all over the place.

Not this land grab of property and back room deals with lawyers and politicians.

Sure, there's enough death going on to keep the Reaper himself busy, but I'm not good at the political shit that Lucifer seems to thrive at. He's been putting blockades around every empty storefront he can that the Russians could possibly be interested in.

If he doesn't buy 'em, the fucking Italians do.

The fucking Italians... What the fuck should I say about those damn bastards? They sure as fuck have paid us back with interest when it comes to being our allies. Ever since we started giving them real estate at the docks, and then the formerly controlled Yakuza areas, they have been at our beck and call.

Yeah, they're helpful all right, but it comes at a cost.

If you ask me, a fucking big one.

We have to be the big brother who fucking protects 'em. Like last night, I had to be the backup for one of their big deals. They shipped some grade A weapons from our docks out to Ohio, where they've been fucking around with the Irish.

It seems to me, for a good while, all the big power houses like the Italians, the Irish, the Russians, the Yakuza, and Lucifer's group in Garden City, have been busting our heads against a wall fighting with each other. It makes me wonder if an actual widespread war will start up like it did back in the forties.

Shit, times like that now could be very bad.

They had guns and firebombs back then. We have the internet, guns, rocket launchers, and credit scores now.

Leaning back against the barstool's seatback, I tip the ice cold bottle of beer back and let the cold liquid wash the shot of tequila I took right before it down. There's a big loaded burger sitting on the plate in front of me, and as I take a bite, I feel like I can finally relax.

I just got back stateside a week ago, and I finally feel like my legs are stable enough to walk. Spending four weeks on a huge fucking ocean freighter had me feeling like I was going to puke every day, all day long.

A month of fucking puke has me on edge. Thank fucking god, I don't have to babysit any more fucking shipping containers.

That motherfucker Simon… just his name is enough to give me heartburn. I called him as soon as I got outside of Neryungri, and he told me he had another job. I was still trying to get my hairy ass out of Russia without fucking dying, and he already had another job for me.

I could have strangled him right fucking then, but no. He wanted me to ride back on a massive ocean cargo ship so I could babysit a fucking container of weapons.

Don't get me wrong, I do what I'm told, but that fucking boat… Fuck me running.

The burger and beer are the first time I'm allowed to

be my normal self. No suit, and by hell's demons, no fucking tie. I've finally gotten into a pair of jeans and a t-shirt.

I'm not Lucifer's polished fucking killer here in my bar. I'm able to let my fucking happy dick flag fly.

My bar is a fucking dive bar. It's always been one, and with my fucking say, it will be one till I die. We don't play fucking hip-hop or fucking pop music. We don't have all them fucking girly drinks, and we sure as fuck don't have the hoity-toity crowd in here.

We have bikers, beer, hard liquor, and guys who just got off at the industrial plants. We serve food that's made to fill the stomach, and beer that gets a man drunk.

Fuck, we even started getting them fucking hipster guys in here for a couple of months until they figured out we really were a working-class bar and not the new trendy location.

Missy's raspy voice lifts my head from my plate as she stands directly in front of me. Her big fucking tits are on proud display and she pushes them out towards me. "Want another shot?"

Shaking my head, I look back down at the fries. Those fucking tits are as real as I was happy on the fucking cargo ship. Even if I was into fake-bodied women, she just doesn't do it for me. It's easy to keep my strict rule of not shitting in my own backyard with her.

"Nah." My eyes look at the now empty bottle of beer. "Just get me a beer."

"Sure. What about a quick fuck in the back?"

"Nah, I don't fuck bar whores."

"Whatever, pencil dick," she says as she pulls a beer from the cooler. Her words may sound harsh, and I'm betting so do mine, but it's our style.

Missy's been here working for me since I bought the place three years ago. Her and Hambone. Hambone is the big motherfucker at the door who sits there watching out for her and my money.

She's been trying to get in my jeans since we first met. But I don't do the relationship thing, or fake tits. She didn't take kindly to being rejected, but now she just blows off my rejections as a term of endearment.

Fucking nutty ass women.

Looking in the mirror, I watch as the two women who came up earlier make their way back towards the bar.

Missy grumbles loudly as the girls come closer. "Fucking Princesses."

We get these types every once in a while. It's always entertaining when they figure out we're not their type of crowd, but far be it from me to turn away daddy's money.

Turning back to my burger, I keep on eating it. The fries on the side can wait. I want to eat something with meat in it. I need the fucking proteins, I guess.

They veer off from us, heading to the now silent jukebox instead.

Turning my head to watch the red-haired girl walk away, I can't keep my eyes from following her ass as it sways back and forth. No, she isn't doing it on purpose, that much is for sure. If anything, she looks like she's trying to minimize the wiggle, but with an ass like that there's nothing that will stop its sexy sway.

I swear she has eyes in the back of her head, though, because she looks back at me with aggravation. Fuck it, if she doesn't want to be ogled for the sex-stick she is, she shouldn't be in my bar.

Giving her a wink, I turn back to my food.

The red-haired, sex-on-a-stick must be the elected lamb sent over to Missy because she walks over to the bar and says, "The sign on the jukebox says we have to use tokens to play music."

"Yep," Missy says with a smirk.

"Well, can I buy some?" She frowns with annoyance in her voice. I think she's the one who the blonde girl called Beth.

"Sure, but you have to get the bosses approval."

Well, shit.

I can just hear the rolling of the girl's eyes as she asks, "Who's the boss?"

Pointing to me, Missy says, "Right over there."

Now Missy can distribute the tokens herself, but she loves to fuck with people.

Looking up from my bottle, I say, "What kind of music are you going to play?"

Beth has this mystified look on her face as she shrugs her shoulders. "Does it matter?"

"Yep."

"Well..." she starts to say before stopping. I can tell

she's weighing whether or not she wants to keep talking to me.

She does, I know it.

It's not like she didn't feel that same fucking jolt in her body I got earlier. It went straight to my cock. I've been sitting here with half a fucking hard-on since I saw that delicate pink tongue come out of her mouth earlier.

But those fucking hazel eyes. Christ on a fucking pogo stick. Those damn things melt my fucking brain.

"Well?" I rasp out at her. Shit.

She smirks at me then. "Taylor Swift, and then probably something melodramatic like Lady Gaga."

"Who the fuck are they?" I ask.

She looks at me as if I'm an alien or something. "What?"

"Who the fuck are those two people?"

Missy starts chuckling loudly. "They're pop music, Johnathan."

"Well, I doubt our jukebox even knows how to spell them then," I say with a laugh.

She gets this blank look on her face and shakes her head. "Okay, give me some tokens and I will play something good."

Lifting one eyebrow at her, I say, "Give her a couple of dollars worth, Missy. Let's see what she's got."

"Great," Missy mutters as she hands over the tokens.

Lifting my hand, I offer it to smiling girl. "Johnathan."

She looks at it for a moment as if it were some type of

snake. Fuck, I got a snake in my pants if she wants to see one.

Finally placing her soft, cool palm into mine, she says, "Beth. Thanks for the tokens."

I swear to fuck I feel a shock of electricity go through my veins as I hold her hand. It goes straight to my cock. *Fuck me.*

A small cough from Missy shakes us both out of our stupor and I reluctantly let go of her hand.

A small smile lights up her beautiful face and she turns away from me. This close, I see that the loose bun she has her hair twisted up in is holding a huge amount of hair.

A quick image of her riding atop of my thick cock as her hair falls down, covering her breasts, streaks through my mind.

Her hips slowly roll as her tight pussy milks me…

Fuck, this chick is so mine tonight.

Turning back to the bar, I grab my bottle of beer and take a long cold drink. I need a cold shower. Fuck, I feel like I have three fucking legs right now.

She walks over to the jukebox and I watch as she gives her friend a hip check so that she can take over the music selection.

"Jesus, you like 'em young," Missy snickers.

"Yeah, you like 'em fucking loaded."

"Long as it's loaded full of cum and money, I'm a happy girl."

Shaking my head with a laugh, I try to take another

drink of my beer before nearly spitting it out onto the bar in front of me.

Both Missy and I stare wide-eyed at each other then we slowly look over at Beth. She turns her head and smirks at me as the opening roar of Warrant's song *Cherry Pie* blasts out of the speakers.

"Oh fuck, she's going to be the death of you, Johnathan," Missy howls with laughter as she gives a thumbs up to Beth.

Shaking my head, I turn back to my beer and drain half the bottle. "I need another shot."

Snickering again at me, Missy nods. "Don't go getting whiskey dick on the young girl."

Beth does a good job of picking old rock and hair metal. I've never been a big fan of some of the stuff she chooses, but it opens my eyes. Either she's got good taste in music or she's so fucking lucky that she should be shitting out gold.

More of our regulars come into the bar, and at first, they give the girls a wide berth. They know not to fuck around with anyone in my bar.

Don't matter who it is, people don't fuck with each other in my bar unless it's me doing the fucking around.

Soon enough, though, they're treated just like everyone else. I see a couple of the guys eyeing the girls up, but none try to approach.

Might be the vibes I'm giving off. The Beth girl is mine, least for the fucking night she is.

Me and her got a thing we need to work out.

She disappears to the bathroom and I can feel the ache of my bladder begin to push on me. Standing from the bar, I head back to the hallway leading to bathrooms. Walking in quickly, I do a once over in the mirror after I take care of business.

I'm not the best-looking bastard on the block, but I did get my father's strong Viking features. Running my fingers through my beard to get the scragginess out, I stare at myself for a moment.

Looking in my eyes, I can see tonight won't be enough with this girl. That touch of her skin was just too fucking much for it to be a one-nighter.

Maybe a two-nighter will work…

Walking out the door, I see the women's opening at the same time.

Both of us stop there, together in the hallway.

She has a slight blush to her pale skin as she gives me a nervous smile. She may have been confident earlier with the music, but now she seems timid. It could be that I tower over her, maybe by a foot. She isn't a tall woman, probably five seven, hundred and twenty pounds.

She's delicate and beautiful.

"Hey, good choice in music," I say.

"Oh! Thank you… I love music. Just about any kind is my favorite. It's a passion for me."

I nod my head. "You picked a good list. Anytime you come here, you get free reign on the jukebox."

Her eyes twinkle as she says, "Thanks!"

I take a step toward her and she takes a step back,

bumping into the wall. Leaning close to her, I can't help but grin as I watch her eyes widen and that blush deepen.

Yeah, I got her right where I want her.

I put my hands on the walls, caging her in.

Being closer to her, the difference couldn't be clearer. I smell like guns, oil, and motorcycle engine grime. She's the opposite of me, smelling of lilac soap and a faint hint of perfume wafts through my nose. It's not overpowering, like what her friend Sophia has on.

It's something else... maybe her body's natural scent.

"Wha..." she starts to say before I lean in even closer.

"What?" I ask as I stare into those soulful, hazel eyes.

"What are you doing?"

"Figuring out how many days it's going to take to get you out of my system."

Her eyes widen. I think the confusion on her face makes it obvious that she's not as experienced as I first thought. She has this innocent air about her that makes my blood rush to all the right places.

She smells so pure and right.

Leaning in until our foreheads are barely touching, I give her a smile. "You and me had a spark back there at the bar."

"We did?" she squeaks out, and I nod.

"Yeah. You can't tell me you didn't feel it too."

"I... I..." she stammers.

I can't control myself any longer as I stare at those plump, pink lips. My mouth pushes down hard against hers. Her lips are so soft, so smooth and inviting.

She pulls away from my kiss and gasps. "What are you doing?"

"What you've been dreaming about," I say with a smirk.

She wanted that kiss as much as I did. She may have pulled back at the last moment, but right before she did, she pushed against my lips.

Leaning in again, I kiss those lips and this time she doesn't pull away. Her hands reach up to my chest and she grabs my shirt.

Tonight is going to be a good fucking night.

Our tongues glide against each other as I slide a hand off the wall. First, I run my hand along her back, then I grab her juicy ass and pull her hard against my cock.

My cock is going from a semi to a full fucking raging hard-on of steel.

She moans as she shifts one hand away from my chest and brings it up behind my neck. She holds me in place as we spar with our tongues. I feel her leg wrap around mine as she tries to get even closer to me.

It's only our need to breathe that stops us from ripping each other's clothes off right now and here.

"So what are you do—," I start to ask her when a horrible screech comes from the front of the bar.

Her friend Sophia comes running back to us with a wide-eyed look of terror. "Amanda just blasted all over the place... It's like a nightmare or something."

I have no clue what *blasted* means until I get a small

whiff of Sophia. Looking her up and down, I see a wet circle at the bottom of her jeans.

Yep, blasted must mean puke.

"Shit," I grumble at the same time as Beth.

We look at each other and she laughs. "This is going to be gross."

Heading towards their table, I see a huge puddle of liquid with what looks like tissue paper in it. "Who the fuck pukes tissue paper?"

Giving me a nasty sneer, the brunette puke girl says, "You're an asshole!"

"Yeah and you puked up tissues," I growl as I feel all the arousal sliding out of my cock.

Grabbing at her friend, Sophia starts dragging her up from the chair. "We need to get you home."

The other nameless girl nods her head and she helps from the other side.

Beth gives me an embarrassed smile and says, "I'm so sorry."

Digging through her purse, she pulls out a one-hundred-dollar bill and tries to force it into my hands.

"What do I want that for?"

"Because of the mess. I feel horrible... but we have to take her home."

Ah, I get it.

Fuck.

Suddenly a hot wave of possessiveness rolls through my body and I feel my muscles tightening up. I don't want to let her go. No, I want to keep her right fucking here with me.

We still got shit to work out, god dammit.

I look her up and down, the wheels spinning inside my head. She's so small, she wouldn't be able to put up much of a fight. I could throw her over my shoulder and lock her up in the back room... but I'd never get away with it in front of her friends and a bar full of witnesses.

Shit.

Shaking my head, I point to Hambone. "Give it to him. No way am I cleaning that shit up."

The patrons all move out of the way as three of the girls begin to make their way towards the door.

Laughing, Beth turns to go but I gently pull her back.

"Wait," I say.

She looks startled. "Huh?"

"I want to see you again... though maybe without your friends. Come by tomorrow night."

"I... I can't. It's not that easy..."

"Do you have a boyfriend?" I ask.

"No..." she starts to say.

"Then I'll see you tomorrow night."

She shakes her head some more. "I can't, really..."

Does she really think I'm going to let her get away that easily?

"Look, what's your last name?"

"Norton," she says and then frowns. "I shouldn't have just told you that."

"Beth Norton."

"Yeah..."

"Okay, Beth Norton," I smile at her. "If you don't show up tomorrow night, I'm going to come find you and drag you out of your house."

Blushing, she says, "I'll try, okay?"

"*No*. I'll see you tomorrow night."

She stares at me for a long time, her hazel eyes measuring me up. I know she can tell I'm fucking serious. If she doesn't show up, all I have to do is call Simon.

After I pay the fucker, I'll know everything about her.

Where she lives, where she works or goes to school. Where she likes to shop.

When she's most likely to leave her house...

"Ok—" she starts to say.

"Elizabeth!" the unnamed blonde girl who didn't puke everywhere snaps.

"Okay," Beth says to me and then hurries to her friend.

I watch her walk away and my stomach gives a small clench. Whether it's from letting her leave or the smell of puke, I'm not sure.

She stops at Hambone and I can just see the big man's huge shoulders slumping as she hands him the cash. Big guy isn't scared of anything, but get him near puke and he's like a little baby.

Chuckling, I head back to the bar. I'm more than willing to bet that Simon can help me find her if she doesn't show. Fuck, maybe I should just call him later tonight.

Right now, tomorrow seems too fucking far away.

Sitting down at the bar, I start talking to Missy about how the bar's been doing for the past couple of months I've been out of town, when one of the regulars comes in asking if anyone left their car running outside with all the doors open.

Walking out to see what he's talking about, I feel something I can't explain... I feel off in the head.

I know a car in my parking lot shouldn't be left unattended.

When I see it's a Lexus with a purse abandoned on the ground beside it, I feel a deep growl rumble through my chest.

4

BETH

Walking out of the bar, the cool breeze hits my face, dulling some of the buzz I had going on. Glancing up at the sky, I see that there's a bright full moon out tonight.

A shiver travels down my spine and I cross my arms over my chest, resisting the sudden urge to turn around and walk back into the bar... where it's safer.

Safer? I don't even know where that thought comes from. It must be because I've been holed up for so long, trapped in my father's house.

"Beth, come *on*," Lindsey grunts as she helps Sophia support Amanda's weight.

With a sigh, I rub my hands over the bumps prickling over my arms and follow after them. For safety reasons, we parked under the only light on the street, so we have to cross the entire dark parking lot to get to the car.

"Ugh, with all those tissues you eat, you'd think you'd be a little lighter..." Lindsey grumbles.

"Fuck you," Amanda snarls.

"*Lindsey*," Sophia drawls out with annoyance. "Can we not do this right now? Let's just get to the car and go home, okay? I've heard enough bitching tonight to last me a year."

Lindsey mutters something under her breath but nods her head.

Amanda gets one last, "Bitch," in and then we fall into an uncomfortable silence.

To say tonight hasn't gone the way we expected it to go is a gross understatement. It's been more than a year since I've hung out with Amanda and Lindsey, and they've either grown more stuck up and nasty over the year or I just never noticed it before.

"Do you feel like you need to puke again?" Sophia asks Amanda once we reach the car.

Amanda shakes her head *no,* so we all pile into the car. Lindsey and Sophia help Amanda into the back, and I climb into the front, taking the passenger seat.

Once Sophia has Amanda secured in her seatbelt, she climbs into the driver's seat and starts up her silver Lexus. The headlights beam out, lighting up the entrance of *The River Waters,* and I find myself trying to peer through the window to catch another peek of Johnathan. The place is packed now and the music is booming. I can feel the bass of the jukebox vibrating the car from here.

Sophia pushes the shifter into drive, and just as we

start rolling forward, Amanda cries out, "I'm going puke again!"

Sophia hits the brake and we all jump out of the car. There's a mad, fumbling rush to help Amanda out of her seatbelt, and then she stumbles out of the car.

Bending over, Amanda begins to dry heave and I have to turn away, feeling my own stomach start to weaken.

"Here, don't get it in your hair," Sophia says softly, and I glance over to see her pulling Amanda's long, brown locks back for her.

"Fuck, tonight is never going to end," Lindsey grumbles and reaches into the car, grabbing her purse off the backseat.

Lindsey begins to dig around in her purse, and I just stand beside the car awkwardly as we wait for Amanda to stop puking. I'd help, but Sophia seems to have a handle on it.

No reason to add my own puke to the mix.

"You know," Lindsey says, looking up at me as she fishes a pack of cigarettes out of her purse. "You're a lot quieter than I remember."

"I am?" I ask as she withdraws a cigarette and pushes it between her lips.

"Yeah." She bobs her head up and down. "You used to be a lot of fun. Now, you're turning into a mute or something."

She lights the tip of the cigarette and then takes a long drag. Tipping her head back, she exhales a cloud of smoke into the dark sky and asks, "Want a hit?"

I shake my head and glance to the side as a pair of headlights light up the dark night to my left.

A white, unmarked van cruises past us and all the little hairs on the back of my neck stand on end.

"Hey? How's it going?" I call out to Amanda and Sophia as I watch the van reach the end of the street and come to a stop at a stop sign.

Maybe I'm just overly paranoid, but I don't like the looks of that van. There's nothing about it that screams *rapists and murderers on the inside*, but it's made me suddenly aware of how vulnerable the four of us are standing out in the dark parking lot like this.

I look around, searching for anyone else around us, but everyone must be in the bar.

"I think she's almost done," Sophia calls back as Amanda starts to heave again.

The red brake lights of the van are joined by a sudden flash of white as the van starts to reverse back down the street, heading straight for us.

"Oh shit," I cry out, all the little alarm bells going off in my head. "Hey, we need to go!"

"Maybe they just need directions or something," Lindsey says with a shrug and takes another drag off of her cigarette.

"What's going on?" Sophia cries out from the other side of the car as the van squeals to a stop. The two back doors fly open.

"Get in the car!" I scream and dive into my side.

"Shit!" I hear Lindsey curse and see her fumbling inside her purse as I slam my door shut.

"Get in! Get in!" I yell, but Lindsey seems to be too focused on getting whatever she wants out of her purse.

"Fuck you!" Lindsey screams as I watch a dark mass appear in front of her.

Fuck, I'm the only one in the car, and I can hear Amanda still heaving as Sophia tries to push her into the backseat.

Lindsey screams again as the black mass moves closer to her, grabbing her. With a surge of adrenaline, I push open my door as hard as I can, clipping the black mass.

There's a loud, male grunt and then some words are said angrily in a foreign language as the guy stumbles back.

I can't just sit in the car and watch my friends get grabbed so I jump out, meaning to help Lindsey get inside, when she suddenly produces a little black tube in her hand.

It's pepper spray, I realize too late as she pushes the trigger.

A thick stream of fluid shoots out, hitting me on the cheek.

I immediately double over, coughing and crying in burning agony.

Two strong arms wrap around my waist and haul me back.

"Let her go, you asshole!" I hear Lindsey screech and then the screech turns into a scream.

I'm dragged across the parking lot, my heels scraping against the pavement.

I'm in too much pain and misery to even fight back.

"Get your fucking hands off me!" I hear Lindsey squeal.

I start to rub at my eyes but it only seems to make the burning worse. My entire head is on fire. My eyes, nose, mouth, and throat burn with every breath I take. The spot on my cheek where I was hit with the pepper spray feels like it's swelling up like a giant bee sting.

"Help! Help!" I hear Sophia scream. The third help is suddenly cut off with a sickening crack.

The arms tighten around my waist and then I'm lifted into the air.

"Help," I try to croak out but end up only coughing on the word.

I go flying through the air and crash into something hard and unforgiving. More pain lances through my body. The side I landed on throbs and aches from the impact.

Then another set of hands grabs me, dragging me back by my arm and hair.

I can't see, I'm completely blind. I didn't take a direct hit to the eyes, but my eyes are still burning and swelling shut. I reach up, trying to claw at the hands dragging me, but then they suddenly disappear.

"Come on, let's get the fuck out of here!" I hear a deep voice bark.

There are two more thumps. I'm pinned and squished

up against something hard as a warm body is pushed against me. Is it Lindsey, Sophia, or Amanda? I don't know.

Whoever it is isn't talking or moving.

"Please," I hear Amanda whimper at my feet. "I'm going to be sick."

Okay, so whoever is next to me isn't Amanda.

"Shut the fuck up, bitch," another male voice says, his words thick with a foreign accent. "If you puke I'll make you eat it."

There are two loud thumps as if someone is hitting the side of the van, and then a breeze hits my legs as the back doors are slammed shut.

"We got 'em. Let's go!"

I try to move, try to escape my pinned position, but then the van starts moving.

The van squeals out of the parking lot and the body next to me rolls into me, further squishing me against the hard thing that must be the side of the van.

It feels like we're flying down the street.

The tires squeal loudly as we take a sharp turn and then we burst forward.

"Please stop, please," I hear Amanda whimper again before she starts to heave.

"Fuck!" someone curses in disgust. "Get her the fuck away from me."

As I listen to Amanda cry, heave, and sniffle, I struggle with the horror of our situation. We didn't just get grabbed off the street... we didn't.

This kind of shit only happens in the movies or to other people...

Yet it just fucking happened to us.

Shit.

∼

THE VAN FLIES down the street for several minutes before starting to slow. I wiggle and struggle and finally manage to push the body crushing me away. Now that my ribs no longer feel like they're about to collapse, I gulp in air through my mouth, take stock of myself, and try to figure out the situation.

My eyes still burn and are swollen nearly shut, but it's starting to fade a bit. I can't breathe out of my nose because I have so much snot clogging up my sinuses, and my face is burning like I have the worse sunburn ever, but otherwise I'm okay. I suppose it could be worse. I could have taken a direct hit to the eyes.

We just got grabbed off the street, that much is a given. But why? Perhaps this is merely a ransom situation. Given who we are, there's no way this is completely random...

"Fuck, looks like we got the trifecta here, boys. Blonde, brunette, and redhead," one of the men says.

"Yeah, no thanks to you, asshole."

"Hey, I can't help it those other girls ran off..."

"We would have had them if you didn't fucking spook them."

"Hey," a new, deeper voice interjects. "It doesn't fucking matter now. We got some girls, some fucking hot ones. Alexei will be happy."

Shit, so this isn't a ransom situation? We're just some random girls they grabbed because they couldn't grab some others? They don't even know who we are?

"Happy?" the guy with the foreign accent snorts. "We'll see about that."

"What do you mean?" the first guy that spoke asks a little nervously. "We got some girls, we're good."

"Yes," the one with the foreign accent agrees with disdain, and I finally place it. It's Russian. "You got some girls, but not the *right* girls, so we're not *good*."

"Who the fuck cares where they came from?" the first one argues.

"Alexei cares," the Russian says with some finality and there's a tense moment of silence.

Who is Alexei? I wonder. I've never heard that name before. Is he the guy behind all of this?

Rubbing at my eyes, I try to blink them then hiss as a new wave of stinging pain radiates from them.

Suddenly, I feel eyes upon me and freeze.

"What the fuck is wrong with her? Why does she have all that snot coming out of her nose?" the guy with the deep voice asks.

"Her friend fucking maced her," the second voice snickers.

"Fuck, she's ugly," the deep voice says. "Maybe we should just throw her out..."

"Yeah, toss her out with this puking one."

"No," the Russian says firmly. "No throwing out. We've already drawn enough attention to ourselves. This was a huge risk. Alexei does not like risks."

"There's been nothing on the scanners," deep voice argues. "We're free and clear."

The Russian makes an annoyed sound in his throat and says, "We'll see."

"Fuck, man, you're such a buzzkill," the first guy whines. "All you Russians are so fucking pessimistic."

"Yeah," second guy agrees. "We got some babes. Alexei is going to get top dollar for their asses. Just look at this blonde..."

There's some shuffling to my left and my ears strain as I try to figure out what the hell is going on.

"Look, the carpet even matches the drapes," he says and I feel suddenly sick. Are they lifting up Lindsey's or Sophia's skirt? Oh god. "Alexei will get at least six figures for her."

"Get your fucking hands off the merchandise," the Russian says angrily and I sense someone standing up.

"Okay, okay, man! Fuck." There's some more shuffling to my left and then it sounds like whoever is over there is moving away. "I was just making a point."

"Fuck your point," the Russian says angrily.

Deep voice mutters something unintelligible and the van falls back into a tense silence.

Blinking my eyes, I will them to open, to work so I can fucking see. I need to figure out a way to get us out of this but I can't do it blind. Through the slits of my eyelids, all I can make out is darkness. I can't even make out any shapes.

The van begins to slow and then comes to a stop. Fuck. Is it just a traffic light or are we at the destination?

I nudge the body next to me but get no response. I'm pretty sure it's Sophia, and she's so still, so unresponsive, it's starting to scare me a little. What did they do to her? How did they knock her out? My hand starts to roam over her, searching for a pulse or a heartbeat, when I'm suddenly grabbed.

I let out a startled little scream and my throat throbs and aches. That one little scream was enough to make it feel like I just gurgled with razorblades.

Someone backhands me across the face. "Shut the fuck up, you ugly bitch."

My head whips back and my lip throbs painfully. My already abused face flares with heat and the pain is so strong I'm momentarily stunned by it.

"No damaging the merchandise," the Russian hisses.

"This one was already hit with the ugly stick. What's one more hit?" deep voice says as he begins to drag me back. "Open the fucking doors."

The doors swing open and the cool air that hits my face is a welcome relief. Someone passes by my right and there's a thud as they jump down. I'm swung out and then a new set of hands grabs me, pulling me down.

"No, please, no," I hear Amanda whimper, and there's a bunch of movement. "Please let us go."

"Fuck, these two are more trouble than they're worth," deep voice says from above me. "Move it or I'll give you something to fucking cry about."

I start to fight against the hands gripping my upper arms, wiggling and twisting as I struggle to get free of them. Even blind, I need to figure out a way to get away. To get to help. If I could just scream, if I could just fucking see, I know I could get us out of this.

The hands around my arms tighten, the fingers biting down through my flesh until they reach bone.

"Stop fucking fighting or I'll knock your ass out," the man holding me says menacingly. The grip of his fingers is so hard, so harsh, I feel myself start to weaken.

I slide down as my knees start to give out.

There's a thump to my right and then the grip around my arms loosens as I'm yanked back up. "Can you walk or do I need to carry you?"

I lick my lip, tasting blood. "Walk," I rasp, the word feeling like a hot knife slicing up my throat.

There's a grunt and then I'm dragged forward. My feet trip up under me as I struggle to both walk and try to open my eyes.

Little by little, I stumble and peel them open. The fresh air feels almost as good as a splash of cold water hitting my face.

"No, no, I'm going to be sick," I hear Amanda sniffle behind me.

"Don't you fucking da—" deep voice starts to threaten and then there's the loud, stomach-twisting sound of

Amanda coughing and something wet splashing. "Fuck! You got it on my fucking shoes!"

The man dragging me starts to chuckle as we stop and he pulls a door open. I try to look back, to get a glimpse of Amanda, but then I'm shoved through the door.

"Keep moving," my escort commands.

The door slams behind us as he grabs me again and drags me forward.

The light is dimmer here inside and my eyes struggle to adjust to it. What I'm walking on feels softer, it must be some kind of carpet.

It's also quiet. Almost too quiet.

He drags me down a long hallway, takes a left, and then stops at a door. Opening the door, he gives me a hard shove, forcing me through it, and then the door slams behind me.

I stumble forward, almost taking a knee, before I find my balance and spin around.

The light in here is brighter and harsher on my eyes. Tears blur my vision, and I have to look down at the floor to keep the pain at bay.

I don't know how long I just stand here, trying to get my shit under control, before the door opens again. Amanda is shoved roughly into the room and then the door slams behind her.

"Elizabeth!" she cries out and rushes up to me, throwing herself at me.

Sobbing, she wraps her arms around me, and shudders against me. It's everything I can do not to push her off. Not only because she's almost toppling me over, but also because she reeks like something sour.

"What are we going to do? What do you think they want with—" she chokes out, and then the door bursts open.

Amanda sucks in a breath, freezing against me.

I can tell it's two men walking in by the big, black combat boots they wear. I follow the boots as they stomp into the room and drop two bodies to the floor.

One of the bodies starts to moan as the men stomp right back out the way they came. Once more the door slams and then I hear the click of a lock turning.

"What the fuck is going on?" Sophia asks, her voice sounding strained.

"We were grabbed!" Amanda wails and starts sobbing again.

"What do you mean we were grabbed?" Sophia asks.

I'm miserable myself, but the way Amanda is clinging to me and crying, I feel the need to try to comfort her. Tentatively, I start to pat her on the back, but I have no soothing words to offer. For one, my throat still burns like hell, and for two, I don't want to give her false hope.

As far as I can see, there's no silver lining to this situation. We're completely fucked. All we can do is try to stay alive and avoid being raped or killed, and I'm not sure we can prevent either from happening.

"Oh my god, Beth. What the hell happened to you?!" Sophia gasps.

Amanda stops crying long enough to peer up at me. She blinks her green eyes slowly, as if she is seeing me for the first time, and then says, "Yeah, you look like shit."

I feel hysterical laughter starting to bubble up in my throat and have to swallow it back down, because frankly, I know laughing is going to hurt like a bitch.

"Lindsey pepper sprayed me," I croak out and instantly regret saying that much.

"Oh fuck," Sophia says with some surprise and then shakes her head. "Of course she did."

"Why did she pepper spray you?" Amanda asks, a wrinkle of confusion appearing between her brows.

Slowly, but surely, my vision is returning to me, and it's becoming easier and easier to breathe.

I just look at her. I could tell her it was an accident, that Lindsey didn't intentionally hit me with the spray, but the question just isn't worth the pain it would cost to answer it.

"I'm sure it was an accident," Sophia says after a moment, answering for me. "Damn, she's still asleep. Lindsey. Hey Lindsey, wake up."

Lindsey starts to groan as if she's in pain.

"Come on," Sophia says impatiently. "Wake the fuck up. We're in deep shit here..."

"What..." Lindsey moans groggily.

Loud, stomping footsteps sound outside the door and then the lock clicks open. Amanda jumps back, startled, and begins to shake beside me.

I tip my head up, focusing on the door as it swings in.

Three men dressed all in black march inside and then I feel Sophia beside me.

"No," Amanda immediately starts to sob.

"Shush," I hear Sophia whisper. "Stay calm."

The three of us squeeze together as if we could somehow protect each other. There is strength in numbers. Maybe we'll make it out of this if we stick together.

I slide my gaze across the three men's faces, taking in their bad haircuts and smirking lips.

"What the fuck is going on? Who are you?" Lindsey demands with righteous indignation.

"Shush," Sophia whispers harsher.

Lindsey shoots her a look full of loathing and shakily gets to her feet. As she tugs her skirt down, I notice one of the men begin to chuckle. I wonder if he was the one who lifted her skirt up in the first place.

"So, let's see what you've brought me, Sasha," a smooth, husky, Russian voice says in the hallway. I don't know what it is, but there's something about that voice that sends a shiver down my spine.

A fourth man steps into the room, but unlike the other three, he's dressed in an expensive designer suit and not black combat fatigues. Immediately, I recognize him as the man who holds all the power here. I've grown up around these kind of men, I've been surrounded by them all my life. It's not only in the way he's dressed, his charcoal grey suit is impeccable, it's also in the way he stands and exudes dominance.

The other three men in the room are bulkier and obviously stronger, but the way they watch this man, you'd think he was an all-powerful giant.

"I can take no credit for these girls," the Russian voice from earlier says and the man himself appears in the doorway.

"Oh?" Mr. Smooth asks with interest as he lifts a dark brow. He looks at us, his dark eyes slowly perusing over Amanda, Sophia, then me.

When he gets to me, he looks a little taken aback.

"Who the fuck are you?" Lindsey fairly seethes as she stalks forward, drawing his attention.

Mr. Smooth's head turns towards her.

"Who the fuck are you?" Lindsey repeats when he doesn't answer.

His dark eyes light up with amusement and he grins a feral grin at her. "I'm your new master."

"Master?" Lindsey sputters and stops besides Sophia. "Master?" she repeats, and gives us a look like '*can you believe this guy?*'

The amusement vanishes from Mr. Smooth's face.

Lindsey shakes her head and our new '*master*' seems to hone in on her. She has his undivided attention now.

The way he's watching her reminds me of a predator watching its prey before it strikes, and Lindsey has no fucking clue it's happening. She's so worked up, so insulted and full of indignation, she can't see the warnings he's giving off.

"Do you know who I am? Do you know who my

father is?" she asks, her voice growing higher and shriller by the second.

"Shut up, Lindsey," I hear Sophia whisper-hiss in warning. She must be seeing what I'm seeing.

These men, I have a feeling they don't give a fuck who we are. If they did, they wouldn't have just snatched us out of a parking lot.

"No, I do not know who you are," Mr. Smooth says, taking another step into the room.

He inclines his head to the side and there's an open, interested look on his face, but in his eyes I can see something cold stirring. "Why don't you tell me?"

No, I mentally urge Lindsey. *Don't tell him, please.* I don't know why the fuck we're here, or what these guys want with us, but I've got the most awful feeling that they're not going to like finding out we come from powerful families. We're probably better off just going along with this while we wait for someone to rescue us.

And someone will rescue us, I know it. Someone had to have seen what happened... they had to. And when our families get wind of this, they'll find us. They'll spare no expense to get us back.

It's better that these guys don't know who they're fucking with.

Lindsey narrows her eyes, and she must not see the warning in his eyes, because her lips twist with a mixture of pleasure and disdain. "I'm Lindsey Hawthorne, and my father is Michael Hawthorn, as in Hawthorne Real Estate. Ring a bell?"

Mr. Smooth slowly nods his head and he frowns as if he's not happy to learn this new information. "Yes, I've heard of him."

Lindsey's eyes light up and she looks almost excited as she says, "Then you know you're in deep shit for kidnapping me. You'll be lucky if my father does—"

A loud bang rings out, assaulting my ears, and Lindsey just drops.

She doesn't try to stop her fall.

Her arms don't come out.

She just drops to the floor with a thump.

I didn't even see the gun appear. Everything just happened so quickly, and I was too busy mentally pleading with Lindsey, to pay attention to the other men.

Beside me, Amanda screams.

Sophia gapes.

I look to Mr. Smooth, then to the man beside him with the gun in his hand. The man with the Russian accent.

I look down at Lindsey.

Did that just happen? I wonder as a cold wave of shock washes over me.

Lindsey's blue eyes stare lifelessly up at the ceiling, but I just keep staring at her, expecting and urging her to blink.

Get up, Lindsey, get up.

But she doesn't move.

She doesn't twitch or blink.

She just keeps staring.

The light that was in her eyes just a moment ago has flickered out.

Somehow her eyes have dimmed and emptied.

A dark pool of blood begins to spread around her, staining her white blonde hair.

Then I see it, the gun shot. The hole in her forehead. And it registers. What just happened finally sinks in.

I can't stop myself, I scream.

"Lindsey's dead, oh my god," Sophia mumbles beside me. "He killed her, he fucking killed her!"

Mr. Smooth turns back to us, his grin spreading. "Would you three like to tell me about your famous fathers too?"

Amanda shakes her head, sobbing and sputtering out, "No, no."

A spike of fear slams through me as I meet his eyes. Oh my god, if he finds out who my father is I'm going to die.

Just like Lindsey…

Mr. Smooth stares at us long and hard, and I feel fucking petrified. I can't breathe. I can't think. I can't speak. "You are *no one* now, yes? You are my pets."

Amanda nods her head up and down, and Sophia whimpers. Fuck, her father is the Chief of Police. She's screwed even more than I am.

"Who's responsible for this?" Mr. Smooth asks, turning to face the three men in black fatigues.

"Ronny," the Russian answers. "It was his idea to grab

the girls from the parking lot after botching the first grab."

"No, boss, I—"

Again the gun goes off and the guy in the middle drops to the floor.

The other two jump away, startled.

Oh fuck, oh fuck. I seem to be incapable of thinking anything but *oh, fuck*.

Amanda's little sobs start to turn into loud, blaring wails.

Mr. Smooth turns back to us and orders. "Take the girls to the holding room."

The two men in black fatigues hesitate for a moment and then jump forward to do his bidding. They have to step around their fallen comrade and Lindsey to reach us.

"What about the bodies?" the Russian with the gun asks as the two guys start to shove us forward. "How would you like me to dispose of them?

Mr. Smooth glances down at the bodies and turns away. "Feed them to the pigs."

5
JOHNATHAN

Four girls missing from my parking lot. Four fucking girls someone had the balls to take from my fucking property.

Do they not know what my property is? Do they not know who the fuck I am? Who the fuck I work for?

My mind doesn't like the answers it comes up with.

Whoever took the girls from my lot doesn't know a god damn thing. They don't know that my property has become a neutral zone for the city. That no one fucks with anyone on my property.

I fought Lucifer long and hard on this place. He didn't want it, he didn't like it, and he ensured I knew the cost of keeping a neutral zone in his city.

A neutral zone for anyone to come talk without worry of being ambushed. A place that isn't owned by anyone but me.

Sure, I work for Lucifer, and I'm in his inner circle.

But this is a place that is outside of that realm. It's mine. And some stupid fuck just took four girls off my property.

I'd call them women, but fuck, they're barely out of their teens, if I'm guessing right.

Pulling my cellphone from my pocket, I dial the one fucking person I fucking hate calling.

"Yes, Johnathan? What is it now?" Simon's bored tone comes through the phone.

Fucking prissy bastard.

"You need to get down to the bar. I've got a problem."

"Your bar, your problems. You know the rules, Johnathan. I could care less if someone is puking in your beer cooler."

That's about fucking typical of him. He doesn't give two shits. Doesn't even want to know.

"Yeah, well, get your ass down here. I've got a few purses here and the names on the IDs are odd. I can't place 'em, but I know 'em."

"So underage drinking happens all the time, Johnathan. Good night."

"They got yanked from my parking lot, Simon."

"Hmmm. Well, you did say you wanted it outside of.... what was it? Everyone's hands but your's?"

"Simon, listen to the fucking names. You owe me for the fucking shipping container."

"Give me two of them."

"Elizabeth Norton... and Lindsey Hawthorne. I recognize the Hawthorne last—"

"I'll be there in nineteen minutes, don't touch a thing. In fact, drop the purses where you stand."

Hmph, now he listens to me. The fucking asshole. Who the fuck did I just name off?

"What the hell?" I ask as I look down at Beth's ID.

Her long, red hair in the picture is flowing down past her shoulders, her smile is so awkward. It's her bedroom eyes though, those damn eyes. The ones that can break a man's will in an instant.

"Do as I say! Now!" The line disconnects and I'm left standing there in my parking lot with a small circle of people forming around the scene.

Looking around me, I raise my voice. "Back into the bar or leave, those are your two fucking options!"

Dropping Lindsey's purse after I shove the ID back into it, I don't know why, but I can't seem to let go of Beth's. It's not that I want to hold onto her stuff like a fucking teddy bear, but just being able to look down into her eyes brings me a sense of calm. A sense of calm before the fucking hurricane that is about to take over my little piece of the world.

I can sense it coming, with Simon at the fucking wheel.

The parking lot is dark by design. I don't like assholes thinking this place is inviting. I left the one street light alone, and it's cost four fucking girls something.

Their lives? Maybe. Fuck.

Waiting like this is going to fucking kill me. I don't even know why I should fucking care beyond someone doing it on my property, but the thought of Beth being taken makes my heart turn cold and angry.

Someone took something from me.

I watch as a large black Escalade pulls into my parking lot, and I want to shake off the skin-crawling sensation I get knowing Simon is here.

The vehicle stops next to where I am standing, and it's not long before I hear the high pitched whine of a BMW racing down the main road, towards my bar.

Simon hasn't gotten out of his vehicle yet, so I can only assume he's putting on the human mask he wears to fool everyone into thinking he's not a fucking robot, or some ancient spider, biding his time until he takes over the world.

The black BMW with blacked out windows skids to a stop and parks besides Simon in his own blacked out vehicle.

I watch James climb out of the car with a look of annoyance as he scowls at the Escalade.

Coming over to stand by me, he mutters, "I was on a fucking date tonight, asshole. You two better have a good fucking reason..."

He stares at the situation in front of us then looks down to the phone in his hand. Dialing some number, he puts the phone up to his head. "Yeah, babe, it ain't going to work tonight. I'll call ya later."

Growling, he looks over the scene while Simon finally makes an appearance. "Gentlemen."

I can just feel the scowl on my face when Simon says

that. He's so fucking aristocratic... not to mention a fucking germaphobe from hell.

"You want to come into the bar for a drink?" I ask with a laugh.

"I'd rather spend my night getting deloused," Simon says as he walks around the car.

Looking to where I dropped the purses, he squats down by an oily smear on the ground and turns his head to the side. "Someone tried using mace."

Standing up, he walks over to me and opens his hand. "Give me the purse and ID."

Grudgingly, I hand over the purse and ID, but I make sure to take one last look. "I don't have any CCTV footage of this spot, Simon. It's an oversight I'll be looking into. But I want to know everything you can get on these girls and whoever the fuck took them."

Turning from me, he walks over to the other purses, making sure to take a wide step around the various puddles of water and puke.

Picking each one of them up, he says, "I know what you want, Johnathan, and I've already informed Lucifer of the issues at hand."

"Why the fuck did you do that? This was an IOU you owe me from the fucking container ship babysitting project," I growl as I take two large steps forward.

I can sense James matching my steps just before he grabs onto my arm.

"Back down, John," James says quietly.

"What the fuck for?" I ask.

"Because your boss has taken offense and issue with whatever happened to these girls. Lindsey Hawthorne, daughter of realty mogul Michael Hawthorne."

Now I know why her named seemed so familiar.

Bending down, he picks up a purse. Pulling the ID, he says, "Sophia Cronin... Well, I hope it isn't Police Chief Cronin's very daughter, but I don't doubt it."

Well, fuck. The sinking feeling in my stomach drops even further down. Beth Norton, I know the last name, but it's escaping me.

No doubt since Simon hasn't said her name yet it's going to be a fucking big one.

"Amanda Brower, hmmm... No name from memory. I'll have to check on her."

He stops pacing around the car and stands directly in front of me. His eyes pinch around the corners as he gives me a head tilt. He's studying me with those ice blue fucking eyes behind his glasses. He's looking at me like I'm some sort of specimen under a fucking microscope.

"And Beth Norton," I say.

"Norton as in..." James starts to say.

"Yes, as in Richard Norton. Senator Richard Norton."

Oh.

Well, I was about to fuck a senator's daughter. That's a first.

Fuck, who am I kidding? I want her still, and some soon-to-be-dead motherfucker took her from my place.

Took my fucking property from my fucking place.

I can't fucking take it when someone touches my stuff.

I'm feeling a cold rage just thinking of her name. I could give two fucks that she's some senator's daughter.

She was taken from *me*.

I growl into Simon's face, "Fucking find her, Simon. I'll give you a personal favor for this. No questions."

"That's a good thing you offer, but the senator's daughter and Miss. Hawthorne are of value to Lucifer, and as such to the inner circle."

"Whatever the fuck you say, just find the fucking girl."

His phone starts ringing as he is about to reply. Stepping away from me, he puts it to his ear. Listening for two minutes straight, he looks over to me and frowns.

Tapping the phone off, he says, "Keep this shit to yourselves. The police have no clue the girls are even missing. Meaning, we are in the clear of it blowing back on ourselves."

He snaps his fingers at James and says, "Get that car around back. Remove any personal belongings and the plates. I'll have someone come by to remove it in a few minutes."

Smirking at Simon, James says, "Please."

Looking at him in confusion, Simon asks, "Please, what?"

"Say please, Spider, or you can move it yourself. Lucifer called me into this gig, you can say please."

Simon's face goes completely smooth. No frown, no smile, nothing except the cold eyes as he says, "If you would please, James, move that fucking car now."

Snickering, James nods his head. "Sure, who's got the keys?"

Shrugging my shoulders, I head over to the car and start looking around. "You got them in the purses, Simon?"

"No," he says in a clipped tone as he stands there. He hasn't moved a muscle since James started fucking with him. I think saying *please* might have broken all those computer parts in his brain.

"Was this an attack of opportunity or planned, Simon?" I ask as I switch my phone's flashlight on.

Shaking himself, Simon says, "I highly doubt it was planned. These girls never should have been in a dump like this."

James looks over at me at the word *dump*. "You gonna let him call your bar a dump?"

"It's not far off the mark. I prefer to call it a dive bar, though." Frowning at the thought, I look over to Simon. "You know, a couple of them were pretty uptight about being here. Beth was especially, at first. I got the vibe this was completely out of the norm for them."

"Did they stay long?"

"About two hours. No one but regulars came in. No sketchy cars or shit was mentioned till someone came in asking about the car outside."

"Well, we won't be able to keep a lid on the car being left here, or the missing people. But with luck, no one will figure out who they were until it goes on the news that the girls are missing."

"You thinking ransom?" I ask. It seems highly unlikely to me. If it was a ransom gig, why take 'em all? And why not have someone on the inside of the bar to make sure they came out the front? Someone to keep 'em in sight?

"No. It wouldn't fit the scene before us."

"Got the keys," James says as he scoops them up from under a car. "Pretty big scuffle if they made it over here. To add my two cents, if it was a pro job, they would have taken this Lexus or at least hid it from here."

"Sloppy if they just left it here. Doors open, signs of a scuffle," Simon says as he peers around us.

"Sloppy..." Something about this whole thing rings a bell in my head, but the connection isn't there yet. I can feel the connections coming, but I'm missing a piece of information.

"We need to know where they're going," Simon says.

"Yeah, and I'm willing to bet they won't be sending out a ransom note."

Looking at me, Simon nods his head. "You and James get rested up. Then get gear ready for whatever might come up. I'll get my hooks into the traffic lights around here and see if I can spot anything."

~

Beth

"Stop your fucking crying," one of the men in black fatigues barks as they push, shove, and drag us through the hallways.

We're lead down a set of dark stairs, and I nearly fall twice as I struggle with the change of lighting. Sophia's grip on my arm is the only thing that keeps me from wiping out completely.

Once we reach the bottom of the stairs, we're lead down another dark hallway lined with doors and marched up to the third one. The door is unlocked, pushed open, and then we're pushed inside.

I hear one of the two men mutter, "Fucking worthless bitches." Then the door slams behind us and once more we're locked in.

Trapped.

The three of us just stand where we're left for a moment before Amanda collapses to her knees.

"We're going to die, we're going to die," she keeps repeating, and I don't know how to comfort her.

I don't know how long I just stand still, listening to Amanda crying, waiting. Expecting the door to open again and for the men to reappear.

Waiting for them to come tell us they know who we are.

They know our fathers.

Waiting for them to put a bullet between our eyes.

My ears still ring from the gunshots, and it's a long time before I realize Sophia is talking to me.

"What do you think they want with us?" Sophia repeats, looking at me. Her face is red, blotchy, and her makeup is running with tear streaks.

"I don't know," I croak out, but inside I think I know.

I just don't want to say it out loud.

I don't want to voice my fears and give them life.

"What are we going to do?" Amanda sobs, breaking down completely. "They killed Lindsey!"

My throat tightens up and fresh tears flood my eyes. Lindsey's dead, she's really dead, and a part of me wants to collapse, to breakdown like Amanda. But there's another part of me that wants to make it out of this.

That wants to survive.

Wiping the back of my hand across my face, I take another step into the room, and look at what we have to work with.

The walls appear to be made out of concrete and there's no window. We must be in a basement. There's one bare twin mattress on the floor, a bucket… a fucking bucket… and a gallon jug of water.

"What are we going to do?!" Amanda repeats, crying hysterically.

I drop down to my knees and Sophia follows me.

Pulling Amanda into a hug, I fight back my own sobs, my own despair, and whisper, "We wait."

TIME CRAWLS BY. Hours must pass. Sophia and I manage to get some water into Amanda, and then use some of it to rinse off my face. After awhile, Amanda curls up into a little ball and falls asleep on the mattress.

Even in her sleep she whimpers and cries.

Sophia and I sit on the floor, up against the wall, side by side.

"You know," she says, her gaze far away. "I overheard my father talking about a surge of disappearances recently."

"Oh?" I ask, looking over at her.

She nods her head and tucks a blonde curl behind her ear before looking at me. "Yeah, but most of the disappearances were college girls. He warned me to be more careful and to avoid campus after dark..." She shakes her head and the curl she just tucked behind her ear pops out. "He's always warning me of one danger or the other, so I didn't take him seriously."

"We weren't grabbed on campus," I say quietly and look away.

A strong surge of shame slams into me.

"Yeah, but—"

"It's not your fault, Sophia," I say, my throat wanting to tighten around the words to keep them from leaving. "It's mine."

"How is this your fault?" she asks, turning towards me.

"If it weren't for me, if I would have just stayed at home, we wouldn't have been at that dive bar in the first place," I say and hang my head. "Amanda and Lindsey didn't even want to be there." I start to choke up and tears prick at my eyes. "Lindsey wanted to leave... if we would have left earlier..."

Sophia's arms come around me and I feel myself weakening. I feel myself filling with self-pity and self-loathing.

"It's not your fault. It's *not*, Beth. You're not the one that pointed the gun at Lindsey's head..."

The memory of Lindsey just dropping to the floor flashes through my mind. Her dull, lifeless eyes. The blood staining her hair red...

I shake my head back and forth, fighting a losing battle against the tears and sobs that escape my mouth.

"We live in the most dangerous city in the country," Sophia murmurs as she rubs her hand in circles on my back. "These guys... these guys are to blame. And they will pay for this."

"But it won't bring Lindsey back," I shudder.

"No, it won't bring Lindsey back," she agrees reluctantly.

We hold each other and cry for a few minutes.

When our sobs lose their strength, and the tears start to dry, she leans back, wipes her eyes and says, "You know, Lindsey could be a bitch sometimes, but she didn't deserve to die."

I nod my head in agreement and choke out in a half-sob, half-laugh, "She could be a real bitch, but she also had lots of awesome moments."

"Yeah, like that time she pulled Tommy Baron's underwear all the way up to his ears for picking on me," she sniffle-snorts.

I laugh a little. "Yeah, I remember that. Miss Wilson had to cut them off and he walked funny the rest of the week."

"Or that time—" she starts but stops, her eyes widening as we both hear the lock on the door rattling.

We both jump up and walk backward, pressing into the corner of the back wall.

The door swings open and one of the goons dressed in black marches into the room.

He looks at us, then he looks down at Amanda.

Dammit, we just left her lying there, unprotected. He takes a step toward Amanda and I cry out, jumping forward. "Don't touch her!"

He shoots me a dirty look and turns back to Amanda, ignoring me. He walks up to the mattress and starts to bend down, as if he's going to pick her up, and I rush him.

I can't let him touch her, I can't.

I try to shove him away but he doesn't budge. He weighs a fucking ton, and I feel like I just tried to push over a building.

Growling, he turns towards me and shoves me back, knocking me down to my ass. "Back the fuck up, bitch."

The second goon in black steps into the room, lingering by the door. The first guy bends down again, grabbing Amanda and lifting her up.

"Beth, don't," Sophia murmurs quietly, coming up

behind me. I feel her hand on my shoulder, gently restraining me, as I pant angrily and watch the guy march out of the room.

Amanda wakes up with a startled cry and starts to fight the guy as he carries her. "Let me go, please!"

"Stop fighting," the goon grunts, shifting her around in his arms. "Or you'll end up like your friend...with a bullet between your eyes."

That warning seems to suck all the air out of Amanda. I watch helplessly as she sags in his arms and cries.

"The same goes for you two," the guy at the door says as he eyes Sophia and me. "You fight us, you die."

The guy carrying Amanda marches out of the room and the door slams behind him.

As I hear the lock clicking into place, I burst into a fresh round of tears.

I've never felt so fucking helpless.

6

JOHNATHAN

"Johnathan, I've got more information. I need you and James to be at my office as soon as possible. Lucifer will be with us, so make sure to hurry," Simon says in that unhurried voice of his.

It's always even tones with him. Doesn't matter the time of day, he always sounds so fucking infuriatingly calm.

"Got it," I growl as I check the clock on my nightstand.

It's three in the fucking morning.

Pushing disconnect, I look over at the window. It's the dark of night out there. Spider's favorite fucking time, if you ask me.

Calling James, he sounds aggravated when he answers. "You and your fucking troubles. I swear to fucking hell."

"Good morning to you too, sweetheart."

He's in a good mood.

"You guys have shit timing…" he says, and I hear a female's sleepy voice in the background, asking what's going on.

"Get to Simon's office. Lucifer will be there too."

"Fuck. When the hell did Simon figure out that we need the big guy's fucking attention?"

"When the stakes got raised. Police Chief's daughter, senator's daughter, realty mogul's daughter, and some fashion queen's beloved daughter. All money and power families."

"See you there," he says before he disconnects.

Grabbing my jeans off the floor, I stand up and pull them on. These are the least dirty ones I have right now, or well, I should say the cleanest. Walking into the kitchen, I grab my keys off the counter.

It's going to be a long fucking day; I can just fucking see it.

It's a little cooler right now out in the dark of night, but the cold metal of my 1956 Harley Davidson panhead feels good against my calloused hands as I run my fingers over her.

"I know you're cold, baby, let's get you all hot and bothered," I purr to her as I crank her up.

The loud thrum fills the night air as I let her rumble for a couple minutes. I don't know when I'll have a chance to just sit back and enjoy the feeling I have right now. I get the distinct impression from the way the world feels around me, things are about to get rough.

"WHAT THE FUCK ARE YOU WEARING?" Simon hisses, and for the first time in a long while I've achieved my happy place.

I've taken his calm from him.

Fucker looks livid with me as I stroll right into his office.

I'm surprised to see Andrew here as I walk over to one of the chairs by Simon's desk.

"What the fuck are you doing here?" I ask as I slap Andrew's shoulder.

Rubbing his eyes, Andrew grouches, "Fuck if I know. This is your shit show, I'm guessing."

"If you dare sit down..." Simon says to me in a cold voice.

"Gentlemen," Lucifer says as he walks into the room. He looks like he's just been on a vacation. He's completely relaxed and not showing a single sign of it being three-thirty in the morning.

"Matthew," Simon says to Lucifer, calling him by his real name.

"Boss," I say.

James follows right behind him, heads to a chair and slumps down into it.

"Let's all be seated and get this started," Lucifer says.

Grinning right in Simon's face, I lower myself into his plush office chair and scoot around until I find that perfect, comfortable spot.

Simon's eyes are on fire as he looks to Lucifer and then back to me. I can see a small vein on his neck beginning to stand out.

I think the prissy fuck is about to have a stroke.

"Johnathan," Lucifer starts as he sits in a chair facing us. "You seem to have fallen into a dirty world that has been darkening the corners of our city."

Lifting my eyes, I ask, "What do you mean?"

Simon takes over. "While this is more speculation than I'm used to, I was able to gain CCTV footage surrounding your area of town. From the surrounding traffic light cameras, I have a better understanding of who took the girls from your bar."

Turning his screen around, he shows a video of a white van driving along the road leading to my bar. The picture changes and then shows the same van at the light about a quarter of a mile away from it. My bar is on a long stretch of road with nothing else out there except for old, closed up industrial plants.

"This van was traveling on the street at the time intervals you gave me. No other vehicles came during that time except for a pickup truck that stopped at your bar."

I look at the video of the pickup truck. "His name is Jack. He doesn't have any part in this."

"Agreed," Simon says.

"So, what the fuck happened?" Andrew asks as he yawns again. "The girls have me getting up early for soccer practice this morning. Let's hear the meaty bits."

Simon and I quickly do a rundown of what happened

three nights ago at the bar. We start from my point of view then Simon shifts it back to the white van.

"Here's the interesting piece of the story," Simon smiles. "The information you pulled from Yuri added pieces to the Russian puzzle we've been working on, but the white van adds a whole corner of the puzzle we didn't know was taking shape."

Lucifer asks, "How did we not know they would be doing a slave auction in my city?"

Raising my eyebrows, I look over at Andrew and James. This is news to us all, and from the pained frown on Simon's face, I take it he's not too happy about the answer he's about to give.

"It's a floating market. They've been doing this in Europe for the last century. They move their chattel from city to city. They often pick up their merchandise from the cities they plan to have an auction in. Their pickups start anywhere from a month ahead of time to a couple of days. It depends on the influx of what is being called for."

"What are they selling?" James asks.

"Women and children. Never men. Females range from three years old to thirty. The male children no older than eleven."

James looks like he's turned green. He's not the newest member to our family, but he's from a different side of the criminal underworld. Previously, he worked as a very skilled cat burglar. I'm not sure where the ability to use a sniper weapon came from, but for both jobs, he is the one person I trust to get them done. He's way too good with a mile of distance and a rifle to be a civilian, if you ask me. But he hasn't dealt with the shit side of life like this. Things like these usually don't come up on his side of the family's business.

Rolling my neck in a circle, I hear it click twice in loud pops. "So what they don't sell they take with them to the next city?"

"Yes. According to my sources, they move into an area a couple of days ahead of time. Either the Russians, or the local crew, target pickups days or weeks beforehand. Everything is planned ahead of time, if possible, from what I can see. They spend time with the local boss of the area, and then leave a nice cash incentive. Sometimes they'll go back to the same city, if they did particularly well."

"Why are we just now hearing they are coming here, Simon?" Lucifer asks before I can.

"Because the Russians are getting restless again. The money flow they previously had is declining. Alexei Rastov is trying to expand his options. My thoughts are he doesn't know or care of our rules barring slave auctions in our city."

Nodding my head at Simon, I say, "He's keeps his cards closer to his chest than the previous guy did. He's the new wave of boss from Russia. No more of the old, reliable bear."

"Precisely. He has brought a revolution to the front. He's connected through the newest methods of criminal enterprises. Cyber warfare, investment terrorism. You name it, he's willing to try it. But he's not stopped the old proven methods, either. Slavery of the right flesh brings in a strong flow of money."

"So, what do we know?" I ask.

"The van drove a long route for a short distance. Whether they were hoping to grab more girls, or worried about being followed, both seem possible. They eventually made their way across the city to their industrial complexes. As far as I can tell, they've made one of their unused warehouses the spot for the auction."

That's the reason we're here so early in the fucking morning. Fuck. And fuck. They kidnapped my girl and they are going to try to sell her off to the highest fucking bidder.

For fuck's sake, when did my mind switch to her being *my* girl?

Shaking my head to clear the thoughts, I ask, "How is this set up?"

"They have a few methods they use, from what my sources say. And trust me, the information I received about the auctions has been very hard to come by. Squeezing and bribing wasn't easy. From what I gather, they are very selective about who comes to their auctions, and they are very choosey with who gets to buy."

That's probably bad news right now for me.

"Their operation is simple in some aspects. They use websites to advertise their merchandise, but it's a darknet site that utilizes encryption that rivals most government databases."

Laughing, Lucifer says, "So it was easy to get into?"

Simon winces slightly. "Perhaps I should rephrase that. They rival databases that I would encrypt. It was not easy in the least."

"From there, they show pictures of their goods, a sort of what's up and coming with special details. Whether the goods are virgins or not. What their backgrounds are. Some of the women they snatch are from higher education backgrounds. Political science majors, chemical engineering degrees, computer database architects. They don't always go for the everyday slob."

"Do we think they took these women on purpose?" James asks. He's staring at the whiteboard on the back wall of Simon's office.

There are four photos of the women that were kidnapped. Beth being at the front of the line. The next three are in order of importance, I would guess, but there's a red question mark next to each of their pictures.

"Doubtful. They haven't started the higher profile abductions in the states yet."

"What do you mean?"

"Over in Europe, South Africa, and the Middle East, they've done high profile grabs. Remember the second and third place women from the Miss World pageant last year?" Simon asks as he quickly does something with his mouse and keyboard.

Pictures pop up on his screen of two beautiful women.

There's an itchy spot in the back of my brain, but I

can't remember where I've seen those two women before until Andrew says, "Yeah, they went missing on the tour. Somewhere in Tripoli, right?"

"Correct," Simon says.

"Wow," I say. "That's ballsy."

"Not according to them. They have a private wish list section where a client can create a list that's only available to the administrator. There, from what I can tell, is where clients are able to ask for a specific type of woman. Or a specific woman."

"Hmmm," comes from Lucifer, and I can't help but chuckle. He's seeing dollar signs and power right now, I can guarantee it. Whether it's to take over something like this, or sell the information out, I have no clue.

Nodding my head, I start to get an idea of just how sophisticated this line of business has become, and I can see in Lucifer's cold, calculating eyes he's fully aware of the capabilities something like this has.

"What's with the question marks?" I ask.

"They've listed three new girls as of this morning."

"But four went missing."

"Four went missing," Simon agrees. "That doesn't mean they will sell them all or can sell them all."

A new wave of nausea hits me. Beth.

"They've listed two as virgins, and one as... how did they put it? I think it's spirited. No pictures yet."

Virgins. Fucking bloody hell. Their price will be astronomical.

"What's the news on the girls missing?" Lucifer asks.

"Nothing public yet. Although, from what I've heard, the Police Chief wants to make an announcement. The Police Chief is making serious waves trying to go around Senator Norton, but Norton has him locked down tight."

"What the fuck for?" James questions, his incredulity is plainly showing. "Why not have them on milk cartons already?"

"Because Norton has a campaign to run. He's running again this November for office, and he has very high ambitions. From the mouths of his understaff, he has dreams of hitting the Oval in the next twelve years."

"That crooked bastard?" Lucifer scoffs at the notion, but I can see it doesn't surprise him.

"Yes, and anything that could reflect badly, or show a lack of control, is not being let out to the public. And with the way he treats his daughter, he very well could have it leaked he isn't the greatest of fathers. Even his security staff have been heard to whisper of his iron-fisted ways."

Makes sense. Beth and the girls were out for a night on the town. Bet they didn't want to be caught up in the limelight that can happen when some of the semi-famous visit the central strip downtown.

"So, when it goes public they're missing..." I start off, thinking out loud. "If the Russians don't already know, it will either be ignored that they're big names or it could get messy. But, they probably already know... maybe that's why only three are being sold?"

"That's the unknown, why they only listed three girls.

I'm very interested to know what happened to the fourth."

"What's the security like at these auctions?" Andrew asks.

"I would liken it to having the National Guard surrounding a warehouse with the Secret Service inside."

"Oh," Andrew says with a grimace. "That makes things interesting."

I can only agree. "How are we going to take this place out?"

Simon looks to Lucifer then to me. "We can't. It would take too many men and too much time."

My eyes widen. "There can't be that many issues with something like this?"

"There is. And if we let the proper authorities know, it's not unheard of for them to go dark with the auction... or throw a couple of grenades into a holding pen with all the livestock inside."

"What do you mean go dark?" James asks.

"They skip the auction if they hear even the faintest of whispers suggesting that they are being looked at. Then it's another couple of months before they resurface. Usually with a completely new crop to sell."

Fucking hell.

"Okay, so what's that mean for us then?"

"You will be going in alone. I've got you set up as a buyer's proxy. The guy I tapped for this did not come cheap, nor did he want to give up his seat for a special verified virgin auction."

Christ, this is fucking insane.

"By myself?"

"Yes. Andrew, you will be in operational control of it all. James, you will be backup in case we lose any of the girls. Peter will be backing you up with a car of his own to stop any from getting out, if possible."

"How the hell will I get into a place like this? They probably know what I look like, you know."

"That's the beauty of modern day cosmetics."

He pulls up another picture on his computer and for a few seconds I'm confused. There, on the screen, is a guy who looks a lot like me except I have blue eyes and my hair isn't cut short like some fucking hipster.

Then it dawns on me.

Fuck that shit. The girls are going to new homes, if you ask me.

"I ain't cutting my fucking hair, bitch boy," I yell.

Everyone except Simon is laughing at the picture, even Lucifer.

Simon isn't though.

"Think of Beth," Simon says like he has a needle and is trying to stab it in my eye.

It's six in the morning before we finally leave the office space downtown. My eyes hurt from watching the damn screen the whole time, and I still don't have a good feeling about the whole scheme we have in place.

Especially the part of me going in solo.

Andrew has said he'll have more guys in place to try to get me out if shit goes sideways, but I already know I'll be leaving my weapons at the door.

This is going to be a fucking crap-shoot.

Pulling my phone out of my pocket, I dial the one person I know that can do what I need right now.

"Missy," I say as soon as she answers. "Meet me at the bar in two hours. I need you to put your cosmetology license to work. Bring your haircutting shit."

7

BETH

Hours and hours pass with no sign of Amanda. Sophia and I are forced to relieve ourselves in the bucket and then we share what's left of the water.

Sitting side by side on the thin mattress, we have nothing left to do but wait and fret.

"What do you think they're doing to her?" Sophia asks quietly, breaking the silence.

She looks to me, her eyes full of desperation. I know she wants me to reassure her, to give her some kind of hope we can get out of this situation, but I have no hope left to give.

"I don't know," I answer just as quietly. I don't want to think about it, I don't, but I can't help it.

They could be raping her, interrogating her, torturing her, or she could be dead.

Sophia's face crumbles for a moment, and then she

looks away. I listen to her draw in a deep breath, let it out, then suck another in.

"Do you think we've made the news yet?" she asks after a couple of minutes.

"God, I hope not," I exhale in a burst. The last thing we need is our faces blasted all over the media. Once these guys find out Lindsey wasn't the only one with powerful connections, we're dead.

"I bet my father is freaking the fuck out."

I nod.

"Yours too."

"Only if his men have reported it," I sigh.

I feel a little sorry for the guy that has to break the news to him. There have been many times I was able to get away with stuff, like sneaking out for an hour or two to hang with Sophia, just because the guys assigned to me were too afraid to admit they fucked up to my father.

"Maybe they'll be able to find us. My father is the police chief, for Christ's sake. He has to have some idea... some clue about what is happening."

"Shush," I hiss and glance towards the door and then around the room. "They could be listening to us," I whisper.

They could even be watching us. Maybe I'm a little paranoid, or I'm simply used to my own father spying on me, but I wouldn't be surprised if there's a camera or two hidden in this cell.

And that's exactly what this little room is—it's our

holding cell. They're keeping us here until they do god only knows what with us.

"Fuck," Sophia mutters, and then she slumps against the wall. "I'm sorry."

We've gone through a hell of a few days. We were grabbed off the street, watched one of our best friends get murdered in front of us, and have been trapped in this room ever since. I think the waiting, and the heavy weight of the situation, is starting to get to the both of us. I, myself, feel like I'm barely keeping it together.

Either one of us could snap at any moment.

"Don't worry about—" I start to tell her then clamp my lips together when I hear the familiar, terrifying sound of the lock rattling.

Fuck, were they listening in on us? Are they coming to kill us now?

We both jump to our feet and press together as the door swings open. The same goon from before marches into the room, dragging Amanda with him.

"No, please, no. Let me go," Amanda whimpers and pleads, dragging her feet as he pulls her into the room.

The goon ignores her and gives her a hard shove causing her to trip forward before she falls to her knees.

Then he looks to Sophia and I.

My heart freezes behind my ribs and my lungs forget how to breathe.

"You," he says, looking me in the eyes. "Come here."

"No!" Sophia cries and jumps in front of me before I can take a step forward. "Take me instead."

The goon's lips curls up in a sneer and he all but leers at Sophia before saying, "You'll have your turn, blondie. Now get the fuck out of the way."

"Take care of Amanda," I whisper, and try to take a step around her.

"No," Sophia says and shakes her head in defiance. She steps in front of me, blocking me from moving.

"Sophia, don't," I hiss into her ear and nudge her out of the way.

I don't want her getting hurt or killed on account of me.

"But..." Sophia protests, and her bottom lip trembles as I step around her.

"It will be okay," I try to reassure her, but the truth of the situation is in my eyes.

It's not going to be okay, but if we fight, we die, and I don't want Sophia to die.

Right now we need to do whatever it takes to stay alive. Even obey their commands until we can come up with some kind of plan to get out of here.

"Take care of Amanda. She needs you right now."

"Beth..." she says and reaches out as if to stop me.

"I don't have time for this shit," the goon says angrily. "Get your ass over here or I'll take it out on your little friend."

He nudges Amanda's side with the tip of his boot and she cries out, curling away from him. "Bitch has already given me a headache with all her whining."

That does it, there's no more arguing over this. Turning away from Sophia, my spine stiffens when I hear her whimper, but I don't stop walking as I approach the goon.

He grabs me hard by the arm and pulls me close. My lips press together and I resist the urge to cry out. I know from experience that these guys are more likely to let their guard down if we pretend to be cooperative.

"Let's go," he grunts, and even though I'm not trying to fight him, he starts to drag me out of the room.

"Beth," Sophia says, and I glance over my shoulder to see her crying.

She looks terrified and helpless.

It hits me now, hard in the chest, that there's a very real chance that I might not come back.

That I might never see her again.

"Don't worry," the goon grins just before slamming the door behind us. "It will be your turn next."

The goon drags me down the hallway and up the dark set of stairs.

My eyes are no longer irritated and this time I have no problem seeing where we're going. I take everything in, burning it into my memory. If we can get away, if we can get to someone important like Sophia's father, the information will be invaluable.

Behind the doors, I hear others crying, whimpering.

Some of the cries sound like women, but some of them also sound younger...

A sick sense of unease travels down my spine, curling in the pit of my stomach, and lifts all the little hairs across my flesh.

Do they have children here? Locked behind those doors?

I look to the goon, my eyes boring into the back of his head.

What kind of sick fucks are we dealing with?

Up the stairs, he tugs me and then takes a sharp left. I'm led down a dimly lit carpeted hallway and then through another door into what looks like a locker room. The carpet gives way to tile and the air here is moist from a recent shower.

The goon's grip on my arm relaxes and then he just starts to push me forward with a hand at the small of my back.

"Remove your clothes," he orders coldly.

I'm given one more push around a tiled corner until I'm face to face with a long row of open showers.

I look to the showers and then back to him. Is he serious?

"Remove your clothes," he repeats, and crosses his bulging arms over his chest. "Or I'll do it for you."

I take a step back, away from him, and my mind races for a way to get out of this. The thought of removing clothes in front of him, of being completely naked and vulnerable, is just too terrifying at the moment.

I've never been completely nude in front of a man before, and the clothes on my back are the last shred of dignity I have left.

The goon uncrosses his arms and takes a menacing step toward me.

"No, please," I hear myself say and immediately hate myself for saying it.

I don't want to beg. I don't want to be weak or pathetic. But god dammit, how can he just expect me to strip like it's nothing?

I take another step back, eyeing my options. I could try to make it past him, make a run for it... Then I see his fingers brush his waist. He's carrying a gun.

Shit.

If only I had my own weapon, I might have a chance. I glance behind me then side to side, searching for something to use, but there's only showers, a bench, and lockers.

"I had to help your little friend undress," he says with a smirk tugging at the corner of his mouth. "I don't think I have much juice left in me..." He reaches down and adjusts his crotch. "But I'm sure I could find something for you."

I stare at him, frozen in horror at the implications of what he just said. He undressed Amanda? What else did he do to her?

What will he do to me?

He takes another step forward and I quickly decide I

much rather strip naked myself than have his hands on me.

He takes another step and I nearly jump out of my skin.

"Wait, no!" I say and start to tug my shirt over my head.

He gives a grunt of approval as I pull my shirt off and then clutch it to my chest. I start to shiver involuntarily as the moist air hits my skin.

"Remove the rest," he says, his voice sounding gruffer, and crosses his arms over his chest again.

My fingers don't want to release their clutch on my shirt, but I have to if I don't want his hands on me. Forcing my fingers to open, I let my shirt drop to the floor then reach down and unbutton my jeans.

I hear him make a sound of appreciation as I have to wiggle to get my jeans over my hips. Bile burns the back of my throat and I consider letting myself get sick. But did that stop him from abusing Amanda? I doubt it.

Straightening, my jeans pool at my feet and I toe my shoes off, stepping out of them. Nearly naked now, I cross my arms over my chest and shiver as I stare at him.

His eyes narrow. "Do you not understand fucking English? I said remove all of it."

With tears stinging my eyes, I uncross my arms and reach behind myself, unsnapping my bra. I can't even look at him as the straps slide down my arms. Sliding one arm out then the other, I do my best to reveal as little as possible, but it's pretty much hopeless.

The bra drops to the floor and I keep one arm pinned tight against my breasts as I use the other to push down my panties. My panties give way too easily, and once they drop, my hand immediately goes to my mons, covering it.

"Get in the shower," he orders and my eyes flick up. There's an open, hungry look on his face that fills me with cold terror.

"Now," he barks when I don't immediately move, and the harshness of his voice spurs me into action.

Turning away from him, I give him my naked back as I walk up to the closest shower. There's a handle I have to twist to the left to turn the water on. The first spray of water is icy cold and I gasp as it hits me.

"Use the soap in the dish," he orders behind me, and I cast a glance over my shoulder to see that he's moved closer.

Fuck.

Compliance. Pretend to be compliant and maybe he'll drop his guard long enough to give me an opening, I remind myself.

If I can steal his gun I can fucking shoot him with it.

Looking forward again, I reach out, my hand shaking as I grab the little bottle of soap that's been left on the soap dish by the water handle.

One handed, I pop the lid and then just squirt the bottle onto the top of my head. I lather up my hair, scratch my nails through my scalp, and resist the urge to look back again.

Pretending there's no one behind me, I rinse my hair

out and then squirt some more soap into my hand. Just as I start to rub the soap onto my arms, I hear a little grunt behind me.

Glancing back without thinking, I see him rub his hand over his groin.

Fuck, he's getting off on this.

Looking forward again, air puffs out of my mouth in little pants as I focus all of my energy on completely not losing my shit. I want to scream. I want to cry. I want to fucking attack him, and the only thing keeping me from not doing it is the desire not to have a bullet in my head.

I work the soap up and down my arms then quickly over my chest. I stare at the tile wall as I wash myself as quickly as I can. I just want to get this over with now. The more I try to hide myself, the longer I'll have to be naked in front of him.

The air behind me moves and my hackles rise. I cast another little glance over my shoulder and see that the goon is even closer. His eyes are locked on my backside as he rubs his hand over himself.

"Hey, is she done yet?" a new voice calls out, echoing in the room. "The doc is ready for her."

"Fuck. Hurry it up," my guard orders and moves back.

I begin to tremble, unable to stop it. That was close, too fucking close for comfort.

I turn the water off and then wrap my arms around myself as I turn back around to face him.

He bends down and picks a towel off the bench. Then he grins as he holds the towel out.

I have no choice but to walk up to him if I want it.

Teeth chattering from the cold, my eyes remain locked on his face as I approach him. I get only as close as necessary before I reach out to take the towel from him.

He immediately yanks the towel back, out of my reach.

His eyes gleam with cruel amusement as I have to move closer. I reach for the towel again, half expecting him to yank it back, but his eyes drop, locking on my wet breasts.

I yank the towel from his hand and immediately jump back.

"Dry off," he says gruffly.

"Hey! What's the hold up?" the other voice calls out.

"She's almost done," my guard yells back then he glares at me. "Hurry it the fuck up."

I run the towel over my arms, ignoring my hair, and then wrap it around me for protection.

Grabbing me hard by the arm, he drags me around the corner and out into the hallway where another goon dressed all in black is waiting.

The new guy looks me in the face and then seems to do a double take. "Is that the redhead from the other night?"

"Yeah," my guard answers and begins to drag me past him.

"Wow. She's pretty fucking hot without all that snot and shit."

My guard just grunts and continues to drag me down

the hallway. We pass the stairway to the basement, more doors, then take a left. I try hard to remember how I was led in last night, but I was so confused and disoriented, I just can't remember which way the exit is.

He leads me up to another door, pushes it open and pushes me in. I trip a little as I step into the room, but then my escort yanks hard on my arm, pulling me up so I don't fall on my ass.

"Get on the table," he orders.

Looking around the room, I take in the dark panels of the walls, the little stool with wheels, the little table with medical instruments, and finally the table he wants me to get on.

No. *No fucking way*, I think as I stare at the table. It's one of those medical tables with metal stirrups my gynecologist uses, but there are leather restraints attached to it.

"Get on the fucking table now," my escort growls and shoves me towards it.

"No." I shake my head and pull down on my arm, trying to yank it out of his grasp.

I've put up with a lot of shit so far but I've reached my limit. There's no way I can just willingly climb up on that table and allow them to strap me to it.

"Why do they always fight the table?" the other goon chuckles behind us.

"Fuck if I know," the guy holding me grunts. By the arm, he tries to drag me closer to the table but I'm having none of it.

Unable to free my arm, I turn on him and try to push him off. He doesn't budge.

His lip curls up with a sneer and my feet nearly leave the ground as he yanks my arm up harder. My shoulder screams in protest as he drags me closer to the table, my toes dragging against the carpet, and I feel my towel fall away.

"No!" I cry out and continue to fight him. I start to kick at him and lean back against his grip even though the pain in my shoulder is nearly excruciating.

He's going to have to yank my damn arm off because there's no way I'm allowing them to strap me down.

Right now, in my mind, there are things worse than death.

He pushes me up against the edge of the table, trying to force me up on it, but I twist and take a swing at him.

My punch lands against his chest and he grunts softly.

Taking another swing, this time at his face, his hand captures my hand in mid-punch. He applies so much force with his crushing grip, a scream builds inside my throat and my knees start to give out on me.

"Want some help?" the other guy asks, sounding amused.

"Yeah," my escort grunts just before his grip tightens.

I scream and then feel another set of hands at my waist before I'm lifted into the air.

They toss me onto the table but I don't stop fighting

them. I kick and scream and throw punches at them, but they still manage to overpower me.

I've never felt so pathetic or weak. I'm giving it my all but, the two guys aren't even winded as they overwhelm me.

Straps are wrapped around my wrists and tightened until my arms are pinned at my sides. My legs are pushed apart, my feet forced into the stirrups, and then more straps are wrapped around my ankles.

Shaking my head back and forth, tears stream down my cheeks as I push and struggle against my restraints.

My escort takes a step back and his eyes roam over my spread, restrained body, as if he's admiring his handiwork.

"I hate you," I snarl at him.

I hate them all. I hate them for grabbing us. I hate them for killing Lindsey. I hate them for abusing Amanda.

And I especially hate this sick fuck for getting off on all of it.

He only laughs. "They all say that."

"I'm going to kill you," I promise. And in my bones I can feel it, the power of the promise. Maybe not today, but someday… Someday soon.

Two sharp raps sound against the door and then a new, softer voice asks, "Is she ready for me, gentlemen?"

"Yeah, doc, she's all yours," the guy who escorted me in says and then gives my thigh a slap.

Instinctively, my body jerks, and I hiss.

"Good, good," the newcomer murmurs as he enters. In walks a thin, older man dressed in a gray suit. "Clear the room."

~

Tears trickle down my face as my escort from earlier tugs, drags, and pushes me down the hallway.

I feel humiliated and violated after the pelvic exam the 'doc' gave me. He didn't use any of the shiny instruments that were laid on out on the little table for him.

No, he used his fingers, his ungloved fingers, to perform my exam.

"Fucking virgin," the goon gripping my arm growls as we descend the stairs like it's a bad thing.

Pictures of me were taken after the exam. With a gun pointed at my head, I was forced to stand in front of a backdrop while I was photographed from all sides, naked.

Something inside me feels broken. Like a piece inside me is missing. A piece they've taken from me.

I don't even try to fight the guy stomping beside me. In fact, I want to return to the cell, to its safety.

Reaching the bottom of the stairs, I try to tune out the whimpers and cries of the other prisoners, but I can't stop the sounds of despair coming from the youngest ones from affecting me.

There are children here, I know it. Children, for fuck's

sake. I swear I even hear a little boy sniffling for his mommy.

The despair, the humiliation I've been feeling starts to warm until I'm so angry I'm nearly seeing red from it.

The door to my cell is unlocked then pushed open. For a wild, crazy moment, I consider trying to make a grab for the goon's gun.

But then he shoves me inside and slams the door shut behind me.

My shoulders sag and my knees start to give out. I just want to curl up into a little ball and be near Sophia.

Looking around the cell, I spot Amanda sitting up on the bed.

"Where's Sophia?" I ask, my eyes going over the room again, thinking somehow I missed her.

Amanda wipes the back of her hand across her red-rimmed eyes and sniffles. "They took her after you."

8

JOHNATHAN

Placing the small microbud inside of my ear, I shake my head, making sure the transceiver doesn't become dislodged. The little piece of technology is so small, that if not seated properly, it can fall right out with just the slightest movement. When seated correctly, though, it should stay in even if I were getting in a fist fight.

When I don't feel it fall out, I reach in very gently to lightly brush my finger against the microswitch.

"Testing, testing. Touch my testicles," I murmur quietly.

"Fuck you, asshole," comes Andrew's grumble. Thankfully it's at the correct volume.

"If you could stop playing like children..." Simon says quietly.

"What's the range on this again, Simon?" I ask while walking into my bedroom.

"One mile as the crow flies. Thick concrete walls shouldn't be a concern, but if there are too many layers below ground, we might run into trouble."

"I'll do it on the fly then. Any activity on the cameras around the warehouse?"

"Not much. Two limos have entered the property, but nothing has come back out."

Dropping my towel to the floor, I grab a pair of new dress slacks then the new black dress shirt. I've got a lot of suits, but with Simon's insistence, I'm wearing higher quality tonight.

I finish getting dressed and look out my bedroom window to the brand new, blacked out silver Lexus LC. It has all the bells and whistles. How the fuck he got a brand new one of those is beyond me. And while I never usually go for one of these kinds of cars, it sure does have beautiful lines to it.

"Tell Lucifer I'm keeping the car," I say as I turn back to the bathroom to give myself a once-over.

"That car is worth more than your—" Simon starts.

"Now, now, boys, play nice," Lucifer's voice slides through the bud in my ear.

Fuck. I didn't know the big guy was watching over the happenings. He must be doing it from the ops center at his compound. Fuck, that makes three different sets of ears listening in, not counting James and Peter.

Ignoring the elephant in the room, I ask, "James, are you set up yet?"

"In position," comes his soft voice. "I've got eyes on the front."

"Peter?"

"In the rear," he says. "Not much going on, but they've opened up the back gate and I've seen some scuttling. They aren't frenzied, though."

"Move your video feed two degrees to the west," Simon says.

"Stop there," Andrew says. "See those three semi trucks, Simon?"

"Yes. They must have repositioned them. This will be their exit when they are done for the night."

"Agreed. Peter, if they move even the slightest, you need to get behind the one that shows the most strain as it leaves the lot."

"Yeah, I doubt they will have that much hardware in it. So, we're hoping they leave with the slaves in it?"

"That's my guess."

"Simon..." I say as something occurs to me. I'm getting an itchy feeling in the back of my head again. "Or Lucifer. You need to call in more guys. We need to have those trucks tailed, if at all possible. All three of them."

"Why?" Andrew asks.

"A gut feeling."

"Fully understood," Simon says. "I'll pull Phillip and John in. Thaddeus, and James the second, are still in Ohio."

"Have them pulled back as far as possible, Simon," I say. "Use used cars, but not ones that can be traced to us."

There's a silence as everyone on the line begins to work.

Then Andrew breaks through. "You alright, big guy?" he asks me jokingly, but he knows I'm serious.

"Yeah. I got that feeling things are going to get squirrelly quick if we don't have everyone here."

Looking in the mirror, I barely recognize myself. The biggest change to my appearance is my hair being cut short and died a rusty brown. My eyes have gone to a dark brown as well. But there are subtle changes too. The beard has been trimmed in slightly, still shaped long, but now with a kept look to it. Long gone is the look I've carried for so long, and in its place is a man I don't know.

Missy worked wonders on my face, and when I put my contacts in, she said I had a fading resemblance of the real Johnathan, but she could only tell it was me if she looked hard enough.

I suppose it's good I've never tattooed my hands because the neck and body ones are covered easily with how I'm dressed. Slipping on my father's Harvard class ring, I chuckle. Jesus, he would be laughing his ass off now if he could see me.

My old man was one of the rich boy, Harvard elites back when he was young dumb and full of cum. One of those guys from the old-school of business. He and my mom couldn't have been from more different paths of life. She was the daughter of a mechanic and waitress. Teaching in some edge of the city poverty ridden school. They met at some fundraiser where she was pleading for more school supplies, and soon enough, they found that instant-love thing.

I never understood that shit. Instant fairy tale love.

What crap.

"You ready to get moving?" Andrew's voice comes over the earpiece.

"Yeah, give me a second."

Adjusting my tie one last time, I head out of the house and straight to the brand new Lexus. Opening the car door, I get hit by the smell of new leather. Fuck, this thing must have come off the lot as soon as they got it there.

Starting up the engine, I look down at the odometer and see it has less than one fucking mile on it. Holy shit, this is a hot fucking car. I love my bike like it's my significant other, but she's not the warmest of women in the dead of winter.

Just feeling this baby start up so quiet and smooth gets me hard.

Pulling out of the driveway, I look up at my two-story house. It's in the middle of nowhere suburbia. This is the place I rarely, if ever, come to. I don't have a lot of use for a house. The small apartment over the bar suits me more. This is just a shell for me. A mask that Lucifer likes his guys to have to keep up a sense of normalcy for the men.

Especially since Lilith came around.

He likes us to have the family look about us. I think most of us being single guys, who work the darker side of life, don't have much in the family way. I don't. Almost all of the inner circle doesn't either.

Shit, Andrew and Lucifer are the exceptions so far, and all of us have seen how that's been going.

Andrew and his wife are all modern family kind of shit. He's got kids and a wife who fucking adores the shit out of him.

He's been neutered.

Dude's got a ball and chain now on him.

Doesn't go out drinking, only goes to the strip clubs when it's for work. Shit, man, he doesn't do anything fun anymore.

Fucking women and the grip they get on men. I don't know how they stand for it, but they do.

And now I can't quit thinking about Beth. The image of those hazel eyes closing as she leaned in for my kiss.

The way the tequila mixed with something else that tasted dark and sexy, like she was my own piece of dark, dangerous candy.

Her intoxicating scent as we mashed our lips together. Her tongue hesitant at first, perhaps out of practice, but what she lacked in practice she made up for in almost reckless abandon as she pushed her firm breasts into my chest.

Holding herself to me.

Shit and fuck.

She has no right putting herself in my thoughts like that.

They're not the kind I want floating around when I'm getting ready to walk into the fucking lion's den.

Especially since I can't fucking stand the thought of not being the one who buys her.

Not going to lie, at least not to myself. The thought of buying her gives my cock a little jerk, like he's looking up to me and saying, *that's right, big guy, we're about to buy ourselves a fucking little goddess of sexual perfection.*

∽

"Comms check, go for one," I mutter as I bend over, pretending to tie my dress shoe.

"Go for two," James says.

The rest of our crew check in as I stand up, looking around the place.

The security to get into this place was fucking intense. There wasn't a single fucking spot on my body they didn't feel up except my damn ear holes, thankfully.

Shit, even my freshly died hair was ruffled. They got some of that sticky shit Missy put in it on their hands, and I had to crack a grin. Looks like I'm not the only one who doesn't care for the stuff.

As soon as I drove onto the property, I was carefully directed where to park then escorted into the warehouse where the auction will be taking place.

I highly doubt this is the same building they are keeping the merchandise in, though.

They wouldn't be stupid enough for that.

They're going to want a way to protect the livestock as

much as possible from any potential threat beyond their own.

And fuck me. Yep, fuck me with a damn stick.

They're putting me into a private booth.

There's almost a dozen other booths around the one I'm politely, but firmly, shuffled into.

I get a quick look at the other men and women who've arrived around the same time as me and it looks like none of them are freaking out.

But shit, this means I'm more than likely going to be watched and monitored.

The armed man who is escorting me into the booth bows to me with his head before asking in a thick Russian accent, "Would you like a drink?"

Pausing a second, I try to think of a way to get word to the guys listening in about the situation I just got thrust into. "Yeah, rum neat. Will I have a viewing monitor of the live auction from this cube, or will they be strictly online? My... client would prefer that I can see the merchandise alive and moving before I buy."

"It will be on the large monitor." The man points to the screen. "They will be, as you, say moving. It will be on stage."

"Excellent."

"I need the account number we will be taking the money from."

Repeating off the number I memorized to him, I can only hope we have enough in there.

The man leaves the room and I let out just one

grouch. "Fucking stuck in a damn cubicle. How am I supposed to see the merchandise and get a feel for them?"

Simon comes through quickly over the comms. "Clear your throat to answer yes. Are you in a private booth which is most likely monitored?"

Fuck, I feel like a spy or some shit.

Clearing my throat, I hear him curse. "Dammit, this isn't how they normally operate."

"Perhaps they're stepping up the security. The girl's names could have come up to them somehow and they are ensuring this does not go awry," Lucifer's voice comes through in a smooth drawl.

"Find out their bidding method. I was able to hear the representative's words so we should be able to get a better grasp from what he has to say."

It's not long after I take a seat in the comfortable leather chair that the man comes back with my drink. "Your drink, sir."

Accepting the rum, I take a sip only to be shocked by the taste. This isn't a cheap drink. No, the smoothness with which it goes down, and the subtle flavor, lets me instantly know it's a label I probably couldn't afford to drink more than once a year.

"Since my client was not able to attend, I want to become familiar with the bidding methods for tonight's showing."

"I will be with you throughout the bidding, sir. We will bring out the merchandise one at a time. There will be bidding only for that one. Then the next will be brought out. I will be here to send in a bid if you like what you see."

Nodding my head at the small monitor beside the large one on the wall, I ask, "And the second monitor?"

"It will show current price, and it will show lineup. It updates as progress happens."

"Ah, so I'll know what has been bought?"

"Yes."

As if speaking the words were magic, the second screen blinks on. A panel on the left side displays the faces of many women. Under each face is a dollar amount showing what I assume will be the starting bid.

Fuck. There's more faces on there than even I can stomach.

It's only with the grit of my fucking stomach I can ask in an even voice, "How many are for sale tonight?"

"Eighteen, sir."

"What does he mean eighteen?!" Simon hisses in my ear. "It was twenty earlier today."

"Has something changed in the lineup?" I ask as I stare at the one face that has brought me so much fucking heartburn.

Beth is there in front of me, on the small screen, her eyes so lost and haunted. This is not the woman I knew. Not the woman whose bedroom eyes had me feeling like a caveman.

"Ah... We had one bought ahead of schedule. My boss was offered something he could not say no to."

Beth is there, and so is one of her friends. But two of them are not...

"You said one? What about the other?" I ask.

His silence fills the small room and I can't help but clench my fists. Fuck.

"Damn," I hear Andrew through the line.

"We need to know who was bought, and what happened to the other," Simon says.

"Well, I would like to pre-bid on a—"

"It's not possible, I must apologize."

"Is it pricing?"

"No."

Even more fucking silence fills the air as I turn away from the man. I'm radiating calm, cool, and collected.

Fucking radiating it.

But I swear if I could turn around and grab this motherfucker's balls, and yank them all the way up to shove down his throat, I fucking would.

Looking at the small screen, I watch as the faces scroll past.

It's starting up now.

I swear I can feel the fear radiating from the captives through the walls of the cubicle as the main monitor pops on. The background on the screen flickers to life, and there on a pedestal, is the first entry for tonight's auction.

It's a young woman of Asian descent standing there, trying to cover her naked body the best she can.

Watching her eyes darting around in terror pulls at

me, but I'm here on business. And as much as I would like to help, I won't.

The small screen rolls around again and I spot a face has disappeared.

What the fuck?

The Asian woman's face is still there while the bidding takes place, but one of Beth's friends has disappeared.

It's only Beth there now.

There were four fucking women when she came to my bar, and now it's down to her, and I haven't been able to do shit to stop them from disappearing.

Turning my head back to man in the box with me, I ask, "Why am I watching merchandise disappear from the screen? You guys don't want us to all have a shot at bidding?"

"The merchandise has been sold," he says with a shoulder shrug.

Motherfucker. Turning away from him, I know I won't be getting information.

"And it was a virgin. I guess you guys are playing favorites with your buyers," I mutter to the guy.

"Shit," Andrews voice comes over the comm in my ear.

"Peter, look for anyone leaving the property!" Simon all but yells.

"James, try to neutralize any opposition."

"Switch to comms channel two, Peter. James stay on this one," Andrew orders.

Shit, now's when things are going to get dicey.

As if Andrew can sense my unease that things are heating up, his voice comes through the comm. "Keep cool, Johnathan. Nothing to do but move forward."

Fuck! He's right, but I can feel my hand tightening hard around the glass. If Beth disappears off the screen, I have no clue how many people I'll have to kill to get to her.

"Got some movement," James says.

"Roger. Move to comms channel three," Andrew orders.

The bodies flash past me on the screen as I keep my eyes on her picture. Fuck, fuck, fuck.

When it's her turn, my eyes snap up to watch her get paraded out just as all the other women have been. She's been labeled virgin, and it's why my thoughts keep turning back to our kiss. The way she seemed so out of practice…

The bidding instantly leaves the twenty thousand dollar initial reserve price. Fuck, I can see that even if she wasn't a virgin, she would reach higher than most of the women who have been sold.

Without turning my head, I say to the man behind me, "Bid until I've won."

"Sir?" the man asks, and in my ear I hear Simon cursing loudly at me to shut the fuck up.

There's a laugh somewhere on the line, but I can't figure out who it is.

Turning my head from the woman standing there,

naked, her arm across her full breasts with her other hand trying to hide her sex, I say, "I said bid on her until I've won. You've taken options from my client away. *I will win this one.* Do you understand or are you stupid?"

Not bothering to look at him any longer than I must, I turn my eyes back to Beth. Fuck, just the thought of someone looking at her naked form is enraging me. I'm trying to remain cool, but I can feel with each bid from someone else, my blood pressure is rising higher and higher.

The bidding is slowing down, but some asshole keeps bidding up by ten thousand dollars a shot.

Fuck it.

"Five hundred and fifty thousand," I say to the man in the room as I bet past the four hundred thousand mark we're currently at.

It's time to put an end to this fucking shit.

"What did you just fucking say!?" Simon screams in my ear so loudly I can barely keep myself from slapping my ear.

"Five hundred and fifty," the man repeats as he inputs the number into the little pad he's using.

The number was sitting there, waiting for me to bid. And like the fucking asshole I am, I've all but laid my dick out on the table, daring anyone to come and try to measure up to me.

We sit there for a full thirty seconds. I know some asshole out there is probably trying to figure out how high I am willing to go.

"You are the winning bidder. The funds are being taken now."

Standing up from the chair, I say, "Fine."

A flicker on the screen catches my attention, and even though I know I shouldn't bother looking back at it, I do.

God dammit. My stomach drops to the floor and if I could kill every motherfucker here with my bare hands, I would.

There, on the large screen, is a boy no older than six. Blue-eyed, brown hair, with fair skin and freckles. He looks like the Norman Rockwell boy.

The bidding jumps quickly to ninety thousand, but then starts to taper off.

"I want to win this bid too. Put two hundred thousand on the table now," I say, trying not to growl.

"Yes, sir." He must be used to my ways because he doesn't even bat an eye.

"What the actual fuck?" Simon says in disbelief.

Thirty seconds later and I'm now the proud owner of Beth and some little boy.

Looking through the rest of the auction roster, nothing else stands out.

I'm already in way over my head, but fuck it. Sometimes you do what you must.

Standing back up from my chair, I walk over to the man and motion to the door for our cubicle.

"I'm done here."

"Sir, the auction is still going on. I assure you there are more to bid on."

Towering over him, I look down in his eyes. "I said I'm done."

I'll give the Russian prick some credit, he holds out on me for a full second before licking his lips nervously. "I will take you to processing now, yes?"

Motioning to the door, I say, "Yes. Get my client's property ready for transportation."

SIMON CONTINUES to berate me as I stand quietly in a corner office, looking out the small dirty window. Walking to this office gave me a chance to look into the windows of others, and while I'm not the only person waiting in one of these booths, there aren't that many other people.

Behind me, the door opens, and when I turn around I see Beth getting shoved into the office with a black hood over her head. Her body has finally been dressed in a hospital gown. The boy follows behind her in a pair of pajamas.

Fucking hell.

The little boy has his hands clutched tightly on her arm as he whimpers under his black hood.

"Your property, sir," my Russian aid says to me.

"Thanks. Can we leave now?"

I can see Beth's shoulders jerk in response to my words. I don't know if she recognized my voice, but something in her posture has changed.

Fuck, I need to get them out of here.

Nodding his head, he walks forward. He has two chain collars, the kind they put on dogs, in his hands. Dropping them over the two's heads, he gives each attached leash a test pull.

The resulting gagging sounds turn my stomach into a raging inferno.

Snapping the leashes from his hands, I growl at him, "Do not harm my client's property."

Pulling on the leashes, I walk out of the office and head back down the hall they led me through. I don't yank on the leashes, but I make sure they don't have time to lag behind.

Marching through the warehouse then out into the pitch-black night, I head to my car. Keeping them close, I start muttering under my breath when I get close to the car. "I'm out. Two in tow."

"Roger. One is out of building with two friendlies coming out."

James's voice comes through the comm. "Got two Russian dicks watching you through the widows. Another five surrounding the property."

Getting to the Lexus, I push the boy into backseat and fasten his seatbelt as quickly as I can. Then I grab Beth by the arm and pull her to the front passenger seat.

Whatever she thought when she heard me speak back in the office has been forgotten as she quietly tries to struggle out of my hands.

Her flight or fight response is kicking in as I open the car door.

Grabbing the top of the bag, I yank her head close to my lips and growl in her ear. "Beth, calm the fucking hell down."

Her body goes limp and I'm thankfully fast enough to catch her. Lifting her in my arms, I settle her in the seat before strapping her into the car.

When I finally get into my seat, I let out a deep breath. Almost done here, I just need to get the fuck out of here.

In my mind, I feel like some Russian prick is watching us, lifting his automatic rifle to aim it at us as he gets an order to shoot.

Pulling out onto a main road, I say to Andrew, "I need a new car and I need it fast. This one will be tracked, I'm willing to bet my life on it."

"Got it. Will have a rolling trade-off set up. Leave the city going west."

"Roger," I say as I lean over to pull the hood off of Beth's head.

She looks around with a mixture of hope and fear, then we pass under an overhead light.

She looks at me and then her eyes widen in fear. Fuck, my disguise is working too well.

"Beth, it's me. It's Johnathan."

9

BETH

I stare hard at the face that looks somewhat familiar to me. His hair is shorter, his eyes are a different color, and his skin is caked in makeup.

Reaching up, I yank the tape covering my mouth off, wince from the pain, then I blurt out, "What the fuck? What the actual fuck, Johnathan?"

Did this asshole really just buy me?

"Hold that thought," he rumbles at me, and then the car takes a sharp turn to the left. I have to reach out and grab onto the door handle to keep myself upright.

His eyes slide up and lock on the rearview mirror. He stares hard at the mirror as if he thinks someone is following us, and I stare at him.

A million thoughts run through my head. "Why did you—"

"Yeah, I see him," he murmurs and, it takes me a second to realize he's not talking to me.

"Roger that."

We take another sharp turn, this time to the right, and then we burst forward as he guns the gas.

My heart starts to quicken with excitement as we make turn after turn. The way he's driving, the way he's talking to someone I can't see... is this a rescue mission? It has to be.

I take a new, longer look at him, and really burn him into my eyes. He's dressed in a dark, expensive suit and he looks almost civilized now with his beard trimmed.

Somehow, someway, my father must know him and hired him. Or maybe he knows Sophia's father. Or even Lindsey's...

Lindsey, shit.

Gripping the door handle tightly, an image of her lying in a pool of blood flashes through my head.

"ETA two minutes," Johnathan murmurs, pulling me out of the memory.

Glancing over to my window, I take in the night sky and all the glittering lights of the city. It looks like life has gone on as normal while my friends and I were trapped in our own little version of hell.

How long was I held in that little room? How many nights have passed since we were grabbed? It felt like an eternity, but I bet only a couple of nights have passed.

A little whimper comes from the backseat, sending a chill down my spine, and I immediately twist around in my seat.

"Jesus," I breathe out when I spot a little kid with a black bag over their head.

They're curled up in the corner between the seat and the door. They must be the little one I sensed holding on to me when we were lead out to Johnathan.

I glance over at Johnathan but his eyes are still focused on the road.

Is he rescuing this kid too? He better be because if he's not, I am.

The little one whimpers again and my heart squeezes in sympathy for them.

"Hey, it's going to be okay," I quietly try to reassure them.

The car begins to slow before coming to a complete stop. I turn back around to see what's going on. It looks like we're parking in a dark, empty parking lot.

"Yeah, we're at the first rendezvous," Johnathan says, and then looks over to me.

Something dark flashes in his eyes and the air seems to thicken as he stares at me. There's something in the way he's looking at me, something almost... possessive in his eyes.

This is a rescue mission, yes? Yet, if he's my hero, why is he looking at me like he's the villain?

He starts to reach for me and instinctively I shrink away. I freeze up as I press against the door and watch him like a hawk as he reaches down to my lap. I watch his eyes drop, lingering on my legs, the tips of his huge fingers hovering above them.

Then he suddenly seems to snap out of whatever trance he's in and unbuckles my seatbelt.

"Beth, get out of the car," he says, his voice so husky and thick he has to clear his throat from it.

Not needing to be told twice, I reach over, yank hard on the handle of the door, and push it open. Stepping outside, the cool night breeze hits me and causes the flimsy little gown I'm wearing to flutter around me.

I'm not sure what just happened in the car but I'm grateful to escape it.

Before Johnathan can stop me, I step up to the back door and yank it open too.

Reaching in, I immediately pull the black silk bag off the kid and reveal a head full of brown hair.

"Hey," I say softly, and force a smile I'm so not feeling right now for the frightened little boy looking up at me. "It's okay. I promise I'm not going to hurt you."

Despite my smile and reassurance, the little boy still shies away from me. His big blue eyes watch me warily as I reach in to undo his seatbelt.

Dammit, I knew they had children in there. *I knew it.* Yet, a part of me just really hoped I was wrong. If I had any faith left in humanity, this little boy's haunted eyes would utterly destroy it.

"Stop fucking staring, asshole," I hear Johnathan growl angrily and cast a quick glance over my shoulder.

He's not talking to me, is he?

"Hey, sorry, man," someone chuckles. I can't see who it is because Johnathan is standing behind me now, blocking me with his huge body. "I didn't realize there was a full moon out tonight. I couldn't stop looking."

"Keep looking at her like that and I'll tear your fucking eyes out of your goddamn skull."

It takes me a moment to realize they're talking about me. My cheeks ignite with heat as I realize that my ass is out for the whole world to see. Reaching behind myself, I grab the thin gown as best as I can but keep my other hand out for the little boy to take.

"Here, take my hand, please," I plead to the boy.

He shakes his head and begins to scoot away from me.

I swallow down my sigh and keep the smile plastered on my lips. "I only want to help you. I was... sold too."

The little boy stops scooting away from me, and I can tell he really wants to trust me, but he's afraid.

Dropping my voice to a whisper, I lean further into the car to tell him, "I'm scared too."

The boy looks at me for a long moment and then he asks, "You are?"

I nod my head, and cast another quick glance over my shoulder at Johnathan. "Yes."

The boy scoots a little closer to me. "Is he going to hurt us?"

"No," I say and shake my head. I don't know what's going to happen, and I don't know what kind of man Johnathan is, but, "I swear, I won't let anyone hurt you."

The little boy scoots a little closer and his voice cracks as he asks, "You promise?"

"Come on, we gotta go, Beth," Johnathan says impatiently.

My smile grows a little wider as the little boy scoots even closer and reaches out for my hand. "Cross my heart."

Once the little boy places his hand in mine, I use it to pull him out of the car, and then wrap my arms around him. His little arms wrap around my waist and he clings to me like I'm his bastion of protection.

"Come on," Johnathan says, and jerks his chin towards the parking lot. "We gotta change cars."

I nod my head, and with the little boy clinging to my side, follow him across the dark parking lot.

~

There's a moment of awkwardness when we reach the older blue Civic that's been left running for us.

Johnathan pulls open the back door and scowls as soon as I slide into the backseat with the little boy still clinging to me. Our eyes meet and I can immediately tell he's not pleased by my seating choice.

He looks like he's about to argue with me, but I shake my head at him.

With a low, rumbling grumble, he slams the door shut and walks around the car. By the time he slides into the driver's seat, I've got both the little boy and myself strapped into our seat belts.

"We're on the move," Johnathan says as we pull out of the parking lot and take a left.

"What's your name?" I whisper softly, hugging the little boy close to me.

"Charlie," he responds, his body relaxing against me.

"Well, Charlie, it's nice to meet you. I'm Elizabeth, but all my friends call me Beth."

There's a few moments of silence and all the questions I want to ask Johnathan roll through my head.

Why did he buy me? How did he even find me? Just who the hell is he?

I thought he was just a gruff biker guy who owns a dive bar, yet with everything going on, it's clear he's more than that.

"It's nice to meet you, Beth," Charlie says so softly and politely I feel myself smiling in the darkness.

I hug him a little closer and he snuggles up against my chest.

"Did you get eyes on all of them?" Johnathan asks and my ears perk up.

"Fuck," he curses. "There's supposed to be three. Yeah, yeah, I know you can count."

"Three, what?" I ask, looking up and meeting his eyes in the rearview mirror.

He takes another right turn and then holds his finger up at me in a sign for me to wait.

His head slightly inclines to the right as he listens to whoever is talking in his ear, and I press my lips together while I wait.

"Well, where the fuck is she?" he asks angrily.

My stomach suddenly sinks. I just know he's talking about Lindsey.

"Did anyone see her coming out?"

"Johnathan," I say, trying to get his attention.

He holds his finger up again. "Do you think they moved her last night?"

"Johnathan," I say again, more forcibly.

He ignores me. "Well, she's gotta be somewhere. Maybe she's still in there. She didn't fall off the fucking—"

I just can't take him talking about finding Lindsey for one second longer.

"Lindsey's dead!" I hiss and he glances up into the rearview mirror in surprise.

Finally, I've got his attention.

"Hold on a minute," he says as we stare at each other.

Just saying that Lindsey is dead out loud has caused this great big painful hole to open up in my chest.

Charlie squeezes me tighter as I push air in and out so fast I'm nearly hyperventilating from it.

I feel like I can't catch my breath.

Johnathan pulls the car over to the side and we come to a stop. He twists around in his seat and turns to face me.

Mouth pulled down in a frown, he looks genuinely concerned as he asks, "Are you alright?"

No, I'm not alright, I'm fucking far from it, and the words almost pass my lips before I realize they may upset the little guy that's holding on to me like his life depends on it.

I have to be strong, I have to be. For him. Whatever I've gone through... it's probably nothing compared to the nightmare he's living.

Squeezing my eyes shut, I take a moment to compose myself before reopening them.

I look Johnathan hard in the eyes and say as calmly as I can, "Yes."

From the way his lips twist and his gaze narrows, I can tell he's not buying my bullshit, but thankfully he's not calling me on it.

Seconds tick by and we just stare at each other. I finally get my breathing under control and I know he's expecting an explanation, but right now I just can't give it.

He breaks eye contact first, his narrowed gaze sliding over to Charlie before coming back to me.

"Are you sure?" he finally asks, breaking the silence.

I bob my head up and down, and close my eyes again.

"Fucking hell," he growls, and I sense him turning around.

The car starts rolling forward and then I'm pushed back against my seat as he hits the gas.

"All three targets are confirmed," he murmurs. "Yeah, I can count, you fucking dipshit." His voice drops even lower, but it's so quiet in the car it's impossible not to overhear him. "Yeah, that's right. I said three. Lindsey Hawthorne is confirmed deceased."

10

BETH

We drive and drive, and I cling to the little boy hugging me, needing his comfort just as much as he needs mine. The bright lights of the city fade away, replaced by the softer, dimmer lights of a residential area.

We pull up in front of a white, two-story house, and the garage door opens. Charlie tenses against me and I try to keep myself from stiffening with apprehension. I don't recognize this house or the neighborhood.

The car rolls slowly into the garage and then the door slides down behind us, closing us in.

"Not tonight, no," Johnathan rumbles as he turns off the car. "We'll meet up tomorr—"

He snorts and shakes his head.

"Yeah, fuck you, Simon. I know who her father is and he can suck my dick."

Big hand lifting up to his ear, Johnathan plucks something out of it and then crushes it in his fist.

Our eyes meet in the mirror and he smirks as he opens up his hand. Tiny little pieces fall, scattering around him, and then he pushes his door open.

Fuck, what did he mean by that? He knows who my father is... yet he seems totally unconcerned by it... Who is this guy? Who does he *think* he is?

The back door on Charlie's side opens and the little boy's arms tighten around me.

"Come on," Johnathan says, and motions for us to get out. "You're staying here for the night."

I give Charlie a little nudge and a smile. "It's okay," I try to say as if I believe it, but honestly I have no clue what the fuck is going on or what is about to happen.

Now that I know Johnathan knows who my father is, knows who I am, and obviously doesn't give a fuck, he feels like a loose cannon. Normally, I have the power of my father's protection to fall back on, but what do I do with a guy who obviously doesn't give a shit?

Johnathan takes a step back, and with another nudge and smile from me, Charlie starts to slide out of the backseat with me following behind him.

Just as I get my feet under me and straighten, Charlie latches onto my side with a death grip.

Johnathan glares down at the obviously frightened child and I glare up at him.

"Where are we?" I ask, and quickly glance around the empty garage.

There's nothing on the walls. No lawnmower, no tools, no boxes of Christmas decorations. Honestly, it looks like no one lives here.

Johnathan's glare lifts and his eyes lock on mine. There's so much force, so much power in his gaze, it's everything I can do to keep from looking away in submission.

"My place," he says, and the way he says it sends a shiver down my spine.

Why did he bring us here? Why isn't he returning me to my father? What the fuck does he have planned? I want to ask, but something holds me back. Perhaps it's because Charlie is so frightened I feel the need to protect him, but honestly, I think it's more of my gut telling me I'm not going to like the answers I'll get.

Turning away without offering more of an explanation, Johnathan jerks his chin, expecting us to follow him. "Come on."

He walks up to the only door in the garage, unlocks it, and then pushes it open. Then he walks through the door and into the house as if he just expects us to obey and follow him.

And we do follow after him, like two little lost puppy dogs. Really, what choice do we have?

Lights flicker on, revealing an immaculate kitchen. The place is so clean, so shiny, either he has an amazing housekeeper or he never uses it.

"Are you hungry?" he asks, and my stomach clenches

so tight I don't think I could keep anything down even if I was starving.

I look down at Charlie but he doesn't answer. He's watching Johnathan like he expects him to suddenly sprout a second head or something.

"Are you hungry, Charlie?" I ask him softly and he peeks up at me.

He shakes his head once and then he returns his attention to Johnathan.

Johnathan grunts and nods his head, moving into the living area. Even here, there is only the most basic of furniture. A couch, a TV, a table, and a recliner—all looking unused. There's no painting on the walls, no books in the built-in bookcases.

No photos of family or children.

"I'll show you where you'll be staying for the night," he says without looking back at us.

For the night. Those three words fill me with a sense of relief as we follow behind him. This is only temporary, I think. Merely a rest stop until we move on to our final destination.

Wherever that is.

He leads us through the living area then up a set of carpeted stairs. There's a short hallway and four doors. And there's something about those four closed doors that fills me with a sense of dread.

Walking up to the second door, Johnathan pushes it open but doesn't step in. "The kid will sleep in here."

Charlie's steps slow as we walk down the hallway, and once we reach the open door, he freezes.

"It's alright, Charlie," I say softly and give him a reassuring squeeze. "I'll stay with you."

I understand his reluctance. I was locked inside a room for several days. How long was he locked up before the auction?

Johnathan shakes his head back and forth, and jerks his chin. "Your room is down the hall."

Slowly, I lift my chin in the air and look Johnathan square in the eyes. "I'm staying with him."

A look of anger flashes across Johnathan's features, and I almost deflate with regret. I don't know why he's doing this, and I don't know what's in it for him.

For all I know, he saw an opportunity and he took it.

He may have bought me with the intention of returning me to my father for a huge reward, but why did he buy Charlie too?

Is he into little kids?

The more and more I think about it, the angrier and angrier I get. There's no way I'm leaving Charlie's side. I promised I'd keep him safe and I fucking meant it. If Johnathan has good intentions, he shouldn't care which rooms we sleep in.

Johnathan and I have a stare-off. I'm so not backing down from this.

"Fine," Johnathan finally snaps and runs his fingers angrily through his hair. "Fuck," he mutters softer.

He steps away from the doorway, shakes his head

almost sadly, and then gives me a hard look. "I'll be downstairs if you need me," he rumbles, and then the floor is vibrating as he stomps away.

Charlie and I both turn, watching as he disappears down the steps, taking all the tension with him.

"Are you tired?" I ask Charlie.

Charlie looks up at me and shakes his head.

"Me either," I sigh. "But we should try to get some rest."

DESPITE HIS CLAIM of not being tired, Charlie falls asleep almost instantly once I get him tucked comfortably in bed.

I left the door to the room open, for his benefit.

For my benefit.

After what I've been through, I don't know if I'll ever be able to close a door again.

Staring down at Charlie's sweet face, I'm filled with the strongest need to protect him. Asleep, he looks even more precious, more innocent.

Entirely too vulnerable.

I brush a lock of his brown hair out of his face.

How could anyone hurt him?

Anger begins to boil in the pit of my stomach. Anger for what Charlie has gone through. Anger for what they did to me. To Sophia and Amanda.

Anger that they killed Lindsey, killed her like she was nothing. Killed her like they had the right.

Feed them to the pigs.

A tear of pain rolls down my cheek and it sets off a chain reaction. As my body begins to shudder, I roll away from Charlie, afraid I might wake him. Sitting on the edge of the bed, I bend over and wrap my arms around myself.

Trying my best not to lose my shit.

I've been in survival mode for so long, now that we're here, in a perfectly normal house, in a perfectly normal room, I don't know how to process it. I want to feel safe, I want to *be* safe, yet I know we're not out of danger yet.

As if he's conjured from my thoughts, a shadow appears in the hallway. Looming tall in the darkness.

Tipping my head back, I peer up at Johnathan.

Is he an angel or a devil?

Did he save me or does he have some other nefarious plan?

"Beth," he says softly, almost tenderly, but there's a strange edge to it.

Wiping the tears from my cheeks, I take a deep breath. I feel myself standing, some invisible cord drawing me to him.

His jacket is gone and so is his tie. The collar of his white shirt is open, his shirt-sleeves are rolled up. Tattoos twist and spiral up his forearms.

He's a wolf in sheep's clothing, and as I walk up to him, the way he watches me, I feel like a fucking lamb.

Stopping in front of him, I resist the urge to cover myself. Resist the urge to shiver. He's radiating so much tension, so much heat, I suddenly feel cold.

"Did you... did your... people find Amanda and Sophia?" I ask softly.

The need to know that they're okay, that they're safe, is the only thing that matters to me at this moment.

He nods his head.

Relief flows through me and it's so strong, so overwhelming, I nearly crumble from it.

"Are they okay?" I ask, my voice cracking with emotion.

He nods his head again and takes a step toward me.

Thank god. Thank fucking god. Now that I know that they're both safe, I'll finally be able to rest.

"Thank you," I whisper so softly the words sound like a wispy breath.

I owe so much to him.

His eyes slide over my head, towards the little boy sleeping on the bed, then slide back again.

There's so much tension in the air, so much *restraint*, that the air is fairly crackling with it.

The way he's looking at me now, I can't tell if he wants to kiss me or if he wants to break my neck.

Self-preservation causes me to take a step back. Nervously, I lick my lips before I ask my next question.

How do I ask him if he's a good guy or a bad guy without pissing him off?

Something dark flashes in his eyes and without speaking he extends his arm and holds out his hand.

I stare down at the hand, at his offering.

Somehow I know if I accept it, if I place my hand in his, there's no going back.

I hesitate, not yet willing to take the next step that closes the distance between us.

I'm safe here in this room. At least, I think I am…

"Why did you bring me here?" I ask quietly, not realizing the danger I'm in.

Before I can escape, his hand is closing over mine and yanking me back. With a startled cry, he pulls me into the dark hallway.

"Johnathan," I gasp, my senses reeling as he pushes me up against the wall.

His mouth smashes against my mouth, not giving me a chance to protest. His beard scrapes against my chin, against my cheeks.

His leg wedges its way between my legs and I feel his knee pressing against my sex.

His entire being overwhelms me. His size, his scent, his touch. Everything about him wraps around me, flooding my senses.

His lips push against mine. Hungry. Urging. Desperate.

I want to give in, I do, but there's something still holding me back.

Grabbing me by the face, his lips push and push, demanding that I open for him.

Fear wars with the desire coiling in my belly. I don't know what I'm doing, I don't know how to do this.

Everything is happening so fast.

I start to fight him. My hands push at his chest, my head tries to twist and turn away. I just need a minute, but his grip tightens.

"Beth," he growls in frustration, the vibrations tickling my lips. "Open for me."

"Why?" I ask, the word going around and around in my head.

Why did he buy me? Why did he bring me here, to his house? Why is he doing this?

"Because we still got something to work out," he groans, and then resumes his assault on my lips.

His mouth slants over mine, over and over again. He's not going to give up. No, if anything, my resistance only seems to make him that more demanding. That more persistent.

He pushes and pulls, and with each suck, with each growl, I feel like something inside me is about to snap.

Just when I feel like I can stand no more, just when I'm about to give in, his teeth sink into my bottom lip.

I gasp in pain and my lips part just enough for his tongue to find entrance.

He invades my mouth. His taste overtakes me, and his groan of pleasure slides down my throat.

His tongue touches mine and I feel this horrible, wonderful *zing* behind my ribs. With each stroke, with each glide, I start to weaken.

"Beth," he groans into my mouth and presses closer.

His chest crushes against my breasts, and his knee moves only to be replaced by something just as hard. Something that begins to grind rhythmically against my sex.

I find myself picking up the rhythm, picking up his desperation. Our hips roll in tandem as I chase the pleasure building in my core.

"I haven't been able to stop thinking about you," he rasps against my lips.

This is nothing like the first time we kissed in his bar. There, we were just two strangers caving into our drunken lust.

Here, I feel like there's more to it. There's too much need, too much desperation on his part for this to be just a simple moment of lust.

And I don't want it to stop. No, something inside me needs this. Needs him.

I want to let go. I want to get lost in him.

I melt into his body as his hands grip me, squeezing me, trapping me in his tight hold. He continues to push into me, continues to kiss me like he's trying to pour his very soul into me.

He feels so good, so warm. So fucking big and strong.

I rock my hips forward, my clit pulsing and aching, while moaning into his mouth.

Suddenly he breaks the kiss, pulling away, and I cry out at the loss of him. I pant, staring at him in confusion.

Why the fuck did he just stop?

Leaning back, his eyes gleam triumphantly in the dim light, and then he sweeps me up into his arms.

"I've gone through a lot of trouble to have you," he growls huskily into my ear before carrying me down the hall.

11

BETH

Johnathan carries me through the open doorway at the end of the hall and uses his foot to shut the door.

My breathing quickens and my heart flutters with panic. I twist and try to escape his arms as he carries me over to the bed and lowers me down.

"Wait," I gasp as he grabs the bottom of my paper-thin gown. I wanted this, I did, but now that it's about to happen I'm scared shitless. Maybe if he knows the truth it will change his mind. "I've never been with a man before."

The corners of his lips curl up as he grins, "I know."

The pleasure from earlier is nearly forgotten, nearly overwhelmed by my fear.

He's really going to do this... He's really going to be my first.

My gown is yanked up, over my head, and I'm left

with nothing covering my body. Nothing shielding me from his hungry eyes.

Nothing shielding me from him.

He stares at me long and hard, his eyes drinking me in. Frantically glancing side to side, I grab a pillow and use it to cover myself.

He rips it out of my hands.

"Johnathan, *please*," I plead. "I'm scared."

The pillow goes flying and he grabs me by the ankles, dragging me closer to him.

"Don't worry," he rumbles almost soothingly as his knee drops to the bed. "There's nothing to be afraid of."

That's easy for you to say, I think. He's done this before. I bet he's had hundreds of women... and probably in this bed.

I stare up at him, my breasts rising and falling with my panting.

His head dips down and his mouth comes down on my breast. As he pulls back a gentle suckle, all other thoughts go flying out of my head.

God, that feels so good.

His tongue swirls around and around, and the coarse hair of his beard tickles my skin. My nipple tightens in his mouth, becoming as small and hard as a diamond.

Teeth scrape across the tip and something inside of me clenches. He pulls back another suckle, this one harder than before, and I squirm.

Inside me, pleasure and fear continue to war, and I'm

not sure which will win. I want to push him away. Yet, I also want to pull him closer.

As his mouth works me over, laving and worshipping one breast before moving on to the other, I can't help but wonder what comes next. What can he do to me? What can he make me feel?

My skin warms and tingles in anticipation.

"Fuck, you taste so fucking good," he breathes out, his head coming up for air. "I've been waiting three fucking days to do this."

With a growl, he grabs my breasts and squeezes them in his big hands. For the first time, I realize he has callouses. Callouses that scrape and dig into my flesh.

He squeezes and squeezes, molding my globes in his rough hands.

I feel myself arching up, feel myself pushing myself into his grip. I shouldn't want this, I shouldn't, but I'd be lying to myself if I said I didn't like it.

Maybe it's because I was so close to death, but right now, in his hands, for the first time in three days, I finally feel *alive*.

"*Fuck*... these tits. I want to fuck these tits," he grunts, and it's so dirty to me, so scandalous, I don't know how to respond to it.

No man has ever talked to me like this before. No man has ever *handled* me like this before.

I'm more than a little floored by it.

His hips rock forward, and I feel the hard bulge in his pants prodding at my sex.

"Three fucking days," he growls, and his grip on me suddenly tightens. "Three fucking *long* days I've had to wait to get you in my bed."

I cry out as his hardness rubs against my clit.

"Three days I've been thinking about fucking you, Beth," he rumbles with another roll of his hips. "Thinking about how I'm going to take you, how I'm going to fucking *claim* you."

He gives my breasts one last squeeze and then he begins to slide down. His lips and beard drag down my tummy, and his eyes remain locked on mine, full of dark intent.

I start to panic as he nears my belly button.

"What are you doing?" I gasp and start to sit up.

His hands come down on my breasts and he pushes me back down to the bed.

"Enjoying what I bought," he grins and looks down.

I squirm beneath his appraisal, never before feeling so revealed, so vulnerable. And just when I think it can't get any worse, that I can't feel anymore humiliated, his hands come down to my thighs and he spreads me wide open.

"Beautiful," he growls.

"Oh, god," I groan and try to arch away from him.

Hands locked around my thighs, he holds me in place as his head dips down. I feel the tickle of his beard before I feel his tongue dragging through my folds.

"So fucking innocent," he rumbles, and I reach down, trying to push his head away.

He growls and resists my push.

The tip of his tongue flicks against my clit. The jolt of sensation that courses through me is so strong, so intense, I jerk.

"So fucking sweet," he says appreciatively, and drags his tongue through my folds again.

He laps at me and suckles my clit into his hot mouth until I'm coming undone, my reservations forgotten.

I don't even realize when his hand moves. I'm so caught up in the pleasure and new sensations, I'm spreading my legs eagerly for him.

My head thrashes from side to side and all these little throaty moans keep pouring from my lips.

When I touched myself alone in my room at night, it never felt like *this*.

Hands now gripping at his hair, tugging, I try to pull him closer in encouragement.

His tongue presses hard against my clit, swirling around and around, and then something hard is probing at my entrance.

"So fucking *tight*," he groans, his warm breath washing over all the wetness he left.

There's a slight pinch, and then that hard thing slides through my wetness, spreading me open.

I whimper and try to close my legs, locking my thighs around his head. It doesn't stop him. No, if anything, it makes his mouth that more ravenous.

The pain is uncomfortable at first, but then, strangely,

it seems to amplify all the pleasurable sensations I'm experiencing.

"Fuck," he rasps as I feel myself clenching around him, trying to pull him in. He's almost there. So close to where I need it. "You like that, baby?"

The hard thing works in and out of me, gliding along with my wetness. This incredible pressure begins to build inside me, filling me with warmth and neediness.

I begin to rock my hips, chasing... something. I don't know what. An explosion. The end?

I'm so swollen, so tender, I can feel my pulse throbbing in my clit.

Then I feel fuller, stretching wider. It's another finger, I realize.

His fingers are inside me.

Before I can adjust to the new fullness, his fingers curl inside me and I'm crying out, twitching and jerking as he rubs against a spot that's extremely sensitive.

It's more than I can take at the moment.

"Relax," he growls as I tighten around him.

But I can't. The sensation too much, too strong.

"Johnathan, *please*, it's too much," I gasp. I don't want him to stop, but what he's doing is too overwhelming.

"You're still too fucking tight," he grits out like his teeth are clenched, but his fingers uncurl. "I'll split you in half."

I know I should be afraid but somehow I'm not. Just the thought of having him inside me, stretching me, breaking me, has me clenching my thighs around his head in anticipation.

The fear is gone, replaced by something more primal, something more basic.

The need to get off.

In and out he pumps his slick digits, and the pressure inside me expands and expands.

My hips rock up and I find myself grinding myself shamelessly into his face as his mouth comes back down on my clit.

He sucks and sucks, pulling me hard into his mouth. Then his teeth bite down giving me a light pinch.

The explosion begins in my center and ripples out. I cry out, squeezing around his fingers as my limbs twitch and jerk.

Johnathan grunts and makes these throaty noises of approval as he licks me up like he just can't get enough.

Waves of pleasure roll through me, sweeping over me, until I feel weak and rung out. I don't know how long it goes on for but the entire time he's growling and devouring me with his mouth.

As the last little spasm fades away, I release my death grip on his hair and collapse against the bed, almost ready to pass out.

Johnathan gives my clit one last playful lick, and I'm so sensitive, I can't help but squeak before his head pops up.

He hovers above me, staring down at me with a glistening beard and eyes full of hunger and *want*.

What I just experienced, what I felt, I've never felt anything like it before. It was amazing, but at the same time it's absolutely terrifying. This man, this *stranger*, has the ability to strip away all my resistance and make me like it with just his touch.

Staring into his eyes, a little pang of fear spikes in my chest, but then he slowly withdraws his fingers, deliberately drawing the sensation out.

I squirm and writhe against the bed, unsure if I want his fingers to leave me or if I want them slamming back into my core.

"Fuck, I've got to be in you *now*," he groans.

Reaching down, he quickly unbuttons his shirt. A chest is revealed, a hard chest, covered in tattoos and hair.

For too many moments, I'm frozen, my brain still hazy from the orgasm as I watch him undress. There's a rushed frenzy to the process. A couple of buttons go flying. Stitches pop from their seams.

It's not until he shoves his pants down and his cock springs upwards that I burst into action. I start to scramble away, heading for the headboard.

He comes down on top of me.

"Get back here, you," he says, dragging me back down and fitting me beneath him.

His skin meets my skin and I shiver from his warmth.

I just let him violate me in the most intimate of ways, and enjoyed the hell out of it, but now that he's about to penetrate me, I'm scared as hell.

His leg presses against my leg and I can't help but marvel at the hair tickling my inner thigh.

He's so big, so hairy and intimidating, as he looms above me, he's downright beastly.

I look down between us, at his cock pressing into my stomach.

He's hard everywhere I'm soft.

"Johnathan—" I say, my voice breathy and full of uncertainty.

His mouth smothers my mouth, cutting my words off. He kisses me hard and deep, as if his mouth is trying to eat my mouth.

His weight begins to sink me down into the mattress and an unfamiliar need begins to awaken inside me.

Fuck, there's just something about having this gruff man on top of me that is making me hot.

God, I'm so fucked.

A big hand covers my breast, squeezing gently at first, until I start to arch into his touch. His calloused palm flattens my nipple and then his fingers are roughly kneading me until I'm moaning into his mouth.

Gently, he rocks his hips, stroking my belly with his velvety cock.

He eases me into the rhythm, his tongue tangling with my tongue.

Just when I start to rock my hips, my clit reawakening with a needy throb, he tears his mouth away from my mouth.

Looking deep into my eyes, there's an eagerness there

I'm not familiar with. He looks at me like I'm the most beautiful, most desirable woman in the world.

Reaching between us, he takes his cock in his hand and rubs it against me in tight little circles.

I groan, relishing the newly discovered pleasure of feeling his silky flesh gliding against my clit.

"This is going to hurt," he states almost eagerly.

He guides his cock down until the crown is pressing against my entrance.

Before I can pull away, before I can stiffen in preparation, he grabs up my hands and slams forward.

He penetrates me with one deep thrust.

I scream, but his mouth is instantly there, muffling the force.

Searing, agonizing pain burns through my pussy, and I swear he just tore me apart.

I start to fight him. Twisting and turning beneath him. My hands try to jerk out of his grip as my hips try to buck him off.

"I'm sorry, baby," he murmurs as he kisses me gently, but I don't truly believe he's sorry.

No, he looked way too damn eager before he slammed into me, and I tell him just that.

He wanted to hurt me, he wanted to destroy me.

He releases his grip on my hands to cradle my face.

He kisses my lips again and then his lips move to my soaked cheeks. Tasting my tears.

I punch and slap at him, but it doesn't stop him. He

whispers sweet endearments as he kisses and strokes me gently.

He tells me how beautiful I am, how perfect I am.

How good it feels to be inside me.

Gradually, the pain begins to fade away, and the punches and slaps become less satisfying with each tender spoken word.

I allow myself to relax beneath him and the burning in my core dulls to a faint throb.

Sensing my submission, his words take a dirty turn.

"You're so fucking tight," he rasps, sounding almost agonized. Deep inside me I feel something pulse. "Can you feel how perfectly your little pussy fits around me? You were made to take my cock."

I begin to shake my head in denial, but his fingers tighten around my face as he slowly, so slowly, slides his cock out. "Yes, Beth."

Suddenly, he slams back in.

I whimper as the pain fades under a spike of pleasure.

His hand slides up, his fingers fisting in my hair. With a tug, he's arching my head back as he growls, "Why do you think I bought you?"

Out, he slides, only to slam back in to the hilt.

Smashing my clit in the process.

"I'm not your fucking hero," he growls as he withdraws.

I shudder, instantly missing the pressure against my little bundle of nerves.

He slams back in, so hard, so deep, so damn gratifying, I cry out.

"I bought you because I want to own you," he grunts as he grinds himself deep, touching parts of me no one has touched before.

I try to stiffen beneath him, hating that my hips want to rise up. Hating that my legs want to wrap around him to keep him right where he is... right where I feel so full.

He grinds and grinds, rolling his hips as he works himself against me.

And with each roll of his hips, with each smash against my throbbing clit, I feel the walls of my resistance crumbling down.

Just as I begin to tighten up around him, stiffening in anticipation, he gives me one more deep, rolling grind of his hips and then quickly pulls out.

I pant up at him in confusion. I was so close, so damn close.

"I bought you because the moment you walked into my bar, you were *mine*," he states as something dangerous flashes in his eyes.

I try to brace myself for what's to come, but then he reaches down and grabs my hips, tilting them up before he comes back down.

"I bought you because I want my cock to be the only cock you ever know."

He drives forward and the pleasure that slams into me is so strong, so intense, I can't stand it.

I start to fight off the orgasm, willing my body to shut it down.

But there's no reprieve, no chance to escape the sensations he's forcing on me.

I'm pinned beneath him, trapped against the mattress, as he drives himself into me.

Over and over again.

His skin slapping against my skin.

His will threatening to overpower my will.

He fucks me almost as if he's trying to punish me. He fucks me almost as if he's trying to punish himself.

I rock beneath him as his body crashes into my body. Assaulted by pleasure I never asked for, by pleasure I've never known.

"Come," he demands, as his thrusts become harder. Fiercer.

I try to arch away from him, my hands shoving at his chest, trying to push him off. But my hips. My damn hips rock up, pressing into him.

Begging him for more.

"Come," he demands again, the look on his face strained and intense.

But I can't let him do this to me. I can't.

The pressure building inside of me is stronger, different than it was before. Once I go over this edge, I know I'll never come back.

"Come, goddammit," he snarls with determination, and I feel his hand release my hip.

Then that hand is there, between us.

Playing with my clit.

"Beth, goddammit. *Beth.* Come for me, baby," he groans, sounding nearly desperate, and then suddenly I'm there.

I lock up around him and the pleasure that rocks through me isn't warm, liquid waves of bliss.

No, it's a fucking typhoon.

"Fuck," I hear him roar out as my pussy clamps down on his cock.

Squeezing him.

I cling to him as the pleasure threatens to tear me away and destroy me with its force.

"Fuck, fuck, fuck..." he repeats over and over, and vaguely I'm aware of him filling me up.

Pumping me full of something hot.

My orgasm goes on and on, and for a moment I fear it will never let me go.

But then Johnathan is there, pulling me closer as he gently rocks inside me.

"That's it, baby," he coaxes me as I finally start to come down. "Take all you want."

His hand brushes back my hair tenderly, and I realize my pussy is still milking his cock.

Suddenly, a little aftershock rolls through me, leaving me jerking and twitching before I can finally still.

I slump in his arms, breathless and dazed.

"Good girl," Johnathan grins as he slides out of me and nuzzles his nose against my nose.

Despite the little jolt of pleasure coursing up my

spine, I have the sudden, overwhelming urge to punch him in the throat.

Good girl? Seriously?

He chuckles as I stiffen, and then rolls over onto his back, taking me with him. He tries to squeeze me up against his side but I start to fight back.

"Where do you think you're going?" he asks, his voice an amused rumble.

"Home," I croak out.

I just let this guy utterly destroy me and I've suddenly realized there's more to be afraid of than having sex.

My throat feels raw and I don't know why at first. Then my cheeks ignite into flames as I realize I must have done a lot of moaning and screaming.

"Nah," Johnathan says easily as his arm locks up around me. He drags me closer, against my will, and presses me against his hairy chest. "I think I'll keep you right here."

"Keep me?" I repeat a little incredulously and try to push up, off his chest, only to have him push me back down.

"Yeah, keep you," he says looking down at me. Something flickers in his eyes and I feel frozen as my worse fear suddenly comes true. "Have you forgotten already? I bought you, Beth. I fucking *own* you."

12

JOHNATHAN

Normally, when I wake up next to a warm female body, my thoughts are pretty precise—why the fuck is she still hanging around?

Now those thoughts aren't there, and if I hadn't solidified my ownership of Beth last night, I would still be feeling contentment with having her here.

Fuck, that's not good.

I was only joking to myself when I thought I could let her go after a couple of good fucks in the sack. Not now.

No, not now.

She's fucking mine. I bought her and I sure as fuck intend to keep her.

Last night, my racing mind went through all the implications of those thoughts.

Lying next to her kept me from falling asleep. Even when her breathing went slow and deep, her body did this jerking thing a couple times, and I have no doubt it's because she was dreaming of her past few days.

Those dreams of hers are what kept me up.

The thought that she had to go through something like that. The knowledge that she's far from safe right now and she's blissfully unaware, it's going to be a fucking issue.

I can feel it.

She doesn't have the real world awareness to understand that us *'rescuing'* her from the Russians was only the beginning of a shit storm.

Beth's old life is gone. One fucking night of fun and its fucking gone. Fate? Karma? Bad decisions? None of that fucking matters.

It is what it is.

She didn't do anything wrong, she made no bad choices. If anything, she should still be locked up in the ivory tower her father left her in.

I've read the files on her life, I know the tyrannical rule of her father.

She's been fucked from day one of her life. And now she's even more fucked.

Well, fucked by me, and just fucked in general.

She can't go back to her old life, that's going to be impossible. It will not work or happen. The moment the Russians spot her at her father's side, she's dead. She knows too much, has seen too many faces.

I don't give two fucks about Lucifer's plans, she won't be his fucking tool.

The vibrating on my nightstand sounds harsh in the deadly quiet house. Pulling my arm from under Beth's head, I snatch the phone from the table and stand up.

"What is it?"

"So you've finally decided to answer the phone? Do I need—" Simon starts in on me and his voice sounds shitty. Probably using speaker phone.

"Fucking shut up, you fucking arachnid. What the hell do you want?"

There's a long silence and I can hear his breathing come out in a hiss. "You fucking Neanderthal. Do you have any idea what you are doing? You were ordered to specifically bring the woman to us, and you couldn't even do that. You even bought a child. You were expressly told to bring us the woman. Everything else was to be igno—"

My voice is low, but I put as much menace in it as I can. "Simon, if you say one more fucking word about the kid... *I. Will. Fucking. End. You.*"

The long silence between our words rings out. We're both breathing heavily, and I can feel his sheer anger through the phone.

I leave the room as quietly as I can to keep from waking Beth.

I know she's more than likely playing possum. Her breath is too shallow, her body too unnaturally still.

Shutting the door, I walk down the hall, past the room where the kid is curled up in a ball under the blanket. He's so fucking small... It's like looking at a wounded animal turning in on itself.

"Gentleman, I believe we need to restart this conversation," Lucifer's slow drawl comes through the line, and I know instantly he's been listening the whole time, watching the little drama play out.

He's been getting a feel of the situation. Looking at all the angles and lines this little episode shows.

"Yes, sir," I answer first. "What is it you want, Simon?"

"Why did you not bring the woman here?" he asks, and I can tell he is forcing the civility out his ass.

"I bought her, she's mine," I say, and as soon as the words leave my mouth, I figure that right there was stupid.

It lays my thoughts and feelings out bare for the world and the devil himself to see.

"That money was from my accounts, Johnathan," Lucifer says calmly, but I can hear the annoyance in his voice.

"And I have more than enough money to pay you back for both purchases, which I will be doing today. Even with interest it won't be an issue."

"That's convenient," Simon snarls. "But that isn't the issue and you know it very well."

"I didn't bring her back to you because she's mine and I've taken claim of her. Is that what you need to know, Simon?"

"What exactly do you mean by that?"

I stop looking at the child in his bed and walk down the hallway to the bathroom.

Unleashing a fucking torrent into the bowel, I say,

"She's under my protection. No matter how we look at this situation, she would be as good as dead if we gave her back to her father."

"Explain," Lucifer says, and I can tell both he and Simon know exactly what I'm going to say before I even say it.

"They know who she is, there's too small of a chance they don't. The moment she's spotted anywhere near her father, they will be going all in to take her out. The collateral damage would be too big for us to contain, as well."

"Us? What's this have to do with us if they harm him or her?" Simon asks, and I'm not sure if he's pulling my strings or not, but he sounds generally unaware of the most basic answer.

"It comes down to us not being able to contain our fucking problems in the city. We let the Russians get too big of a head and they're going to take a look at all of us. We can't afford that, not right now."

"That's above your pay grade, Johnathan," Simon mutters.

"He's right, Simon."

There's another long pause.

Then Lucifer says, "That's neither here nor there, for the moment. Johnathan, bring Beth and the child to the offices today. We need to speak with them and get what information we can. We also need to know what was happening behind the scenes."

"Yes, sir."

"Good, and we also need to speak about this buying her for yourself."

"We'll see," I say.

The phone hangs up and I put the phone down on the sink.

Flushing the toilet, I head back to the bedroom. Passing the bedroom with the kid, I see he's slowly waking up. His head is turned towards me and his eyes are staring wide-eyed at me.

Shit.

I'm only in my boxers, this isn't going to be good.

He begins to tremble and I can see his mouth opening to scream, but I shake my head.

Hiding my lower half, I say quietly, "Let me get some pants on. I promise nothing bad is going to happen to you."

He doesn't respond verbally, but his mouth closes tight and a small streak of tears erupts under one of his eyelids.

Well, fuck.

Ducking out of the room, I run down the hall to my bedroom

Beth is sitting on the side of the bed. She's sliding a shirt of mine from the dresser over her top, and I really fight with my instincts to stop and look at the bottom of her breasts before they're covered.

Fuck, I'm only a man dammit.

Torture. It's pure fucking torture watching her get dressed.

Shaking my head, I step quickly to the dresser. I was an asshole to the kid last night, and I can only put it down to needing to get the fuck out of there. Well, also needing to lay claim to my woman.

Yanking on a pair of jeans, I zip up. Beth is watching me with a stunned look as I fly past her. "Stay here. I need to talk to the kid."

"What—" she starts. I wonder if she forgot our little guy was in the house?

Coming to a halt outside of his bedroom, I take a deep breath. Making sure I look calm and composed, I knock lightly on the door jamb.

His head snaps up from where it was hiding on his knees. He's sitting now in a small ball on the bed, his knees up under his chin.

Staring at me with his big, scared eyes makes me feel like an asshole. An asshole for being an adult. An adult he can't trust because too much shit has happened.

"Can I come into your room?" I ask him as gently as I can.

Where I attacked first with Simon, I try to play the softer side of my asshole self with this guy. I'm not good with kids.

Fuck, I'm barely good with adults.

"It's not mine," he says quietly.

"It is now," I say, and keep still. I won't enter that room unless he gives me express permission. "Just like mine and Beth's is down the hall. This is your room, so it's your rules."

He isn't buying it, though, so I sit down just outside of the doorway.

Fuck, I'm getting old.

My knees crack as they go into the same position he's in. Mirror, I have to mirror him. Not the abject fear, but the positioning.

It's like when you interrogate someone, or when you're in a business meeting. When you want someone to come to your side of things, sometimes you have to start out with being just like them. Very slowly you change your postures and gestures. It gives them a lead to follow.

"Last night must have been really scary for you," I say. "Fuck, it's probably more than last night. Right?"

He doesn't answer, he's like a small brick wall of fear.

"How long were you with those guys?" I ask.

Nothing.

Fuck it.

"I was kept up like you were for a couple of months back in my early twenties," I say as I shift a bit, this fucking wood flooring is hard on the ass-bones.

It was more than a couple of months, it was six long fucking months.

"You…" he says quietly after a couple of seconds, but doesn't finish.

"Yeah… I was down in Mexico… You ever heard of that country?"

He nods his small head, and I know that's a good step. He's engaging. This could have taken so much longer, and it probably will if he's as fucked up as I was.

"Well, I was down there acting like an idiot. Drinking alcohol and causing as much trouble as I could. Bunch of guys I use to know back then, we were all young and stupid. Stupid, as can be," I growl.

He flinches, but I think he knows I'm not mad at him. More about the shit that happened.

"They have you in a cage, buddy?" I ask.

Again, a small nod.

"Yeah, they ain't no fun," I say. "See, me and the guys were at this tit… at a bar, I mean. Lots of music. Grown up girls dancing around the bar for us guys to smile at and give money to. Well… we were being stupid, like I said, and when I tell you this, I'm probably going to say it when you become an adult too. Don't throw change at a woman dancing and laugh. It's not smart."

His eyes look confused as he asks, "Why would I do that? That's mean, to throw things."

I want to snicker, but I don't, he's probably right. "Yeah, well, I forgot my manners, and so did the guys I was with."

Nodding at me, he relaxes his arms just slightly and so do I. Mirror, have to be a mirror.

"See, we did that stupid thing, and all these guys who were there took offense to what we were doing. They got us thrown out, and they decided to teach us big, stupid Americans a lesson. See, we were too drunk to really understand how dangerous of a neighborhood we were in, especially since we were the only Americans there. We weren't in the places you travel to for a vacation."

"We ended up walking down a dark street towards what we hoped was the shitty hotel we holed up in for the night."

We were too fucking stupid, full of ourselves, and full of youth. You can't say that to a kid, though, that kind of stupid new adult shit won't make sense to them.

"What happened?" he asks, and I can see the smallest of movements from him. He's leaned in.

"We got attacked by twelve guys. Twelve big, mean men who didn't take kindly to our kind there. They came at us from the front and the back, hitting us with sticks and bottles. Beating the life out of me and another guy named Brent. The other three guys we were with ran off. They slipped the trap and got to bright lights, able to make it back to the hotel, safe and sound."

"But? What about you and Brent?"

"We didn't make it back to the hotel."

My body is here, but somewhere in my mind, I can smell the shit in the gutters, the dirty human bodies as they slam fists and weapons against us.

We fought back pretty damn well, but two against that many never wins.

"We got our asses kicked pretty bad. I had a couple of broken ribs, and my right two fingers were broken badly. That's not counting the cuts and bruises. Had a concussion too, I think. That's where your brain takes a really hard hit and it gets all kinds of fuzzy. By the time they were done beating us, we were knocked unconscious."

"When we were finally noticed it was by the local

police. They also didn't take kindly to people like us, so they dragged us to the jail and left us there for three days. Wouldn't say anything to us. Just left us there. Well, they wouldn't answer me. Brent went into some type of coma. I don't know for sure, but I'm pretty sure if he got treatment he would have been okay."

Shaking my body, I motion to him. "If you can come here, or I can come in, I can show you something."

Charlie looks around himself. He's hasn't been paying attention to the fact I haven't moved from my spot without his permission. "Umm. What is it?"

Letting my legs down, I show him my hands, making fists. "You can see where one of my knuckles got flattened by a guard after he slammed a metal baton on it. He wanted to punish me for being a rich, privileged, white boy. That fucker hated me. Hated me with all his being. He hated Brent too, but Brent was dead by the time they transferred me to the closest prison."

Motioning for me to come in, he looks at my hand as I scoot into the room and sit about five feet from him. Him on the bed, me on the floor.

He needs to know he is above me in his safe place. Gotta keep him feeling confident.

"Brent died?"

"Yeah, he never woke from the coma he got knocked into."

I don't tell him, though, how they beat Brent even when he was unconscious. How they punished him for not waking up. I don't know what they did, but the beating I got for trying to protect his dead body nearly ended me too.

"Dragged me to a prison, where I was the only white guy in a prison full of angry men who wanted my death. Two long months and some change, defending myself every single one of those hours. I remember the nights and the showers where, naked men would try to make me do things. Where I had to fight for my very survival. They do stuff like that to you?" I ask.

I try to make it as gentle as I can, but I need to know if they did that.

If they did, I'm going to have to get some kind of mental help here, more than I can hope to do myself.

Shaking his head, his eyes wide. "No... A... Big guy came to play with me, but the other guys wouldn't let him. I... I don't think he really wanted to play."

Fuck. Thank fuck. "I... know that you don't want to tell me a lot of stuff, and you're scared kid. But you need to know I'm here now. I promise you nobody will ever come near you like that again."

His eyes well up in big, wet pools of tears, and it's all I can do not to move. "They killed mama and daddy."

"I know kid, I know." I open my arms up to him, spreading them wide as he flings himself down from the bed and onto my lap.

What the fuck do I do now? Shit.

"I got ya, kid. I promise."

~

I NEVER KNEW a body could rock and shake as hard as his little body did in my arms.

His wails and moans coming from him in great, gasping heaves and sobs.

He's been so fucking tough through his shitty role, but I think he's finally breaking down to the bottom.

I need to build him up now.

Lifting his tiny body back onto his bed, I tuck the covers around him loosely. I don't want to put any constriction around his body.

Looking around the room, I see how bare and Spartan it is.

In my life, I've lived pretty close to having no ties. Nothing that I couldn't leave behind without a second thought. But this kid can't do that, not yet. It isn't healthy.

He needs ties, he needs things to call his own besides a bed and blanket. I know there are kids out there that don't even have that, but then most of 'em haven't had their parents murdered and almost got sold off to some sick fuck.

I want to shake my head at his lot in life, but that ain't going to fix the shit.

Turning away from my kid, I look straight into the eyes of Beth. She's staring at me with those wide doe-like eyes, deep pools of tears primed to spill down her cheeks.

A hitch in her voice gives me pause. "Was that true?"

"What?"

"What you said about being in a Mexican prison?"

"Yeah," I say, and I walk towards her. I didn't give the

kid the full truth, but it was close enough to suit my needs on what he needed to hear. That he wasn't alone, that you can get past it all.

Maybe.

Closing the door, I grab Beth by the hand, pulling her with me.

There, against the wall just inside our bedroom, I push myself against her supple body. She's wearing one of my shirts, and while she's a little taller than most women, it still hangs down low on her body.

She fights me momentarily as I grab her hands, but I'm not in the mood for games and subtlety right now.

Holding both hands over her head, I smash my mouth against hers. Those eyes stare at me in shock. She's not aware of just how much I need her right now.

How I need the feeling of her body against my own.

Kissing her with the rage inside of me, I try to slow myself, but I can't.

My free hand goes to my pants. Unfastening the button of my pants, my cock goes from just awakening to a full-on rod of steel as I push my knee between her thighs.

I need this connection. I need to be a part of someone, of something, anything. I don't know what stops her fighting, but when I pull away from her mouth she is breathing heavily.

My own breath comes out in gasps.

Slowly, her thighs spread with the help of my hand.

The slickness there is growing as I rub my hand against her silky folds.

She's not going to run now, not when I rub my fingers through her growing heat.

Finding the little bundle of nerves, I stroke my fingers across it in small, circular brushes. Her leg wraps around mine as I shift myself between her thighs, pushing my cock against her wet pussy. I know she's going to be sore from last night but I need this.

I need her.

I need to take what's mine in this world.

Pushing the head of my thick cock to her opening, I drop her hands and feel them latch around my neck as I lift her up, pushing her back against the wall. Her legs wrap around me as I hold her there, my cock slowly pushing into her oh-so-tight folds.

She's as tight as she was last night, and I feel some guilt as I give a hard push.

Bottoming out inside of her, the gasp she lets out in my ear makes my cock jump inside of her.

My hands holding her ass cheeks, I lift her up and then drop her back down again, over and over. My cock almost leaving the molten hot squeeze of her tight pussy.

This isn't enough for me; I need more of her.

Pulling away from the wall, I kick the door shut and walk us to the bed. My thrusts all but stopping as I focus on us not falling to the floor and breaking my dick. There must be some friction, though, as she moans quietly as the base of my cock rubs against her little clit.

She has absolutely no clue what the sounds of her being pleasured do to me. It makes my balls ache with the need to plant my seed deep inside of her womb.

Reaching the bed, I fall with her, and we land with me slamming deep down inside of her.

"Fuck!" she yelps, and my moan of pleasure makes her giggle.

"Jesus, you're fucking tight," I growl out.

Her giggles are having the most wonderful fucking effect of helping her already sinfully tight pussy clamp down on me.

"That's... so dirty sounding," she whispers to me.

"There's nothing dirty about this," I say as I pull out slowly then push back deep into her.

"Oh god!" she whimpers as I keep up my slow, forceful pace.

"Nothing dirty about claiming what's mine," I grunt as I push in again.

Her eyes have that hooded with lust look as she tries to stammer out, "I'm not... yours... you can't... just take someone."

"I already have, Beth," I say as I pull far enough out that just the crown of my cock is nestled inside of her.

Then I slam in deep and fast.

I can feel the wall of her womb slam against my cock as she gasps.

"You. Are. Mine. Don't. Fucking. Doubt. It." Each word is punctuated with a stab of my cock.

I don't do it as hard as the first push, I don't need to bruise her, but she needs to know she's fucking *mine*.

Her breath comes in small gasps as I lay myself down on top of her. Her full breasts mashed down between my chest and hers. I wish I had the forethought to remove that fucking shirt of hers so my mouth could latch on her pale pink nipples, but it's too little too late.

Each slam of my cock into her fills my heavy balls, and just the thought of there being more than one way to claim her as mine makes me ache with the need of release.

My right hand reaches up and pulls her neck to the side and I lean down to latch my mouth on her neck.

Biting down gently, I suckle on it.

This must be one hell of a sensitive spot because her legs wrap around my waist so tightly I can barely thrust inside of her.

"I'm.... I'm... oh god!" she wails as I push myself deep inside of her, my own eruption shooting off.

I can feel every pulse of my cock as I shoot my load deep into her womb.

"Christ!" I call out as I collapse on top of her.

Her legs shake as they slowly release their vise-like grip on my waist.

I'm probably some fucked up kind of individual, I think. Just about an hour earlier, I was telling the kid how he's free, and that I would never treat him like those bastards, and yet... I just told Beth, no matter what, she's mine.

No choices in the matter.

And I probably just put a baby inside of her to make sure of it.

~

"Yes, Johnathan. How can I help you?" Lucifer's precise voice comes through my phone.

I'm standing here, completely naked, looking at Beth's curled up form on the bed. She's in that post, just got fucked the hell out of, bliss.

Her naked ass is on display for all of its glorious worth.

"I need to speak with Lilith, sir," I say, and it's the very first time in my life I have ever asked to speak to the boss's wife for anything.

I'm quite sure the questioning tone in his voice is probably the first time he has had to call my sanity into question. "You do? What about?"

"Sir, I have a problem... I need clothing for Charlie and Beth."

"Ah," he says with a tone of amusement. "Let me see what we can do."

I can hear him moving around and then he asks, "So tell me, Johnathan, how is domestic bliss treating you? A woman and child in your home. Will the world tilt on its side now? Surely, it must."

If it was anyone but Lucifer himself saying shit like

that to me, I would probably try to shove their head up their ass. "Fine sir."

"Ah, here's my beloved now. Let me put her on speakerphone so we can both help you as best as we can."

Motherfucker! Asshole is just loving this shit. Rub the fucking dirty biker's nose right in the fucking family life shit.

"Hello, Johnathan, it's wonderful to speak with you," Lilith's pleasant voice comes through the line.

"Ma'am," I say, trying to gather my thoughts. "I seem to be in a... predicament..."

"You do?" she asks with confusion, and I can hear the chuckling of Lucifer in the background.

"Yes... I need some clothes, but I don't know how to get them, or where to get them, without leaving the house."

Sitting down beside a confused looking Beth, I purposely look at her naked breasts. She tries to cover them, but with my free hand I pull her arm away.

Shaking my head *no*, I gently begin to rub on her right one.

Rolling her eyes at me, she pushes my hand away, and scoots away from me, sitting up.

"Well, what kind do you need?"

"Female stuff. Pants and shirts. Little boy stuff too."

"Um... What?"

"I..."

Thankfully Lucifer puts me out of my misery. "He

seems to have found himself like my men are seemingly wont to do these days, with a readymade family."

Lilith's musical laugh comes out in a burst, and it makes me smile. She may well be married to the devil himself, but she's like a little tinkerbell. "I see! I'll have some things sent to you today. What size is your wife and son?"

Ah, fuck!

Looking at Beth, I ask quietly, "What size are you?"

With her eyes widening, she hisses, "I feel like your little dirty secret sex doll!"

"The boy's five or six and very thin. Normal sized, I would say. Could you have them send some toys too?"

"Of course! Any certain kind?"

"Nah, just something he can do with his hands. Lots of stuff. I'll make sure all of the costs are covered."

"Okay, and your wife?"

"My wife..." I say and I swear Beth's eyebrows reach into her hair.

"I'm not your wi—"

I put my hand over her mouth.

"She's a size four to six. Medium shirts and coats."

"What about her undergarment sizes?"

Fuck.

"They're big?"

"What's big?" Beth hisses at me again.

"Your boobs," I mutter back.

"32D, you giant—"

Putting my hand back over her mouth, she works her teeth up against my skin and bites down on my palm.

"Stop biting me!" I yelp out, and I swear on the other side of the phone I hear peals of laughter.

Fuck that hurt.

Releasing my hand, she moves completely away from me, covering her body as she goes. Her self-satisfied smile gives my cock a huge stirring.

Fuck, I love it when she fights.

Pulling my shirt over her head, she says, "My shoes are a size seven, and Charlie will need some too."

"Shoes and socks too, ma'am. Thank you, I really appreciate this."

"It's no problem," Lilith laughs quietly. "I'll send a variety of stuff for your child and wife."

The last thing I hear before I hang up the phone is Lucifer's loud booming laugh.

13

BETH

Charlie grips my hand tightly, and I know my own anxiety is only making him more nervous but I just can't help it. As Johnathan maneuvers the car through the hundreds of street lights that make up downtown, my heart races.

This is it, this is my chance to escape.

All I have to do when I step out of this car is scream my head off and make a huge scene. I'm sure most people will think I'm just some crazy lady at first, but surely someone will have to investigate... And when they do, when they find out who I am and who my father is, Johnathan won't be able to keep me.

But what about Charlie?

I glance over at him and squeeze his hand back. He gives me a little smile and something inside me wants to crack.

When I eavesdropped on the story Johnathan was

telling him, I overheard Charlie tell Johnathan his parents are dead. Does he have family out there? People who will love him and take care of him?

Or would he simply become another kid lost in the system?

Indecision and what-ifs plague me for the rest of the drive. I suppose I could try to plead with my father to let me keep Charlie, and he might even go for it if I spin it in a way that would politically make him look good… but I highly doubt it. My father has made it very clear he has plans for me. Plans that involve selling me off to the ally that will give his career the biggest boost.

Fuck. I just can't win here. Everywhere I turn, someone wants to own me or sell me like I'm not a person. I've somehow become a *thing*.

A body without a mind or heart.

I let out a little breath and sag against the backseat.

If I manage to get away, I'm really only trading one prison for another.

I'm screwed no matter what I do.

Johnathan turns the car down a tight alley and then pulls into a private parking garage. We follow the winding, spiraling driveway up and up.

When we finally pull into a parking spot, my heart sinks even further. There are two men already waiting for us. Two imposing looking men dressed in dark suits.

I guess they're taking no chances here. I don't know what I was expecting… for Johnathan to let us out of the car in the heart of downtown in broad daylight where anybody could see me and recognize me? Yeah, right.

"I'll get your door," Johnathan rumbles, and our eyes meet for a split second in the rearview mirror before he steps out of the car.

The two men step up to him and they exchange quiet words. Nervously, I smooth down the hem of my dress as I watch them.

Though it does feel good to have proper clothing again, I can't help but wonder where it came from. An entire wardrobe of designer clothing in my size was sent to Johnathan's house this morning, along with toys and clothing for Charlie.

Obviously, there are forces at play here, bigger forces that I'm about to meet.

Johnathan cracks a smile at the two men and then the three of them come around the car to my side.

Johnathan opens my door and then reaches in, offering me a helping hand. As soon as I place my hand in his, his big fingers close around mine and pull me out.

Straightening beside Johnathan, I instantly feel the two men's eyes on me, scrutinizing me and sizing me up.

Johnathan and I make quite the pair. He's dressed in ripped jeans and a tight, faded black t-shirt that hugs all his muscles. I'm dressed in a black Chanel dress and Louboutin pumps.

I may be a little overdressed for the occasion, but I don't want these guys to forget for a second where I come from.

Suddenly, the shorter of the two men lets out a low whistle between his teeth as he looks me up and down. "Trying to work your way up in the world, Johnathan?" he grins.

Johnathan's grip on my hand tightens and his eyes narrow as he pulls me into his side. "Shut your mouth, James, before I shut it for you."

James tips back his head and laughs. Obviously, not the least bit concerned about Johnathan's threat.

"Never thought I'd see you, of all people, falling for such a.... expensive skirt," he smirks.

Charlie slides out of the car and instantly latches onto my side. He eyes the two strange men in suits warily and we both jump a little when Johnathan slams the car door shut.

"Keep it up, numbskull," Johnathan growls and cracks his neck. "I could go a few rounds."

"Now, now," James says as he holds his hands up in front of him in a sign of surrender. "I didn't mean anything by it..."

Johnathan stares at James for a long time before he nods his head and starts to turn away.

But then James snickers. "It's just that you're always going on about how all women are leeches, and all they want is to get..."

For a moment, Johnathan's face turns so red I'm afraid he's about to bust all the blood vessels in his cheeks. But then he just chuckles and shakes his head, causing James to trail off.

"What's so funny?" James asks as all the wind goes out of his sails.

"Go on, keep laughing at me, brother," Johnathan says as he tugs Charlie and I along.

"Okay..." James drawls out as he follows behind us.

When we reach the elevator, Johnathan pushes a button and the doors immediately slide open for us. We step inside, and as we all turn, Johnathan and James come face to face.

"You're next," Johnathan smirks.

For a moment, there is only confusion in James's eyes, but then I watch them fill up with a slow, dawning horror.

WITH EVERYTHING GOING ON, I know I should be nervous as hell over the interview about to take place, but with how much James sulks, coupled with the look of pure dejection on his face, I can't help but feel my own smirk tugging at my lips.

I'm not quite sure what the secret joke here is, but it's funny watching the big guy squirm beside me.

"Take it back," James mutters, burning a hole into the back of Johnathan's head with his glare.

Johnathan strokes his beard thoughtfully for a moment and then chuckles. "No."

"Damn you, Johnathan. You of all people shouldn't wish such a fate on someone..."

Johnathan's arm tightens around me, pulling me

closer. I feel his hand wander down, his palm molding around the curve of my waist. He gives a squeeze and then rumbles out appreciatively. "It's growing on me."

It as in me?

I tip my head back and give him my best glare, no longer amused by this little interaction.

Johnathan grins at me, his eyes gleaming. "It also has its perks."

I try to pull out of his embrace, but his beefy arm only further tightens around me, trapping me against his side.

The elevator dings and the doors slide open.

Johnathan's arm finally loosens and we step out first. As he begins to lead Charlie and I forward, I 'accidentally' misstep and end up slamming the heel of my pump down hard on his boot.

"Oops," I blink innocently as he stumbles and curses.

Behind us, James bursts into laughter, and has to brush past us to exit the elevator. "Has it's perks, huh?"

"Shut up," Johnathan mutters as he shakes the pain out of his foot.

James shakes his head, still chuckling, until Johnathan so nicely reminds him, "Remember, you're next, buddy."

James reaches up and uses his middle finger to scratch the back of his head as he walks down the hallway.

Straightening, Johnathan puts his foot back down on the floor, stomps it a couple of times, and then stares me down. I return his stare and have to bite my lip to hold back my laughter.

He leans in close to whisper, "Tonight, you're going to pay for that."

"Pay for what?" I inquire innocently, looking up at him through my lashes.

Johnathan growls deep in his throat.

I smile sweetly, amused by his annoyance.

"Tonight," he repeats as if reminding himself and starts to lead me down the hall.

I follow beside him, feeling pretty damn good about myself until we reach the office door.

Reality crashes back in and with it my best friend panic. I don't know what's about to happen. I don't know why we're really here, only that Johnathan's boss wants to ask me some questions.

Johnathan pulls open the door and motions for Charlie and I to enter ahead of him. Lifting my chin into the air, I steel myself and brace myself for whatever is coming next.

Charlie and I step into a brightly lit, wide open reception area. The walls are a crisp, pristine white, but the long reception desk and the plush waiting chairs are all done in silver.

Above us, recessed lighting beams down on us from a white ceiling, and I have this wild thought that if heaven had a waiting room it would look just like this.

"This way," Johnathan says and motions to the left.

There's no receptionist behind the desk and no

company logo displayed on the wall. I have no clue where we are, though I am somewhat familiar with the building. We're in one of the many sky rises that houses a dozen or so of Garden City's top financial companies. This office could very well be one of them.

The place is eerily silent, the only sounds the echoes of my heels tapping against the white marble floor and Johnathan stomping beside me.

Charlie squeezes my hand and I glance down at him. He's looking around with wide, curious eyes.

"You're doing so well," I say softly, and feel like that's an understatement. He's been perfectly behaved this entire time. So behaved, I almost forgot he was with us.

He offers me a tentative smile and my chest tightens.

This kid, he's going to have me wrapped around his little finger if I'm not careful.

We reach the end of the hall, and without a word, Johnathan pulls the last door open.

I shoot him an anxious look before stepping into a private office. Unlike the rest of the building, this room is done in darker, richer tones. The walls are a cool taupe, but all the furniture is made up of dark, expensive wood.

James and his companion stand off to the side, talking quietly among themselves, and standing in front of the desk is a man I don't know. His suit is perfectly tailored to his tall frame, his hair is slicked back out of his face with not a strand out of place, and poised on the bridge of his nose is a pair of black designer glasses.

With a scowl, he checks the gold watch wrapped around his wrist.

"You're late," he says sharply.

Johnathan just shrugs his shoulders as if he doesn't give a fuck. "We hit some traffic."

Behind Johnathan, the door closes and the air thickens. I suddenly feel like I'm trapped in a room full of well-dressed giants.

Well, mostly well-dressed...

The scowling man's face tightens and his lips pinch together in irritation. I get the impression he's about to reprimand Johnathan, but then he shakes his head and sighs, probably thinking better of it.

Reaching up, he slides his glasses down and rubs the bridge of his nose for a moment. Pushing his glasses back into place, his sharp gaze slides to me.

He seems to stare right through me before nodding and saying politely, "Miss Norton."

Normally, at this time, I'd expect him to step forward, hold out his hand and introduce himself, but he does neither of these things. A little caught off by the lack of proper etiquette, I choose to just nod my head back at him.

His eyes flick briefly towards Charlie and then right back to me, as if he's dismissing him.

And that dismissal instantly pisses me off. Already, I don't like this guy.

"You can call me Simon," he says, finally offering his name.

Oh, can I? I think as press my teeth together and smile back at him.

"Are we ready to get this shit show started?" Johnathan asks, stomping forward.

"We're just waiting on Andrew and Lucifer," Simon says, and then the door to the office opens.

"Speak of the devil," Johnathan mutters.

Everyone turns to face the newcomers.

"Gentlemen," the most beautiful man I've ever laid eyes on grins as he steps into the room. "I'm sorry if we kept you waiting."

I don't mean to stare, I really don't, but right now my eyes seem to have a will of their own. I just can't bring myself to turn away. From his chiseled cheeks, to his piercing light-blue eyes, every feature demands to be noticed and admired for its beauty.

I've heard rumors of him, of a rich and powerful man so handsome he makes the very angels weep, but seeing is truly believing.

"Ah." His eyes alight with... something. Something close to amusement or pleasure as they fall upon me. "This must be Miss Elizabeth Norton"

Johnathan clears his throat loudly and the sound breaks the spell I'm under. My cheeks burn with heat as I pick my jaw up from the floor and nod my head.

"It's just Beth," I croak, and instantly wish a hole would open up below me so I could fall into it and *die*.

Seriously, I've never been boy crazy or anything. Why is this handsome stranger having such an effect on me?

It's kind of annoying and pissing me off.

"It's a pleasure to meet you, Beth. My men call me Lucifer, but you may call me Matthew," he smirks.

I nod, but he doesn't look like a Matthew to me. No, he pretty much embodiments the name Lucifer.

Beautiful, dangerous, powerful.

Someone not to underestimate.

He turns those piercing eyes of his onto Charlie. "And this must be little Charlie."

Charlie bobs his head up and down, and then I sense him taking a step back as Johnathan takes a protective step forward.

"We ready to do this?" Johnathan asks.

Lucifer's smirk sharpens and his eyes glitter with amusement again as he looks at Johnathan. "Yes, Johnathan. By all means, let's begin."

Lucifer takes another step into the room and behind him walks in another man with a little boy.

The little boy steps up to stand beside Lucifer and he looks almost like a little replica of him. He's dressed in a white dress shirt, black slacks, expensive black shoes, and his golden blonde hair has been brushed back.

The boy can't be more than eight or nine, yet he carries himself in way that I've only seen in men much older.

"I think it would be in everyone's best interest if the children were not present for the conversation about to take place. Charlie, would you like to go play in the next room with my son Adam?" Lucifer asks.

I glance down at Charlie. He peers at Adam with a mix of open curiosity and serious apprehension. Honestly, I can't blame him. Adam doesn't look like the kind of boy who likes to play.

Johnathan lays a reassuring hand on Charlie's shoulder. "Come on, I'll walk you over."

I force a happy smile for Charlie as Johnathan peels him away from me, not really giving the little guy a choice. A part of me wants to keep Charlie here with me, where I know I can protect him, but Lucifer is right.

The conversation we're about to have is not one for little ears.

Charlie walks stiffly beside Johnathan and casts one last worried look at me over his shoulder before disappearing through the door.

My protective instincts are at odds. I want him with me, yet I also want him gone.

Hell, I'd happily go play in the next room myself if it was offered.

"Coffee?" Lucifer asks, drawing my attention back to his features.

I nod my head. "Yes, thank you."

Lucifer motions to the chairs and I take the cue. Everyone starts to settle in. Simon comes forward to sit in the chair beside me. Lucifer takes his position behind the desk. James prepares my coffee and brings it over to me, while his companion remains oddly silent.

"Thank you," I tell James, and take my first sip just as Johnathan returns.

Johnathan takes a long look around the room and comes to stand behind my chair instead of taking the open chair beside me.

He lays a protective hand on my shoulder and I'm instantly grateful. I know what they want to know and I'm not looking forward to reliving any of it.

"Miss Norton," Lucifer starts, addressing me from behind his desk. "I know this must be difficult for you, but it would be immensely helpful if you could tell us the events that took place the night you were taken from Johnathan's parking lot."

I take another fortifying sip of my coffee and lift my eyes to meet his. The way he just so tactfully said that it was almost like he meant it... yet it's not quite sincere enough for me to believe it.

All eyes are on me and I feel the pressure to start spitting out all the gory details.

But first, I just have to know, "Why?"

Lucifer blinks his eyes at me and leans back in his seat almost as if he's surprised by my response.

But then a slow, charming smile curves along his lips. "Miss Norton, don't doubt for a moment that we're on the same team here. We both want the same thing—"

"I want justice," I cut in, interrupting him.

Or do I want revenge? Either will do.

Johnathan squeezes my shoulder again, and I'm not sure if it's because he's trying to reassure me or warn me, but I can't stop now. Before I rip myself open again and bare myself to these men, men I don't know but who obviously expended a lot of resources to rescue me, I need to know what they will do with what I give them.

"For Lindsey," I add, my voice starting to crack.

Her face flashes in my mind, but I push it away.

I take a deep breath and steel myself. "For my friends and for myself."

Lucifer doesn't blink as his gaze hones in on me. Staring into his eyes, I watch them harden and then glitter with something dangerous.

For a split second, I'm almost afraid to ask, "Is that what you want?"

I have no doubt this time he's being completely sincere when he leans forward and says almost eagerly, "We do."

14

JOHNATHAN

I feel a strong sense of pride when I look at Beth by my side. She held up so damn well to all the questions we put her through, even the embarrassing ones. That she wants revenge on the fuckers who took her and her friends shows she's got grit.

She especially wants revenge on the fucker she called Sasha.

Every single name that came out of her mouth was quickly entered into Simon's little fucking computer brain. I could see his machinations running overtime as she cleared up some parts of the operation. The doctor coming in to do a check on her was important. I don't see them having one that travels with them. My bets are it's someone close to the Russians, probably has a private practice somewhere nearby.

One thing that I had to put my fucking foot down on was Simon trying to get in to question Charlie.

Not one fucking chance in hell will I let that fucking spider near my boy.

"Lucifer, I've seen how bad the boy's fucked up. We won't get answers like this from him. I've been working with him this morning, and anything we do here will shoot that in the fucking foot."

"We need more answers..." Simon says with some heat. "His information could provide us with valuable intel."

"Look, I'll get the answers, but not here and not like this," I say. "Lucifer, let me work with him. There is no reason to hurt him when we can get the information another way."

"Agreed," Lucifer says slowly then looks to Beth.

"Miss Norton, would you mind terribly if I asked you to go watch over Adam and Charlie?"

"Okay..." she says hesitantly, and I can tell she wants to be a part of what's going on.

Taking her by the hand, I lead her out of the office.

Stopping as soon as we're out of earshot, I say, "Take care of our boy. Make sure Adam isn't boring him to death."

Pressing her tight against the wall, I kiss her hard and fast. "We need to talk tonight."

Letting her go, I usher her over to Adam's office. Yeah, the little fucking kid has an office of his own. Lucifer has been interviewing people lately to become his secretary. Can't fucking believe it myself.

Beth walks ahead of me, and in the dress she's

wearing right now, I admire the regal bearing she has to her step. She's regaining who she once was, or maybe who she'll be. What happened to her has changed her, I can see it. Most of it probably not for the better. No one comes out of something like that unharmed, but she's not letting the bad make her crumble, letting it bring her down in a hole of despair. She's trying to take the fight back to the ones who hurt her and her friends. She's also trying to keep Charlie safe.

Safe like a real mother would do.

Once she's settled in, I head back to Simon's office to face the music.

As soon as I walk in, I ask, "So what do we not know?"

"Far more than I would like to admit at the current moment," Simon says, and I can see that it almost pains him to admit it.

"Yeah, what I walked into wasn't a mom-and-pop type of setup. Too much security and high-end shit going on."

"We're you able to see anything beyond the auction?"

"Not much. I could see a couple of the buyers, but that was it. Never saw anyone besides my handler."

"We figured as much."

"Johnathan," Lucifer begins, and I can tell I'm in trouble. "Senator Norton has been asking around for his daughter. He's even come to me for aid in the matter."

Right to the fucking heart of the problem.

"Tough shit. She goes to him she's as good as dead."

"She's not the only one whose parents are anxious to hear some news," Simon says.

"Yeah, well, one's dead. What happened to the other two?"

"Successfully picked up, though there's a body count now," Andrew says, and I can hear the grimace in his words.

"What kind of count?"

"James and Peter, it seems, took exception to the men they took the girls from. Both dead, and so are their security teams. They've disappeared off the radar for now, but I can imagine it's going to come back that two buyers ended up dead after the auction. The Russians are going to be curious."

Fuck.

"And the dead one?" I ask.

"No sign of a body so far."

"What about the pig feeding thing Beth told us?"

"Could be where the bodies were dealt with..." Simon mutters. He doesn't like things like this, he wants hard facts and cold corpses. He wants to be able to count things up perfectly.

"She was the real estate guy's girl, right?" I ask.

"Yes. He's not going to sit any longer on this issue, either. He's personally come to us and asked for any information we can get."

"I'll be speaking with him, Simon," Lucifer says.

"Are you going to give him the details?"

"Of a sort, but I'll offer to personally deal with the matter. That will keep him in line... At least with us. It will also help form a better bond when it comes to the Senator trying to push his way into the matter."

"You need to turn the girl over to us, Johnathan," Simon says coolly as he looks to Andrew and Lucifer.

Raising his hands, Andrew grunts, "Leave my ass out of this."

Fucking shithead.

"Johnathan... This is going to pose problems if you don't," Lucifer chimes in.

"Don't give a shit. You didn't either, and neither did you, Andrew, when it came to finding your wives."

"That..." Lucifer starts to say, and his cold eyes warm with mirth as it dawns on him. "Is true."

"Same thing floats here. I bought her, I keep her. Her father can suck my hairy ass for all I care."

Standing up from the chair, I finish with, "Think of it this way... We can keep her as a good way of keeping him in line. He wouldn't dare push you too hard. He can't have any of his darker connections come to light, can he? It would be a good deal for us to have a senator, or maybe even something larger, in our pocket for a rainy day."

"Point taken," Lucifer nods his head, and he's being far too understanding of this.

It's giving me the creeps.

"What's happening with the other two girls?" I ask. Beth's going to want to know.

"They will be returned to their families, and the families will be made aware of the work we did to get them back."

More people that will be beholden to Lucifer. Owing the devil himself a fucking favor is not an easy burden to bear.

"I'm going to take Beth and Charlie home. Need to get the house set up for having a family in it."

15

BETH

The drive back to Johnathan's house is tense and quiet. There are too many things between us, too many words that need to be said, but can't be in front of Charlie.

I have absolutely no clue what was discussed after I was asked to leave the room, but when Johnathan finally did come to fetch Charlie and me, he looked stiff, like something is bothering him.

He's been glaring at the road the entire drive back. His big hands gripping and squeezing the steering wheel in a death grip.

Now that he knows what happened to me, is he going to give me back?

I don't know why, but that possibility makes me feel sick to my stomach. It's one thing to want to get away, to escape his prison.

It's another thing completely to be tossed out on my ass.

I want to stay with him because I want to be with Charlie, I convince myself.

It's not that I want to stay with the man who told me he bought me and *owns* me now. No, it can't be that. It can't.

That would be insanity.

We're from two different worlds. Even if for one crazy moment I wanted it to, it could never work out between us.

Despite what happened in his bed last night. Despite what his touch does to me. Despite the way he looks at me like he fucking *needs* me.

We might as well be two completely different species.

We're two opposites that were never meant to attract.

"Are you hungry?" he asks, his deep, rumbling voice breaking the tense silence.

I start to shake my head, but my stomach speaks up in protest, growling in hunger.

That stiffness in his body just melts away. And when he looks over at me, his eyes softening, my heart does a little flip-flop.

I must have finally cracked. That's the only explanation for my reaction to him.

"How about you? Do you like pizza, Charlie?" he asks.

Charlie seems to perk up, sitting up straighter in his seat as he answers Johnathan's question. "Yes."

"What kind of pizza do you like, little buddy?"

Johnathan asks as he makes the final turn onto the street he lives on.

"Pepperoni," Charlie smiles.

Johnathan hits the little button on his visor and the garage door starts to roll up. "Pepperoni pizza it is."

Johnathan parks and we exit the car. I linger by my door, waiting for Charlie to get out. Once he does, I can't help but smile as he steps up to me and slips his hand into mine.

That is until he turns to Johnathan and holds out his other hand.

At first, Johnathan just stares at Charlie's hand as if he doesn't understand what the boy wants, but then a slow smile creeps across his lips. Walking up to Charlie, he ruffles his hair affectionately before covering his little hand with his much bigger one.

And at this moment, something has changed. The dynamic has shifted, and it's all thanks to Charlie.

I can't exactly be angry or throw a childish tantrum because Charlie is reaching out to Johnathan for the same kind of protection and affection that he gets from me. Nor can I drop his hand or pull away.

So I have no choice but to follow along as Johnathan leads us into the house, the three of us hand in hand, like we're some kind of fucked up family.

∼

"What do you think of this room?" Johnathan asks, shoving his open laptop into my face.

I blink down at the picture of a blue living room displayed on the screen.

"It's nice, I guess...." I say hesitantly, not sure if this is somehow a trick question.

Johnathan scowls and yanks the laptop back.

Balancing the computer on his lap, he grabs his bottle of beer and throws his head back, drinking deeply from it.

I turn back to the Star Wars Lego set spread out on the dining room table that I'm helping Charlie build.

Johnathan sets his bottle back down with a clink. "What's your favorite color?"

"Purple," I respond right away as I struggle to separate two pieces I locked together incorrectly.

"Purple?" Johnathan scoffs. He reaches for his beer again and mutters quietly, "I'm not living in no damn purple living room."

"Wait? What?" Did I just hear him right?

"What's your second favorite color?"

"I don't know... I guess red..." I frown at him, and then curse at the two Legos as I bend the tip of my nail painfully back.

Shoving my finger in my mouth, I try to suck the pain away until Johnathan's eyes light up with heat.

With a blush, I pull my finger out and wipe it off on the skirt of my dress.

"Brown it is," Johnathan grunts, and then jams a button on his laptop with a flourish.

"What's going to be brown?" I ask, not sure if I really want to know or not.

"Our new living room," Johnathan answers with a satisfied smirk.

"You mean *your* new living room," I correct him, waving my stuck Legos at him.

Both of his brows slide up and he gives me a look that pretty much says: *Really, Beth? You're going to say that in front of the kid?*

I open and close my mouth, struggling to find the words that correctly explain what I mean but in way that won't freak Charlie out.

"What's your favorite color, buddy?" Johnathan asks, angling his laptop towards Charlie now. "Any characters that you like? Star Wars? Spider-man? This... Minecrap."

"It's Mine*craft*," Charlie says with a smile, gently correcting him.

"Ah, sorry about that," Johnathan squints at the screen. "Minecraft," he drawls out correctly, earning him another smile. "So you like it?"

Charlie eagerly bobs his head up and down.

"You want your room like this?" Johnathan leans closer to Charlie so he can better see what he's looking at.

Charlie nearly shoves his little nose into the screen. "Yeah!"

Johnathan jams the button again. "Done."

Charlie leans back with a beaming smile on his face,

and I'm torn between ruining the moment or just letting it be.

Maybe I should speak up more. Maybe all this pretending that something really fucked up isn't going on is just going to hurt Charlie more in the end.

As if he knows exactly what I'm thinking, Johnathan's eyes narrow and swing to me.

I chew on my lip, staring back at him. How long can we go on like this? How long can we avoid the giant fucking elephant in the room?

Johnathan breaks eye contact first, glancing back down at his screen. "*Our* new stuff should be here tomorrow."

Glancing back up, his eyes meet mine again and my heart starts to race. Oh god, he's really doing this. He's going all in on this farce.

Snapping the laptop shut, Johnathan sets it on the table and downs the rest of his beer. "Time for bed, buddy," he says, rising from his chair.

"Aw, but I'm not tired," Charlie protests and immediately tries to hide a yawn.

Johnathan chuckles and ruffles his hair. "Yeah, sure you're not."

Reluctantly, Charlie sets the fighter jet he's been working all night on down and stands. "Will you tell me a bedtime story?" he asks hopefully, turning his big blue eyes on me.

I force a smile for his sake and nod my head. "Of course. How about the story of the brave little prince, the beautiful princess, and the big, mean bear?"

～

"Big mean bear, eh?" Johnathan grumbles, forcing me to come up short as I walk into the living room.

I spent over thirty minutes dragging Charlie's bedtime story out, and another thirty minutes more lying beside him while he slept before I worked up the nerve to face Johnathan down.

I had every intention of starting this confrontation off with the upper hand. I was prepared to point out every single detail of this situation that is fucked up and wrong.

But one look at him and I've completely forgotten all the shit I want to say.

Johnathan's eyes drag up and down over my body, and shamefully I feel myself warming. I squeeze my knees together to stop the throb that's building in my core, but the movement only reminds me that I'm still a little tender and sore. And that tenderness reminds me of what we did last night and this morning.

Fuck, I just can't win here.

Johnathan sets down the beer he's been nursing. "Come here," he says and pats his lap. "We need to talk."

I don't know what to do without Charlie here to act as my shield. With him around, it's so much easier to pretend that being near Johnathan doesn't affect me. So much easier to turn everything off.

But with just the two of us here, alone in the room, there's nothing to dampen the attraction I feel for him.

No one to stop him from taking what he wants.

"Come here," he repeats, his voice deepening.

I approach the couch slowly while trying to keep my breathing under control. I need to confront him, but every instinct inside my body is screaming for me to flee.

Stopping a whole cushion away from him, I sit down.

"No," he says gruffly and pats his lap again. "Plant your sexy little ass right here."

He can't be serious.

"I'm not a child…" I protest.

"Then stop fucking acting like it," he growls.

I open my mouth to tell him off, but before I even get the words out of my brain and past my lips, he's reaching over and grabbing me.

He drops me on his lap and wraps his arm around my waist to keep me from being able to get up.

"What the fuck, Johnathan?" I squeak and try to stand up.

"Sit still," he says, the hard bicep in his arm tightening around me and pulling me back down. "So we can talk."

I take a deep breath and push it out through my nose. This is not at all how I expected this conversation to go.

"This is ridiculous," I say through clenched teeth.

I haven't even aired any of my grievances yet and he's already managed to make me feel powerless and small.

"You're fuckin' telling me," he agrees, and reaches over, picking up his beer.

On impulse, and maybe even a little bit of pettiness, I snatch the beer out of his hand and tip my head back to chug it down.

Out of the corner of my eye, I watch Johnathan's amused reaction while I finish his beer off.

"Feel better?" he asks with a smirk.

"No," I answer as I peel the now empty bottle away from my mouth.

He takes the bottle from my hand and sets it off to the side, and as soon as he turns back to me I regret finishing it off.

Now there's nothing to stop him from touching me with both of his hands.

"Did Charlie have a hard time falling asleep?" he rumbles, and reaches up to brush a strand of hair out of my face.

The movement is so tender, so damn sweet and unexpected, I freeze in place.

His eyes soften as he stares down at me.

I shake my head, partly to answer him and partly to shake him off.

He frowns and drops his hand, settling it on my thigh now. His big fingers wrap around me and give a gentle squeeze. "Then what took so long?"

"The story," I lie.

"That must have been quite a story."

I squirm uncomfortably. "It was."

He nods his head slowly, and I have to look away because the way he's staring at me is making me feel incredibly uneasy. I almost wish he'd get angry or pissed about something. This gentleness is completely throwing me off my guard.

"So how did it end?" he asks, grabbing my chin and gently turning my face back to him.

I lick my lips nervously and something clenches inside me as his eyes light up. All of a sudden, I'm very aware that I'm sitting on his lap. Very aware of every little part of me that's touching him. My thighs against his thighs. His heat leeching into me.

"The brave prince and the beautiful princess vanquished the big, mean bear and lived happily ever after."

"That's too bad," he sighs, and his thumb strokes my cheek.

"How's that? He was the bad guy..."

He smiles and I still, realizing I was just starting to lean into his touch.

"Maybe the big, mean bear was misunderstood."

I start to roll my eyes and his grip on my chin hardens.

"Maybe the big, mean bear was ready for more from life. Maybe he wanted the brave prince and the beautiful princess because he wanted something of his own."

It's clear now that we're no longer talking about the story I told and we're talking about Johnathan himself.

I don't know what to say, other than, "This could never work."

"Why not?" he growls, his brows pulling down and his lips forming an angry scowl.

There's a million reasons... hell, make that a gazillion reasons that this whole situation is doomed to fail.

And the first reason is because, "Charlie needs to be returned his family."

"His parents are dead," he states coldly.

"I know," I sigh. "But he has to have other family out there. Grandma and Grandpa. Aunts, uncles, cousins..."

Johnathan shakes his head and releases his grip on my chin. "No. I had Simon look into it. His family is shit and he's better off here."

"But..."

"No *buts* on this, Beth. Both sets of his grandparents are dead. His mother and father were into some bad shit, the whole family was, that's how he ended up in this mess."

Fuck. That's the last thing I wanted to hear. I was still holding out hope that there was someone out there waiting for the little guy to come home.

"So you're just going to keep him?" I ask while leaning back.

"Yeah," Johnathan says firmly, his features hardening. "He's ours now."

Double fuck.

"Ours?" I repeat. I must have heard that wrong.

"Yes, *ours*," he says firmly.

I immediately start shaking my head back and forth. "No. No. No. Johnathan, this isn't going to work."

Johnathan grabs both sides of my face to stop my head shaking. Glaring into my eyes, he asks, "And why the hell not?"

"Because I can't stay here!" I blurt out.

He leans close until his nose is nearly touching mine.

"Again," Johnathan says slowly, calmly. "Why the hell not?"

"Because I can't," I say and close my eyes.

He's too close now for me to concentrate. My lips tingle at just the knowledge that his lips are only a breath away.

I take a deep breath to calm my racing heart.

"My father is going to come for me, he always does. And he always finds me. *Always*."

I open my eyes to see Johnathan staring at my mouth.

"You have to give me back," I implore.

Johnathan stares at me for a long moment like he's contemplating what I just said, and I have the wild hope that I'm finally getting through to him.

Then he has to go and growl, "No."

"You don't understand," I groan, and try to lean away, but Johnathan pulls me back. "With all his connections, it's only a matter of a time…"

A wave of hopelessness washes over me. My life has never been my own. For as long as I can remember, everything has been controlled by my father.

"I understand perfectly," Johnathan says, his face

darkening with anger. "Do you want to go back to him, Beth?"

I frown at Johnathan and recoil at his angry look. "Of course not." It's not that I necessarily want to stay *here*. "But I've never had a say in the matter."

Johnathan nods his head and says with a dark look of determination. "Good, because I'm not giving you back. He'll have to pry you from my cold, dead hands, and even then I'll fuck him up for trying."

I shake my head in disbelief. What is he saying? Is he actually saying he'd die to keep me? "You're insane."

Johnathan nods his head and his eyes gleam possessively as he says, "And you're *mine*."

His declaration of possession causes my heart to jump into my throat.

Before I even have a chance to truly process how I'm feeling, he pulls me even closer.

His eyes soften and once more his attention falls to my mouth. I can tell he's thinking about kissing me and my breathing quickens with my own want.

"Your father can come for you, but he can never take you away from me. He'll have no legal recourse if you're my wife."

16

BETH

"Wife?" I repeat dumbly.

My ears are ringing and my brain feels light-headed and full of static. It's like a bomb just went off in my head.

He can't be serious, he can't. I know he was joking about it with his boss earlier, but how could he possibly want to *marry* me after only knowing me for a couple of days? No, no way. Only an idiot, or someone truly crazy, would be willing to do that.

There must be something else to this. A catch...

All at once it hits me, and I nearly sag with relief as I figure it out.

"Oh," I start to smile. It's ingenious really. "You mean like a sham marriage? That would be really awesome of you, but I can't ask you to—"

Johnathan's face darkens and he reaches down, grabbing me by the hips. I yelp as he twists me around and forces me to straddle his lap.

I push at his chest and try to rise up but he yanks me back down.

His fingers dig into my hipbones and then he grinds his hard groin against my sex. "Does anything about this feel like a sham to you?" he rasps.

I arch away, trying to escape the grinding friction.

"No," I breathe, desperate to escape the trap of his hands.

Even now, in my confused, messed up state, my body is responding to the motion of him rubbing himself against my clit.

He rocks his hips up again, and his voice is huskier, harsher as he says, "Has anything I've said left any doubt about how I feel about you?"

"I... I..." I repeat, clawing at his shirt. I can't think properly.

Between the assault on my mind and body, I'm at a total loss here.

"Answer the question, Beth," he demands with another grind of his hips.

I slowly shake my head and nearly sob as I say, "I don't know. None of this makes any sense."

His right hand releases my hip and drags slowly up my body until his fingers are sliding through my hair. He fists my hair in his hand and uses his hold to force me to stop arching away and look at him.

"Tell me," he says, his voice full of dark warning. "What about this confuses you?"

I stare into his eyes, into the face that first drew me in.

He's more than just a gruff guy with a beard.

He's a man marked by the hard life he's been living. There's a dark promise of violence and mayhem in his features that doesn't exist in any other man I've ever known.

He's forbidden... danger and excitement all wrapped up in a sexy package.

And there must be at least a decade between us. Yet, I want him. I can't seem to stop myself.

There's just something about him that gets my blood boiling. Sharing the same air is enough to cause my breathing to quicken.

But I'm just a young, dumb girl who doesn't know any better...

What's his excuse?

"You don't know me. How could you possibly want to marry me?" I ask meekly.

Johnathan stares at me hard, and from the dark, angry look he's giving me, I get the feeling I've somehow insulted him.

"Because," he drawls out slowly. "I know what I fucking want."

What kind of answer is that?

He scowls at the look of disbelief on my face and his fingers tighten in my hair, pulling me even closer.

"I want you, Beth. There's no big fucking mystery to it. It's plain and fucking simple."

Still, I'm not convinced. There has to be more to it than that... there has to be...

"If you want flowery words and fucking poetry, you're shit out of luck."

Is that what I want? Am I holding back and fighting this thing between us because I want sweet declarations of love?

Johnathan growls in irritation and tugs on my hair, forcing me to arch my neck back. "I want you by side. I want your fucking sexy body always with me."

He leans over me, hovering above me and forcing me to look up. "When you're not with me it drives me batshit crazy."

He rolls his hips, the hard bulge in his jeans grinding against my pussy. "I want you always on my cock."

I moan and fight back the surge of desire rolling through me. I know I shouldn't want him back. I know this entire situation is insane. But to be wanted and desired for who I am, not what I am, feels so fucking good.

His eyes drop to my breasts and I feel my nipples harden and tighten. He releases his grip on my hair only to shove the top of my dress down. My sleeves slide down my shoulders, trapping my arms against my sides.

A low, deep growl vibrates in his throat.

"I want you swelling with my babies. Fuck, I want you knocked up right fucking now."

He shoves the cups of my bra down causing my breasts to spill out of my dress.

Eyes flashing with hunger, his head dips down. "I want to see how big these tits will get."

His hot mouth covers my right breast. I gasp and squirm on his lap and his grip on my hip tightens.

He suckles on me like a man who's been starving and I'm the feast that's literally been dropped in his lap.

His tongue licks circles around and around my nipple, and I can feel a jolt of pleasure in my core each time he pulls a suckle back.

Fuck, I'm already so wet.

He keeps making all these deep, rumbling noises in his throat, and knowing that he's enjoying what he's doing, knowing that he's enjoying the taste of me, shatters what's left of my resistance.

Without even really realizing I'm doing it, I start to rock my hips.

I just have to *move*. I can't sit still with all this warm pressure building in my sex.

Throwing back my head, I arch my spine and offer up my breasts to him. His hand squeezes me, his fingers kneading, picking up my rhythm.

"So fucking sweet," he murmurs, his eyes hooded as he leans away.

I pant, my breasts rising and falling, *aching* for more attention, as I stare at him. My nipples are so wet and so engorged, they throb with the thundering beat of my heart.

I could probably come from him suckling on my breasts alone, and almost did.

His hips rock up, and I swear that hard bulge in his jeans has grown even bigger.

He releases his grip on my hip and then his rough palm drags down my thigh.

"I want to be the only man who makes you wet," he rasps, and then his hand is pushing between my thighs.

My panties are pushed to the side and then those wonderful, thick fingers of his slide through my folds.

"Ah, fuck. You're soaking wet, baby," he groans. He slides his fingers back and forth, gliding along my wetness.

I bite my lip and close my eyes, fighting the need to rock my hips. Fighting the need to find a way to work those thick fingers into my needy sex.

His thumb finds my clit and begins to rub in small, tight circles.

"Johnathan," I moan.

His fingers quicken, driving me quickly to the point of orgasm.

"Beth, I want to be the only fucking man who makes you *come*."

His fingers work fast and furious until I'm crying out.

I'm so close. So close.

My muscles tighten in anticipation. The pressure inside me expands and expands.

I'm about to explode.

The world around me starts to turn white and then he just stops.

His thumb leaves my clit, dragging through my folds teasingly. I blink, trying to bring the world back into focus.

What the fuck?

Johnathan chuckles and pulls his hand away from me altogether. Working between us, he unbuckles his pants and pulls his cock out.

I look down and watch as he grips his shaft in a fist and pumps it up and down.

I've never watched a man stroke himself before, and even though I'm a little pissed he just left me hanging, I'm also fascinated by the way his skin bunches up near the head and then smooths back down.

"In this life, if you want something you gotta take it."

Is he serious?

I glance back up.

The look on his face is so hard, so intense, I have no doubt.

"Are you going to take it, Beth?" he growls.

Fuck. Do I want him bad enough to do this?

I glance back down.

His cock is a deep, angry red, and there's this pearly, white liquid leaking from the head.

"Touch me," he urges.

I want to. I want to know what he feels like in my hand, but, "My arms are trapped."

With a sound of annoyance, he grabs the bottom of my dress and then rips it up, over my head.

"Touch me," he urges again, tossing the dress away.

I bite my lip and tentatively reach down.

The tips of my fingers brush against his cock, and when it jerks, I yank my hand away in surprise.

He chuckles. "Come on, it's not going to bite you."

His hand finds my hand and guides me back to his shaft.

He groans with pleasure as I wrap my fingers around him and suddenly I feel so powerful.

I try to mimic what I watched him do. I pump my fist slowly up and down.

His skin is smooth and hot to the touch. There's this silky, velvety quality to it that just glides against my palm.

I work my hand up and down, my strokes coming faster and faster.

He groans as if he's in pain, and a little, evil part of me likes it. That is until his hand moves and his thumb finds my clit again.

He presses his thumb against me, once more working it in tight circles.

The orgasm I was so close to achieving earlier comes back with a vengeance.

My hand quickens, my strokes coming faster and faster, matching the need I'm experiencing.

Once more, I'm so close. So fucking close I can taste it.

Johnathan groans with agony. I can feel his precum leaking all over my hand.

My core clenches. The first tremor is about to hit. I give myself up to it, letting go with abandon, but then I come crashing back down to my senses.

"If you want it, Beth, fucking take it," Johnathan says harshly, and his thumb leaves my clit.

I cry out at the loss.

My body is literally shaking from being cut off.

My clit throbs painfully, and I just can't stop myself from clenching on empty air. My skin is so raw, so sensitive, if I don't do something about this pent up pressure inside of me, I feel like I might literally fucking die from it.

But I just can't do it. With a slow, dawning sense of horror, I realize I don't want to *take* at all.

I want to be *taken*.

Johnathan stares into my eyes and then he grins as if he can read my mind. "If you want something, take it, Beth," he repeats, and I want to scream in frustration.

Why is he making me do this? Why doesn't he just push himself on me like he did last time?

I stare into his eyes, just about ready to slam myself down on his cock as my consolation prize, when I figure it out.

Lowering my lashes, I lean forward and moan against his mouth, "I want you on top."

His eyes flicker. I start to smile but then the world blurs around me, and suddenly I'm on my back.

Johnathan comes down on top of me, and I welcome his weight.

Something dark inside me fucking needs this. Needs him in control.

There's a freedom in submission. There's a freedom in letting go.

His weight begins to sink me down into the cushions of the couch and I open my thighs wide to accept his huge body.

"Is this what you want?" he asks.

Taking himself in his hand, he rubs the crown of his cock against my entrance.

Yes, I think, as I wrap my legs around him.

"Beth," he growls. "Is this what you want? *Tell me*." He guides his cock up to my clit and smashes it down.

"Oh fuck," I blurt out and jerk. "Yes! I want this. I want you, Johnathan."

There, it's out. Now that I've said it, I have to fucking own it.

I want to be under this man. I want to be connected to this man.

I want him to split me open with his huge cock.

"Good," he groans, and his cock slides down until it's poised at my entrance.

He grabs me by the hair and forces my eyes down. "Now watch me take what *I* want."

In one swift movement, he slams inside me. It's brutal, but it's so fucking welcome.

"Fuck," Johnathan roars, blocking out my own moan.

My eyes roll into the back of my head as his thickness stretches me, spreading me wide open.

I'm so wet, so swollen with need, there is no resistance. Just slick, electric sensation.

"Fuck," Johnathan says again, softer this time.

His cock twitches inside me, and I was so close to the edge it's almost enough to set me off.

He grinds himself deep and my eyes pop open in shock.

I watch as his body works against mine.

So big. So rough.

"So fucking tight," he grits out from between his teeth.

I can't stop myself from watching as he slowly pulls out.

His cock is now glistening with my wetness, and he's just about to leave me completely when my thighs tighten around him.

"So fucking mine," he declares before he slams back into me.

I clench down on him and cry out.

His fingers tighten in my hair and once more he grinds deep as if he could somehow push himself further inside me.

"You know it, Beth, you fucking know it," he groans, and I can tell he's close.

I grab at his shoulders, my nails digging into his skin, trying to pull him back in as he pulls out.

"Tell me who owns you, baby."

Only the tip of his cock remains inside me and I squeeze down on it in vain. As much as I want it to be, it's not enough.

"So fucking stubborn," he snarls.

He fights the grip of my thighs and the thought of losing him completely causes me to cry out, "You own me! I'm yours!"

All his weight falls down on me, driving me into the couch.

I can't move, and I don't need to, as my release sweeps through me.

Johnathan grunts and mutters all kinds of dirty things as my pussy milks my orgasm out of his cock.

My orgasm seems to go on and on.

"That's it. That's it, baby," his words break through the haze. "Come all over my cock."

He starts to fuck me hard and fast. Lifting my hips, and stroking against that buried bundle of nerves.

"You're mine. *Mine*," he declares. "I took you and now I fucking own you. I own the rest of your life."

His pace quickens, his grunts becoming more and more frantic.

And as I feel him swelling up inside me and pulsing, another orgasm rocks my world.

"Fuck," Johnathan moans. He fucking *moans*.

The most delicious warmth fills me and I squeeze around him so hard he stops moving.

"Fuck, fuck, fuck," he twitches and jerks above me as I milk the very life out of him.

"So fucking tight," he grits out in agony and then stills with a groan.

His head falls forward and his grip on my hips relaxes. I sag beneath him. I came so hard, so much, my bones feel like liquid.

Together we pant, catching our breath.

When he finally looks at me, there's so much satisfaction in his eyes he's practically glowing with it.

His cock twitches inside me and I realize I still feel full and stretched out around him.

"Again?" I pant.

He pulls me by the back of the head and brings me closer to his lips. "Again."

17

JOHNATHAN

"We've got the doctor's place of residence. You and I need to go over and have a heart-to-heart with the man," Andrew's deep voice fills my ear.

"When?"

"Now. I'm ten minutes out from your house."

"It's two in the fucking morning. When did we get this info?" I grumble as I look over at the clock on the nightstand.

"Simon just got it about an hour ago. He wants us to act now. Get the info and bring the doc in. And get this... Simon wants to be there at the questioning."

"What the fuck?"

"He wants to be a part of it apparently."

"Fuck me."

"Yeah, I got your gear loadout from the compound. See you in eighteen minutes." Andrew disconnects.

Well, fuck, at least I get to put this bastard's head through the fucking wall. Motherfucker touched Beth in a way I can't forgive. Simon, the fucking Spider, being there... Shit. It makes me wonder what the fuck I'm missing.

It's going to be a bloody night.

Rolling out of bed, I push the blankets back around my naked woman. Beth looks too delicious to leave, but if Andrew's right about the address, then we need to move while it's still a good lead. We have the warehouse and we have the trucks tagged.

That doesn't mean shit though, the trucks haven't moved and we don't know why.

I watch as Beth rolls to her side, the naked flesh of her back calling to me to press my chest back against her. The gentle swell of her hip barely shows, but it's enough to make my palms itch.

I want to slide my hand down and pull her juicy ass hard against my cock. Mental images keep flooding my mind as I feel my cock start to stiffen.

Fuck me, living with her is going to drive me to insanity.

I can feel the need to press my body all over her, to keep my scent on her as I much as I can. I need to mark her as mine, somehow... maybe a fucking collar or tattoo... Though, I highly doubt she would go for it.

I quietly go through my drawers and pull out a pair of dark grey cargo pants and an almost black shirt.

All black isn't natural in the nighttime, it creates voids

in people's vision, whereas dark colors of grey tend to blend in with just about anything.

I've had a lot of these nights over the years working for Lucifer. I'm used to the calls for sudden deadly violence.

Tonight, though, feels off. It feels like we're heading for something more than the normal. I don't have the hairs on the back of my neck rising, but that's not always an indicator of something fucking up.

I kiss Beth on her shoulder quickly before leaving the room. I don't need to wake her or the boy, so I wait until I'm downstairs to get dressed.

Outside, Andrew is already waiting for me in an old, but I have no doubt, decked out black Escalade. Lucifer doesn't allow us to go cheap when it comes to our work vehicles. We have to keep them in shape in case of anything.

Jumping into the front, I look to the backseat to see my loadout bag ready and waiting. Goody. He's brought all my favorite toys with him.

Pulling the tactical vest over my chest, I pull the velcro straps tightly around my waist. Patting the pockets, I make sure I have my brass knuckles securely strapped in.

"Where we headed?" I ask as Andrew guns the engine out of my subdivision.

"Over to Derry Township. He's got one of those sprawling mansion type of spots."

"Any intel on what we should be expecting?" I ask as I

start checking the clips I'm going to stuff in my vest and tactical pants.

"Yeah, couple of satellite feeds, but not much. Simon was trying to get a flyover, but couldn't get us up to date, unfortunately."

"Fuck."

"Yeah, bad timing, I guess. We got a couple of drive-bys going to happen soon. Should get a better idea of the security situation."

"What do you think we'll be running into there?"

"Light security, is my guess. Maybe a guard or two in the house. Doubt it will be much, they aren't expecting trouble."

"You know I don't trust easy times," I grumble as I lean my head back against the headrest.

"You're just a grouchy morning person," Andrew laughs.

"I'm going to take a nap. Let me know when we're close," I say as I recline my seat back.

Closing my eyes, I let my mind drift over Beth's naked body. Each curve of her hips. The swell of her breasts capped by pale pink areolas with rock hard nipples. The way her shoulders looked when I pulled her dress down from the top. The barely-there collar bones. Each part of her is a study in beauty and sexuality.

I'm going to spend years and years pushing my thick cock deep into her pussy, and I don't think it will be enough

A rough shove on my shoulder jars me from my

dozing, and Andrew says, "Quit fucking snoring. We're almost there."

Rubbing my eyes, I want to bite Andrew's fucking head off. I was right in the middle of a very good dream of Beth dancing around in a bikini for me.

It's still the dead of night outside. The clock shows three-thirty. I watch as Andrew shuts off all the lights in the car using one of our specially designed kill switches. Even the quiet hum of the engine is barely audible over the rolling of tires.

"Who's all going in?" I ask with sleep still in my voice.

"You and me, baby. Lucifer and Simon think we can keep this a quiet affair, so fix the fucking silencers."

Pulling my HK MP5 to my chest, I start screwing in the silencer. "No, backup?"

"I got James on the rifle out past the subdivision. Heh, fucker is in a cellphone tower."

With how fucking windy it is, it really does warm my heart to hear he's fucking suffering with the rest of us.

Handing over a small plastic box, he says, "Ear comms."

Taking out the little piece of plastic, I place it carefully in my ear and say, "Yeah, must have lost my other one."

"Dude, we heard the fucking crunch of it."

"Yeah, probably stepped on it or something."

Shaking his head, he says, "You give Simon indigestion."

"Good."

Stopping a half of a mile away from the house, Andrew hands over an iPad with pictures of an aerial view of the house. Yeah, he was right, this guy's got a fucking mansion. Probably has ten bedrooms in the house alone.

"Got a basement?"

"Keep looking at the pics, dickhead."

Swiping my fingers across the screen, I look at models of the house from when it was up for sale. Pictures of the house with infrared body spots.

Swiping further, I don't see anything that answers our questions. Only old, outdated pictures that show nothing but empty rooms. Getting to the end, I find an old blueprint of the house and see it does indeed have a basement.

Goodie. More places to fucking search through.

"This shit's outdated as can be."

"Yeah, I know. Simon sends his regrets, but he couldn't find much else. Whether by design or simply not enough available information, I don't know."

"Fuckers. This is going to be interesting for just the two of us and a guy in a cellphone tower."

"Yeah, Lucifer has been talking lately about our numbers having being spread too thin. Wants to start recruiting."

"Shit, that should be fun for you guys." I can just imagine the files Simon and Lucifer already have on whoever the fuck they are looking at.

"You're included in the fun, asshole. Lucifer wants

you to let him know if you still have contacts with those crazy IRAs, or the French Foreign Legion."

"For the Irish Republican Army, no chance. They have shut all their doors to me. Too much turmoil going on internally and externally from the wars over in Ohio. Lots of splashback. The FFL? Shit, man, I ain't talked to those fuckers in three years."

"You've been out what, six years?"

"Yeah, next month."

The French Foreign Legion. Years of sand and heat. Lots of fights for a country that wasn't even my own. My adult life was pretty fucked up after Mexico. By the time I was finally able to pay my way out of a dirty Mexican prison, I had spent half my family's inheritance, been stabbed twice, and shot once. Got too many stitches to count, and more than enough time behind bars to last me a lifetime.

Getting back to the states was almost just as bad. I couldn't stop seeing all those stabbing knives, the dark eyes full of menace.

They haunted me no matter how much I drank.

So I set off to run from all the fucking demons that were chasing me in my head.

Women, lots of fucking booze, and a string of wrecked hotel rooms landed me in front of a French judge. Salty old hag saw me all fucked up in the head and still reeling from a long bender of booze. She asked me what in the world I was doing. Gave me an offer—join the Legion or get kicked out of the country.

Stupid me was too drunk to understand I wasn't even in America.

I said the Legion.

Joined up and spent five glorious, shit-filled years with sand in places I can't even think about without tears welling up in my eyes.

It wasn't all bad, though. I learned enough shit to keep myself out of trouble and to stay alive. I also found a shit ton of contacts that weren't the best of people. Lots of unsavory fellows.

I went into the FFL a spoiled brat, and came out almost a hardened criminal.

That's where Lucifer picked me up. I was running guns in his city and hiring out protection services for anyone who had the money. Some things you can shake when you leave the military, but a taste for danger wasn't one of them for me. Instead of getting rid of the competition, Lucifer brought me in for an interview.

I'd heard of him, and the deal he made me had enough zeros on the check to make sure I wanted in. Then he showed me how well he treated his guys and what we could do.

I haven't looked back.

"I'll put out some feelers. See if anyone over in the Legion are disreputable enough to work with us."

"Make sure they aren't Russians. Lucifer is pretty fucking hard up about the fuckers right now."

"Dude, I ain't saying the French are picky, but the Russians haven't been welcome with them lately."

Placing the tiny bud in my ear, I nod my head. "Check on comms one."

"Comms command, good to go," Simon's voice fills my head.

Andrew puts the car back into drive and slowly eases us towards the house.

"Next time, could you try to stay awake, Johnathan?" Simon grouses at me through the earbud.

"How the hell did you know I was sleeping?"

"We heard your loud snoring through the damn ear mics."

Snickering, I look to Andrew. "How long was I snoring?"

"Five fucking minutes. I don't think you damn Legion boys were taught anything about staying ready for upcoming ops."

"Eh, it was more of keeping in a good frame of mind."

"Yeah."

Pulling up in front of our stopping point, we both exit out of the SUV as quietly as we can. We're trying to keep this a quiet op, hence we're coming from the east of the house on a side street between two houses.

"James, what's on the thermal scope?" Andrew murmurs.

"Six bodies, possible seventh underground."

"Repeat that shit?"

Stopping next to Andrew, I nudge him with my elbow. "Basement, asshole. What's in the fucking box type of shit."

Shaking his head, he says, "Simon, we might need another team. I don't think we have the spots we need to get in and out without causing an issue."

"No time," I quietly say to Andrew. "It's three-forty."

Growling, Andrew says, "Let's see if we can get thermal on the outside guards, then we'll see what we've got."

"Why the fuck are we going into this so empty-handed, Simon?" I ask quietly.

Through the earbud, he hisses, "The doctor had been considered a minor player. Having four guards and a seventh unknown in the basement was not in the data files."

"What the fuck? You're the fucking Spider... how do you not have this information?" I want to shout but instead I murmur as quietly as I can.

"It's being looked into, Johnathan. I promise you that. I also promise you we need this man."

"Got it. There's going to be a body count on this. You said four guards? Possible fifth? That leaves one or two unknowns. What have you got on that?"

"One in the basement I've got no information on. The one in the bedroom, I would say with nighty-nine percent accuracy, is his lover Jeffery Rogers."

"Is he a player in our happy little fucking theater?"

"No, but we can't use him as leverage either. Leave the body at the house. Gather as much intel as possible."

"James, how loud is that cannon you have? Any chance of muzzling the volume?"

"Eh... not too bad. We don't have many houses for the sounds to bounce off of. I've got a suppressor on, but I'd prefer not to though, if we don't need it. It's still going to make some sound."

Nodding my head at Andrew, I point to our planned path. We move off at a slow run, no sounds coming from us except for our quiet footfalls.

Splitting off to the front of the house, I go hunting for the guy walking a slow pace around the front yard.

Murmuring quietly, I say, "Eyes in the sky would be helpful. Get a fucking drone next time."

Removing my tactical knife from my hip harness, I slowly sneak up on the man and wrap my hand over his mouth, then I shove the blade straight into his chest.

Dead center on the heart.

Tipping us to the side, we fall with barely a sound. Pulse check gives me nothing. Pulling him to the row of hedges, I squat down beside the body.

"Target number three down," Andrew comes through the mic.

"Target number one down," I say as well.

"Stay still, John, you have a roving guard coming your way," James says with urgency.

Holding my breath, I watch a guard pass by my location. He's taking his time as he walks, his face buried in a fucking cellphone of all things.

Stupid shit.

Doesn't he know that will kill any chance he had at seeing me in the dark?

Slowly stepping away from the dead body, I bring the knife back up.

A couple of duck waddle steps later, I stand quickly behind him. Holding my hand over his mouth, I quickly push the blade though his chest, just like the last stupid fuck.

"Target four down, pulling body towards house."

"Target two on the side of house, lighting a cigarette."

"On my way," I murmur.

The fucker I'm carrying isn't exactly light, so by the time I drop him near the front door, I've started panting. Fucking fat bastard.

"Target two down. Target's location in house?"

"Two in the bedroom, from the heat signatures I'm getting on my thermal scope. Nothing on the third in basement," James says through the comms, and I can hear the wind starting to kick up through the microphone.

Walking three-fourths of a circle around the house, I meet Andrew at the door to the library that has a porch attached to it.

Nodding my head to him, I notice he's got a splash of blood on his chest and face.

"What the fuck?" I ask with a harsh whisper.

"Fuck off," he growls right back.

Snickering, I murmur, "I thought you SEAL boys were professionals."

Bending down to the lock, I pull a set of picks from my vest. It's a quick jiggle and then I'm in like a flash.

"You and James need to go rob a vault or something. Not natural how well you do that."

"Yeah, your mom said the same thing."

"She's dead, ya dumb fuck."

"I broke her hip, what do ya expect?"

Moving through the house, I head to the basement door leading off from the kitchen.

"Hurry up, I'll post myself outside of the master bedroom," Andrew says.

Opening the door, my hackles instantly rise. Something's off here and I can smell it from a mile away.

There's a fucking steel, prison-type door at the bottom of the stairwell.

"Gonna need more time," I murmur.

"What the fuck for?" Andrew asks back.

"Simon, you seeing this shit?"

"Affirmative. Andrew, get ready to take the main target. James, move in. I need you to make your way to basement with Johnathan."

"Moving, but I'm ten out at a dead run."

"Take your vehicle and move to the house. I'm calling in Harrold for clean up."

"Tell him to bring his torch crew. Simon, this shit is smelling to high heaven."

"Agreed."

"I'm heading down the stairs. Going to work on the door."

"Careful, Johnathan, check for traps," Simon says

quietly. I don't think he knows what to expect any more than I do.

"Will do."

Heading slowly down each stair, I look for anything out of place. I mean out of place besides a big fucking steel door that could be used in a prison.

Standing in front of the door, I look at the lock—it's a big fucking deadbolt. Those are never an issue, anything can be picked or broken.

"James, how far out?"

"A minute."

"Got a deadbolt."

"Break it."

"Gonna try."

Pulling my picks up, I work for a bit, but nothing's feeling right. "Got a drill?"

"Yeah, I'll bring it in."

Heading back up the stairs, I wait for him to come through the door. As soon as I see his face, I motion to the stairs. "Wait for us. Going to secure the targets first."

Nodding his head, James silently moves past me and then down the stairs. I've never seen someone move like he does.

It's part predator, part fucking ghost like shit.

Moving through the house, I notice how full of fancy shit it is. I mean, like even I know how expensive this shit is, and it's beyond shit my rich ass parents ever had.

This doctor must be more than we know.

Going up the stairs, I finally reach Andrew and nod.

Pointing to the door, we both move as one. Reaching out to the handle, I test it very gently.

No sense in getting our heads shot at if the doc or his partner have a gun.

Giving the nod of my head, I twist the knob slowly open and then quickly move through the doorway.

Andrew steps past me, raising his rifle as I raise my own.

Quickly moving to the sides of the bed, I pull a suddenly shrieking man's head from the pillow.

Not the doctor.

Putting the barrel of the weapon to his head, I pull the trigger twice.

A loud scream of fear comes from Andrew's man as a wall of blood splashes across his face. Cuffing the guy soundly across the back of the head, Andrew and I watch as his eyes roll to the back.

Good, he knocked the bitch out with the first shot.

"What the fuck is so important downstairs?" Andrew asks as he begins to zip tie the man's hands together.

"Fucking steel door at the bottom of the steps, like a prison kind of steel door."

"Shit."

"Yep. You want to get the SUV for dipshit?" I ask.

"Yeah, I'll drop him near you guys so you can keep an eye on him."

"Gag his ass."

"Always do."

Walking down the stairs, I take a moment again to

notice how wealthy this guy is. He's in the fucking money. He's got original paintings on the walls that look all kinds of abstract and completely expensive.

"James, you notice how expensive this guy's taste is?"

"Yeah, the library alone has some shit I could move at premium cost. He's not the usual doctor."

Something about him helping the Russians sounds odd to me. "Andrew, he have any tats?"

"Let me check."

I can hear a shuffle of noise through his mic and then he says, "Nope, nothing."

"Simon, who the fuck is this guy?"

"Former doctor out of Siberia. Got his start in the prisons there as a medical doctor. Moved up the ladder with his willingness to do anything. He makes Stalin look like a school girl."

Lovely. So the basement isn't going to be fun.

Heading down the steps, James follows me as I open the steel door up.

There, in the middle of what looks like a makeshift surgical room, is a man strapped down to a table. Tubes of all sorts run out of his body. IVs, catheters up his junk, and a breathing tube fixed to a machine pumping his lungs full of air.

What the actual fuck?

Moving over to the man, I push my body cam to cover his face. "Who the fuck is that?"

"Damn. I can't tell, but it looks like the doc is keeping him alive," Simon says.

James moves around the room and starts picking up scraps of paper. "I'll start on data collection. You mind if I take some of the artwork, Simon? Lots of shit upstairs I can sell."

"Data comes first," Simon says with annoyance.

"Will do."

"Check for safes and hidden shit," I call after James.

"Andrew, get down to the basement. We need to see if you can figure out what's with this man and if he can be moved or not."

"Will do. How far is Harrold out?"

"Thirty minutes."

"Good enough."

This is not my kind of bag. I don't do the medical, keep-someone-alive shit. Backing up out of the room, I head back upstairs for the doctor's office.

WE'RE about a mile out from the house when a large whooming sound bursts through the night. A fireball explodes up to the sky.

I guess that's what usually happens when you make it a gas line explosion.

Harrold has one of the best cleanup crews around, if you ask me. They're quick, clean, and completely silent on who they work for. Doesn't matter if it's Lucifer, or the Italians, it's all the same to them.

The fact that he won't work for the Russians, though, is a good way to stay in business with us.

The drive out to our own shutdown warehouse is fast thankfully. It's been a long night, and seeing the sky starting to lighten on the horizon, is making me want my bed and Beth.

Fuck. I should have woken her up enough to at least let her know I was leaving for a bit.

The good doctor has enough intelligence to at least try to play at sleeping as we pull him from the back. He tries the same damn thing every other motherfucker does when he feels the ground beneath his feet, he tries to fight and run away.

Fighting with us never works, ever.

A sharp punch to his kidneys and the fight goes right out of him with a muffled screech.

The smell of dust and grime fill my nose as we drag the man through the empty sheet metal shop floor.

This place hasn't had workers in it since the eighties, and it looks it.

Dust is thick on every surface except for the ones that have been used for 'different' purposes. Sometimes you have to take a hand off through a machine, it puts the fear of the devil himself into people.

Dragging the man back to the old office area, we slam him down into a steel chair that's been bolted to the floor.

Securing him isn't too hard after we hit him in his gut.

"Thank you for bringing the good doctor to me," Simon says as he comes into the room.

Fuck me, he's not wearing a suit. No tie, no freshly starched shirt for him. No, he's wearing fucking medical scrubs. Just seeing him in those things is bad. When he dresses up like a doctor, shit's about to get bloody.

I think I'm going to fucking vomit.

I've seen this only once before, and it was way back when I was just starting out in the family. Fuck and shit. This isn't going to be pretty.

"No problem..." I say, as I start to back out of the office area.

Andrew gives me a dirty look and says, "We're not leaving yet, playboy."

Hanging my head, I grimace as I walk back over to the doctor.

Ripping the hood off the doctor's face, I give him a sad smile. "Doc... I got bad news for ya."

He doesn't look at any of us with the due fear he needs to have in his soul right now so I continue. "You're going to die in pain. Lots and lots of pain. No way around that. Wish I could tell you differently, trust me, I ain't going to want to see this either."

The man screams something unintelligible through the gag in his mouth, and though I can't quite make it out, I'm pretty sure it has something to do with my mother.

"I'm going to take this gag out of your mouth now. You can scream and yell all you want, but it's just going to get you hurt. So think real carefully about what you want to say, buddy."

Hearing some rustling behind me, I look over to see

Simon setting up a black leather bag on one of those old metal frame desks.

Yep, this is going to get messy.

Pulling the gag from the man's mouth, he screams just as loud as can be expected. I really wish one of these assholes would change things up for once.

Just one fucking time.

My ears are tired of the screams by the second deep breath he takes. Grabbing him by the throat, I just squeeze my hand.

Squeezing till his stupid fucking face turns purple.

"Stop fucking screaming, asshole," I growl.

"Thank you, Johnathan. I'll take over from here," Simon says smoothly as he walks up to the doctor.

My hands still on the fucker's neck. I loosen my grip only enough for him to speak.

"What the fuck do you want?" the doctor yells.

"Now, now, Doctor Mirov, that's no way to start off our morning together." Simon sits down across from the man and folds his arms across his chest.

Taking a moment to gather up his courage, the doctor launches a massive ball of spit at Simon's chest. The sound of it splatting there makes me want to laugh so badly, but even I know not to fuck Simon when he's wearing scrubs.

Jumping up from his chair, Simon hisses, "You stupid little man, you'll pay for that, I promise you."

"Gentlemen," Lucifer's voice comes from behind us and I grit my teeth.

Yay, the gang's all here.

Color me fucking purple with unending happiness.

I just want to go home and get in bed with my wife. Now, I'm going to need a very long cold shower to get the dirtiness off me.

Perching on the corner of a desk, Lucifer gives the doctor a feral grin. "You really shouldn't anger Simon like that."

Shaking my head, I can't hold it in. The chuckle I have in me forces itself out of my chest and even Andrew has to look away.

Someone spitting on the germaphobe, Simon, is just too priceless. I only wish I had recorded it.

"Can someone tell me why I had a medical transport for a mystery man this early morning?" Lucifer asks, and as soon as the words leave his mouth, Mirov noticeably goes stiff.

"Found some guy hooked up to all kinds of life support. Whoever the fuck he is, Doctor Mirov here was making damn sure he stayed alive."

"Is he still? Alive, that is?"

All of us noticed how Mirov reacted to the question of the man.

When Andrew shrugs, Mirov pales.

"Don't know. I did my best, but..." Lifting his hand, Andrew tips it to one side then the other. "We'll see."

"You must..." Mirov starts before he thinks better of it.

"Now, now, Doctor Mirov, don't be shy with us. I won't be with you," Simon coos at him.

And now I have the creepy crawlies going down my spine.

Leaning down to the man's ear, I whisper, "Now's the time to talk, asshole. Spill it all out for us so you can save yourself some pain."

"Fuck you! I say nothing!" he spits again, this time at Lucifer.

"Wrong answer." My fist connects with the side of his face with as much force as I can put behind it. His head whips to the side then slowly turns back to Simon.

"You need an introduction, I see," Andrew says. He points to himself then me, "We're not too well known, Johnathan and Andrew. The first one you spit on is Simon..."

Pointing to a bored looking Lucifer, he says, "And the big guy right there? You know his name very well. Every single person in this city knows his name—Lucifer."

Wide eyes and a look of pending doom? Check.

Distinct smell of piss and a large wet spot on his pajama pants? Check.

"What is it you want?" Our favorite little shitstain now asks as he stares at the faces surrounding him.

"Tell us who was on the medical table in your basement."

"I... I can't."

"Wrong. You can and will. Hold his hand still, Johnathan," Simon says.

Nodding my head, I watch as Simon pulls a pair of pruning snips from his bag. A loud snip and a bloodcurdling scream later, and the man has tears streaming down his cheeks.

I don't think the doctor thought we would go through with it.

"There will be no warnings, Doctor Mirov. Each time you fail to answer a question, we will remove a part of your body."

Maybe in my old days, I'd feel sympathy for the stupid bastard, but I just don't have it in me now. He touched my girl. He scared the woman I call my own. He has to pay for that.

Nodding my head to Andrew, I motion for him to come hold the thrashing man for me.

Walking over to Lucifer, I take a seat next to him on the desk and say, "I get the death blow, Boss."

Looking sideways at me, Lucifer says, "I do believe he spit on Simon. You know how touchy he is about that."

I shrug my shoulders. "Yeah, well, he touched my wife. I get the kill for that. Rules is rules."

"Funny, I don't remember that being a rule..."

I give him the stink eye. "Lilith, Amy... Rules is rules. Simon can be the killer when someone touches his girl."

Laughing, Lucifer says, "All too true. But do you seriously think he'll ever find a wife?"

Shaking my head, I say, "No, but James sure is scared as fuck that I cursed him with the *'you're next'* comment."

"You're next?"

"Next to get wifed up."

"Really? Whatever for?" Lucifer asks.

I shrug my shoulders. "Don't know, but you know how them southern boys are about curses. He's upset something fierce."

"He's Alexei's father!" screams out Doctor Mirov.

"Well, well, well." Lucifer stands up from our conversation and I move with him as we all circle around the crying man.

"Alexei holds his power because the man is hidden. If he was to die, there are splinters in the group who would break off."

"Do tell doctor, do tell." Simon smiles at the man.

THE MAN before me resembles nothing like the one we brought into the warehouse.

He's missing quite a few fingers and toes.

His tongue, just recently removed, rests on the floor.

Simon is a fucking sadistic motherfucker.

As soon as he discovered he wouldn't be the one to deliver the death blow, he made damn sure he caused this man enough pain to soothe his bruised ego.

The doctor has one good eyeball left. His ears are missing, and his nose is half gone.

That's not to say Simon only worked on his extremities and face.

No, his chest is a patchwork of missing skin, and even his intestines have been pulled slowly out of his body.

Fuck, this has been one long morning.

Walking up to the barely breathing man, I lean my head down and whisper in his ear, "This is for Beth."

Moving to the front of him, I release the lower half of his body and slide it down until his pelvis is hanging off the chair.

Taking the scalpel from Simon's hand, I quickly slice off the man's tiny dick and balls.

Grabbing the bloody mess in my hands, I shove it into his mouth and watch as he slowly chokes to death.

When his body finally stops moving, I hand the scalpel back to Simon.

"Harrold will be here shortly," Simon says. "He'll remove the trash."

Nodding my head, I follow Andrew out of the building. We watch as Simon and Lucifer leave the property and then wait for Harrold to show up.

"Long fucking night."

"Yeah, but it's been a productive one."

18

BETH

Johnathan left me.

At first, when I slowly awoke realizing the spot beside me was cold, I thought perhaps he just got up to do something. But as the minutes ticked by and he didn't return, I had to get up to investigate.

I've searched the house from top to bottom and he's nowhere to be found. His car and motorcycle are both still in the garage.

It's four in the morning and he's gone out to do... something.

I check in on Charlie. He's still tucked under his covers, clutching a fluffy brown teddy bear to his chest, and sleeping peacefully.

I could wake him. I could get us both dressed, use the house phone to call someone and we could get away.

Yet, I hesitate.

Would that be the best thing for Charlie? I can't guarantee I'll be able to keep him with me. I could strike out on my own, even call Sophia to help me, but eventually my father will find me.

Throwing his life back into turmoil and uncertainty just feels like cruelty at this point.

Johnathan may be a lot of things, a lot of bad things, but he honestly cares about Charlie. I know deep in my heart he'd do anything to protect the boy.

And what about me? Would leaving be the best for me? As much as it hurts me to think about it, I could sneak out now and leave Charlie behind.

There's nothing at this moment to stop me from returning to my old life.

Nothing, that is, but me…

I don't know what the hell is wrong with me.

The phone is right there, hanging on the kitchen wall and taunting me. It would be so easy to pick it up, so easy to dial a number, any number, and leave.

This is my chance; the chance I've been waiting for. I may never get another opportunity. But I just can't bring myself to pick up the phone because a sick, twisted part of me wants to stay.

God, that feels so awful to admit, but it's a desire I can't seem to change. I don't want to leave Johnathan.

God help me, I don't.

And I don't want to leave Charlie. I'm already crazy in love with the little guy.

We're starting to build something here, something special.

In just the few days I've known them, we've already created a family.

And, fuck, what if there's already a baby growing inside of me?

Johnathan has made no attempts to hide the fact that he's trying to impregnate me. After our third round of sex last night, I fell asleep with his cock still buried inside me. I'm not on birth control and he sure as fuck hasn't used any protection.

But it's not just the possibility of a baby that makes me want to stay. I could totally be a single mother if I had to. It's that the longer I spend with Johnathan, the more and more I have to accept he likes me for *me*.

He didn't have to rescue me. He didn't have to keep me. I know he spearheaded the entire mission to buy Charlie and me. I know that he was supposed to hand me over to my father, but he defied his bosses and risked their wrath to keep me.

For whatever reason, he fucking wants me and protects me.

Here, in his house, I know I'm safe. If I let myself, I can breathe easy. If I let myself, I can let him do what he's been trying to do ever since he bought me that night.

I can trust him and let him take care of me.

Having made my decision to stay and give this crazy relationship a chance, I climb back into bed and eventually fall back to sleep. I'm not sure how long I sleep, but by the time I feel the bed dipping and Johnathan pressing up against my side, sunlight is bleeding through the blinds.

Johnathan's arms wrap around me and I roll into him. I snuggle up to his bare chest and breathe in deep. He smells just-showered clean.

"Where did you go?" I murmur sleepily.

His chin comes down on the top of my head and there's a long pause before he answers, "Got called out to work."

He's so warm, I can't help but press against him for his heat.

"In the middle of the night?"

"Yeah," he grumbles, then his voice lifts to a teasing tone. "Did ya miss me?"

He stiffens with surprise and sucks in a deep breath when I answer honestly, "Yes."

I smile against his chest and then he's moving. He pushes up on one arm and nudges my chin up to meet his eyes.

"Say it again," he demands softly, staring into my eyes.

His gaze is so intense, so dark and *needy*, I'm tempted to look away.

This is it, once I give these words life there's no taking them back.

My smile fades away and my cheeks feel hot as I give in and say, "I missed you."

"Fuck," he groans, and then his head dips down. He kisses me hard and deep. By the time his head lifts back up, I'm flushed and panting. "I missed you too, baby."

His hand strokes my hair back and we just stare into each other's eyes for the longest time. Memorizing each other's face.

This is a huge turning point for us, and as much as I want to revel in this new direction we're taking, I can tell he's tired and had a long night.

"You should get some sleep," I say, breaking the silence.

Johnathan's mouth softens and he pulls me close again. Our hips lock then his knee begins to push between my knees.

My eyes widen and he laughs at the surprised look on my face. "I can sleep when I'm dead."

"But—"

With a growl, he leans in and smashes his mouth hard against my mouth. "I fucking need you, Beth."

I don't get a chance to reply, and god knows I don't want to stop him. His lips are on mine again, hard, demanding, relentless.

Pressing and pressing, he uses the force of his kiss to push me until my back hits the bed.

His weight coming down on top of me, I spread my legs eagerly for him.

Just knowing what's about to come has made me soaking wet.

Reaching down, he manages to shove his boxer-briefs down without breaking the kiss.

Fitting himself between my thighs, he stiffens in surprise as his skin touches my skin.

"No panties," he groans, finally giving me a breath.

He rocks his hips, his hard, velvety cock gliding against my slick pussy lips.

"No panties," I grin at him, my face feeling a little raw from his beard rubbing all over me.

I'm wearing one of his favorite faded band t-shirts, with nothing else on beneath it.

"Fuck, the things you do to me," he groans as if he's tortured.

Before I can even think of responding, he's thrusting himself inside me, pushing out all other thoughts but *him*.

He's so big. So damn thick.

Every time his big cock slides into me, it feels like he has to fight his way in.

We've done it a lot over the past few days, and I mean a lot. Sometimes his hands are on me before I'm even sure Charlie has fallen asleep.

You'd think by now that I'd get used to the size of him.

"I'm going to fuck you so hard for this," he snarls as he bottoms out and my walls instinctively squeeze around him.

"For what," I pant.

He pulls out, my pussy clenching him, sucking at him, trying to pull him back in.

"For fucking teasing me," he answers right before he slams into me so hard, his cock driving through me with such force, I feel a deep ache and momentarily lose my breath.

"For fucking driving me crazy," he grunts, working himself in and out, faster and faster.

Still fighting my tight clench.

"For fucking being amazing," he groans, and even with all the pleasure he's slamming into me, I feel my heart fluttering behind my ribs.

"Because you're mine. In this bed, in this house, in my world, you're my fucking wife," he says, and at this moment I totally believe him.

He leans forward, pushing more of his weight down on my chest.

"And my wife always deserves a good fucking," he rumbles as he reaches down and pulls my legs up until my knees are nearly touching my head.

"Johnathan," I gasp as the new position causes him to slam into me even deeper.

The spike of pleasure he drives into me is so good, so strong, my eyes start to roll into the back of my head.

"That's it," he grunts, and somehow manages to slip my knees over his shoulders without losing his rhythm. "Take your husband's cock."

He starts to pound into me so hard I can feel his balls slapping against my ass.

"Johnathan," I moan, and he pushes me down, forcing me to take more of him in this new position.

Something starts to build inside me, something so strong, so overwhelming, I'm a little terrified of it. I start to fight it, but in this position I can't escape the intense sensation.

I shove at his shoulders, but it only causes more of his weight to come down on top of me.

"Stop fighting it, Beth," he orders, the force of his body nearly crushing me to the bed.

"I can't," I whine, my head thrashing back and forth.

Each time his cock pounds inside me, he's hitting a spot that threatens to drive me mad.

"You can," he declares, breathing heavily.

The sensation builds and builds. It's an intense pressure that feels like no other pressure I've ever felt before.

"Johnathan, please, it's too much… I can't," I nearly wail in my desperation to escape the thing threatening to overtake me.

But he won't let me get away. He's forcing me to face it head-on.

Suddenly, his relentless pace increases, and he's grunting and groaning loudly with all the effort it takes.

"I've got you. Look at me," he demands, and somehow I manage to open my eyes.

"I've got you," he repeats, and I believe him, I *trust* him, as I focus on his face.

Knowing he's there to catch me when I fall gives me the courage to let go.

A mind-blowing orgasm rocks through me, totally

destroying me. Every muscle in my body locks up as I scream out his name.

Gush after gush of pleasure bursts through me.

And Johnathan doesn't stop. No, he keeps driving into me as if he's trying to fucking kill me.

I claw at him, part of me trying to pull him closer and part of me trying to push him away.

"Beth," he finally roars, and I feel him swelling up inside me.

Then there's warmth. So much warmth. His warmth mixing with my warmth.

His pace begins to slow to deep, grinding thrusts, and the orgasm ravaging my body finally begins to abate.

"Fuck, Beth, *fuck*," he shudders and stills, trapped in the grip of my convulsing pussy.

I tremble beneath him helplessly until the last tremor of my release fades away.

"Holy fuck," I whisper, and Johnathan grins down at me before collapsing, crushing me with his weight.

"Baby, I think you've finally milked all the cum out of me," he groans.

I smile and press my lips to his ear, "I'm never wearing panties again, just so you know."

∼

WRAPPED up in Johnathan's strong arms, it feels like my eyes just closed when his phone starts ringing.

"Fuck," he grumbles, and rolls me with him to grab

his phone off his nightstand. His eyes squint at the screen and he mutters another "Fuck," before swiping it on.

"Yeah?" he snaps, lifting the phone to his ear.

I can hear a muffled, deep voice speaking on the other end.

"Now? Shit. Okay. Give me ten."

Johnathan fumbles with his phone before just tossing it back to his nightstand. His hands run down my back, lingering at my waist, and then slide back up.

I stretch and feel like purring beneath his touch.

Without warning, he rolls me over onto my back and grabs up my hands. His stretches my arms above my head, keeping a firm grip on my wrists.

I blink up at him in sleepy confusion as his weight comes down on my thighs, pinning me to the bed beneath him.

"What's wrong?" I ask, not liking the scowl on his face.

This morning, I thought we had come to an understanding.

"I have to leave," he says, hovering above me.

His body is taut. The muscles in his arms flex as he stares down, and still I don't understand what I did to make him so mad.

His grip on my wrists remains firm and the way he has me stretched out is far from comfortable, but I don't dare try to fight it.

"Okay," I say, trying to stay calm as I stare up at him. Something is obviously wrong here. "More work?"

"Yeah," he confirms, his eyes hardening.

I have no clue what 'work' means to him but from the look he's giving me it must not be pleasant.

"I don't know when I'll be back," he goes on to explain, and his grip on my wrists further tightens.

It's not painful, yet, but it's obvious he's trying to send a message. The same damn message that he's been drilling in my head ever since he bought me. He's bigger, stronger, meaner, and I'm *his*.

"You are not to leave the house, Beth."

I open up my mouth to tell him I won't, but he cuts me off by growling deeply, "Promise me. Promise you won't leave the house. Promise me you won't make a fucking run for it."

I stare up into his eyes, and though I still don't know why he's so pissed off, there's something vulnerable about the way he's looking at me.

Is he afraid he's going to lose me?

I could have left last night and didn't, but I get the feeling right now is not the time to point that out to him.

"I promise I won't leave," I assure him.

He stares deep into my eyes, searching out the truth of my words before his grip and posture begins to relax.

"I don't want to leave you," he finally admits. "I've got a bad fucking feeling about this."

I curl and uncurl my fingers, fighting off the numbness caused by his grip.

"If I had time, I'd drop you off at the compound..."

I stiffen. "Compound?"

His eyes drop to my mouth and he frowns thoughtfully. "Yeah, where Lucifer keeps Lily."

I can just imagine what kind of horrible dungeon that place is.

His right hand releases his grip on my wrist completely and he drags it down to tenderly stroke my cheek.

His head dips down and his beard tickles my chin as his voice thickens. "Promise me again."

Aw, the big guy really is afraid I'm going to take off on him.

"I promise," I say easily, finding his worry kind of sweet. It would be even sweeter if he didn't have me pinned down beneath him…

But I guess I have to take what I can get.

His mouth comes down on mine and he gives me a slow, lingering kiss before pulling away with a look of regret. "I'll be back as soon as I can."

I nod as he rolls off of me and stands from the bed.

I sit up to watch him pick up the pair of jeans he wore last night off the floor and shove his legs into them.

The room is quiet, too quiet as he gets dressed. I start to think of what I'm going to do today trapped in the house with Charlie without him.

Once he's got all his clothes on, he grabs his phone off the nightstand, and leans over to grab me by the back of the head.

He gives me another quick but meaningful kiss.

"Take care of our boy for me," he says, and straightens.

I nod and promise, "I will."

He starts to walk out the door, stops, and turns back. "There's a gun under the bed if you need it."

19

BETH

The phone is taunting me, just begging me to pick it up and dial Sophia.

I haven't seen or talked to her since I was taken from that room we were held in. Johnathan told me she's safe, that they rescued her and returned her to father, but I need to hear it from her own lips.

What happened to her? What happened to Amanda?

I pace and pace in the kitchen. With nothing to do and no one to distract me, the not knowing is driving me a little crazy.

I've spent all morning hanging out with Charlie, trying to keep busy, but now he's doing his own thing. He's currently sitting at the table, playing with all the Lego sets I helped him build yesterday.

Completely oblivious to the little war waging inside me.

Johnathan made it very clear that I'm not to leave, but

he never said a word about phone calls... But even so, I know he'd be pissed if I called someone without asking for permission.

Honestly, I don't know why he's so hard up about keeping me in his house, cut off from everyone I know. We don't want my father to find me, of course, but Sophia would never betray me and give my location away.

Besides, if we're just talking on the phone, she won't know where I am anyway.

Fuck it, I know I'm probably making a mistake, but what Johnathan doesn't know won't hurt him.

Or me, for that matter.

I just need to hear her voice. I just need to know she's *safe*.

Picking up the phone, I quickly punch Sophia's cell number in before I lose my nerve. The phone rings once, twice, and then she picks up.

Sophia's voice comes through the line, and it's so damn beautiful I almost cry. "Hello?"

"Sophia?"

"Oh my god, Beth!" she bursts out. "Where have you been? Where *are* you? Everyone has been like freaking out!"

Ugh, that is exactly what I was dreading. I don't even have a plausible excuse ready. How do I even explain that the guy who rescued me decided to keep me? Even in my head the whole thing sounds insane.

"Beth? *Beth*?" Sophia repeats when I don't answer immediately.

"Uh..." I draw out. "I've been lying low for a while... waiting for things to cool down." Shit. I hate lying, especially to Sophia, but I honestly don't know what else to say.

"Are you okay? Are you somewhere safe?" she asks, and she sounds so worried, the sudden guilt I'm experiencing intensifies.

Has she been worrying about me this whole time? Wondering what the fuck happened to me, just as I have about her?

"Yes, I'm fine," I say, and try to change the subject. "And I'm safe. Seriously. Are you okay? Are you safe?"

"Yeah, I'm home and I'm safe. But it was crazy. I almost ended up in the Middle East!"

"Oh my god," I exhale. "I wondered what happened to you but Johnathan wouldn't tell me anything."

"Johnathan?" she squeaks and I cringe. Shit. I'm fucking up already.

"Yeah... it's a long story..."

"Okay, you *so* gotta tell me."

I lean around the wall and glance towards the dining room, checking in on Charlie. He's still playing happily with his Lego sets, but I wouldn't be surprised if he's listening in on me.

"Yeah, now is not a good time. Listen, I'm only calling because I was worried about you..."

"Is there somewhere we can meet? Can I come get you?"

"I'm not sure that's a good idea. I can't leave... I'm kind

of babysitting."

"Okay, now you really gotta tell me what's going on! How are you hiding out and babysitting?"

Shit. Shit. Shit. I'm just digging myself deeper and deeper here. This would be so much easier if I could just tell her everything, but I don't want her to freak out.

"Look," she says, getting that tone of voice she always gets with me when she's about to put me in my place. "We need to talk, *pronto*, and I'm not going to take no for an answer. You've been missing for days, and everyone, including myself, has been worried crazy. So you need to pick a time and place to meet."

She stops, and I think she's done, and I open my mouth to start giving her an excuse on why we can't meet when she threatens, "Or I'm just going to call up my dad, have him trace this call, and I'll find you anyway."

Fuck, this phone call really was a bad idea. I totally forgot how bossy she can be.

"Sophia..." I plead.

"No, this is happening. You're totally giving me weird vibes and I need to know that you're okay."

I throw my hands in the air. When she gets all bossy like this she almost always gets her way.

But not this time.

"I'm sorry! I didn't want you to worry, and I would have called you if I could. But now is really not a good time." Because I made a promise, a promise I totally intend to keep. "Look, I'll call you later..."

"Okay. Well, I'm just going to ring up my dad..."

"Sophia, don't!"

"And tell him you've been kidnapped again and you called me..."

Gah, she just has to play dirty!

"Then I'm going to get your address, call 911, and tell them it's an emergency..."

Damn, she's really going all in here. And I don't doubt for a second she won't do exactly as she just promised.

"Fine! You win! We can meet!" I cry, and fight back the urge to bang my head against the wall. "But you have to come to me. And you can't tell anyone where I am. I don't want my father to find me."

"I can do that. I won't tell a soul," she agrees, sounding calmer and more relieved.

I rattle off Johnathan's address, the address I noted yesterday when he took me to meet with his boss.

"I'm not far. See you in twenty."

"See you," I say, and hang up the phone feeling like I just made an epic mistake.

∼

"BETH!" Sophia cries out when I open the front door, and flings herself into my arms.

We squeeze each other *hard*. God, I missed her, and it feels so good to see her. Now that I know she's safe with my own eyes, I'll be able to rest easier.

"I was *so* freaking worried about you," she frowns as she pulls away.

"Ditto," I say, and all I can do is make more apologies. "I'm sorry. Things have been rather crazy for me..."

"Is this Johnathan's house?" she asks as she walks in. Her eyes go wide as she takes everything in. All the new furniture. "I really didn't peg him for the boring, suburban type."

Her eyes finally land on Charlie, and she gives me a *'what the hell'* look before offering him a smile. "Hi there."

"Hi," Charlie says shyly and sinks back into his chair.

"Charlie, this is my best friend Sophia," I explain. "You can trust her. She's practically my sister."

Sophia nods her head up and down and her smile widens. "Hi Charlie, it's nice to meet you. And you can totally trust me."

"Okay..." Charlie says, and I can tell even with our reassurance he still seems uneasy. After all the poor guy has been through, it's probably going to take him a bit to warm up to her, but I'm hoping one day he feels just as safe with her as he does with me.

"Are you thirsty?" I ask Sophia and look pointedly towards the kitchen.

She gets the hint and nods. "Yeah, I could use a drink."

She continues to look around curiously. I try to see everything through her eyes, and can only imagine what she's thinking.

As soon as we step into the kitchen, Sophia grabs me by the arm and whisper hisses, "Oh my god, you have to tell me everything. Is Charlie Johnathan's kid?"

"Not exactly..." I whisper back. "He is and he isn't. Johnathan kind of... bought him when he bought me."

"What?!" she gasps.

"It's not like *that*," I immediately say in Johnathan's defense so she doesn't get the wrong idea.

She shakes her head in disbelief and asks, "What is it like then?"

In a rush, I quickly explain everything that went down that night Johnathan bought us and finish with, "He couldn't just leave him there with those monsters. I thought the worst at first too, but he's serious about taking care of Charlie and protecting him."

Sophia rocks back on her heels and gives a soft, surprised, "Wow."

I nod my head and smile at her. "So, like I said, things have been kind of crazy for me..."

"Yeah, no shit," she agrees and grins. "So, you and Johnathan are kind of like a thing now, yeah?"

My cheeks warm and I can't stop my own grin when I say, "Something like that."

"Okay." Her eyes sparkle with amusement. I know she just loves to watch me squirm. "Now you really gotta spill it. What's going on with you and him?"

I shake my head slowly, and honest to god, "I don't even know how to explain it."

Not backing down, she leans close and says eagerly, "You can start after he bought you. Why didn't he take you home? Did you ask to stay with him?"

Shit. I'm afraid if I tell her exactly what went down,

she might hate Johnathan. And I really don't want her to hate him, it's important to me that she likes him.

He's quickly becoming one of the, if not the most, important person in my life. I don't know what I'll do if the two of them hate each other.

"Not exactly..." I say tentatively and bite my lip.

"You really got to stop saying that," she says with a huff. "Come on, you can tell me, Beth. I'm your best friend!"

And that's exactly why I can't tell her. If I tell her that Johnathan has kept me here against my will, she'll flip her shit. And then I'll have to explain how I want to stay with him now while trying not to sound like an idiot.

"We're still figuring it—" I start to say, but then I'm cut off by a very sharp, "Elizabeth!"

What the fuck? Did I really just hear that?

I look towards the living room, and then I look back to Sophia.

All the color has drained from her face and I know she heard it too.

"Beth!" Charlie calls out in distress, and I don't even think about it, I just book it.

I run for the living room and then come to a screeching halt when I see my father, of all people, standing in the middle of it.

"Oh my god, Beth. I swear I didn't tell him anything," Sophia rushes out behind me as my heart races a mile a minute and my brain tries to figure out how the hell this happened. "He must have tapped my phone, or had someone following me."

Fuck. I totally believe her. She'd never rat me out, and having someone tail her sounds just like my father.

"Elizabeth," my father repeats coldly as his gaze falls on me.

He's dressed in his usual ready-for-live-TV way. Dark suit, polished black shoes, hair brushed to the back in an artful wave that he has done by his own personal stylist.

He looks so out of place here in Johnathan's living room, yet I can't help but think if we were back at that office he'd fit right in.

"Father," I say cautiously, steeling my features. "What are you doing here?"

"Beth!" Charlie calls out and runs up to me. He grabs me by the waist and hides behind me, clearly terrified.

I can't understand his fear at first, and then I notice movement at the open front door. Dammit all. My father brought his personal security, aka hired goons, with him. Three huge guys nearly popping out of their suits smirk as they stand ready to carry out my father's bidding.

My father's lips curl with a look of disgust as he takes another look around the room. When his gaze finally comes back to me, his eyes are blazing. "You've had your fun, Elizabeth. It's time you came home."

Now would be the perfect time for Johnathan to come storming in, I think, as I assess the situation.

I'm not sure how I'm going to get out of this without divine intervention.

My father is a man who never accepts the word 'no', especially when it comes from my lips, but I say it anyway. "No."

My father's face darkens and he takes a step towards me. "Playtime is over, Elizabeth. I've been more than patient. It's time for you to return home to your *obligations*." He hisses the last word and I wince.

My obligations being that I'm to sit around in my room like some object that's being stored until it's useful to him.

I shake my head, and before I can speak again, Sophia speaks up for me, "She doesn't have to go anywhere with you. She's a grown damn woman and she can make her own decisions!"

God, I love her, but I really wish she didn't just do that. Any hope that I had of temporarily placating him has now gone down the drain.

My father's face starts to turn an angry shade of tomato red.

"Father..." I say softly, pleadingly.

I know I shouldn't have to plead for my freedom, and it makes me sick to my stomach, but what other choice do I have? I can't take on him and all his goons, and I sure as hell don't want anybody to get hurt for trying.

If I can reason with him, maybe I can still defuse this and come to an understanding. "I can't leave. So much has happened, and if you would just give me a minute, I can explain it all."

"Do explain," he says, his face somehow turning even

redder. "Explain how you lied to your guard and left the house so you could go whoring at some dive bar in the shittiest part of town."

His words are like a slap to the face. I can't even count how many times in my life he's called me a whore, but each time hurts just like the first.

He takes an ominous step towards me, and Charlie's grip on me tightens. "Explain how you were rescued from your predicament, a predicament you *deserve* for your whoring ways, and instead of returning to me immediately, you decided to remain here and continue to play the whore."

"You're a bastard!" Sophia screeches behind me. She starts to take a step forward, but I throw my hand out to stop her.

My father turns his attention to Sophia and again his lips curl back with disgust. "And you're the little blonde slut who's corrupted my daughter."

Sophia sucks in a sharp breath.

This is getting out of hand fast and it needs to stop. Neither of us deserve this, and I don't want Charlie to have to listen to it.

"Stop, please," I plead and clutch Charlie close to me. "You've said enough."

My father's attention turns back to me. "No, I haven't said nearly enough, but we'll finish this conversation at home."

I shake my head. "I'm not going home. I have obligations and responsibilities here."

His face tightens, and he's so red now I'm afraid his head might burst. "Your obligations are to your family. To *me*."

I don't know why he thinks I owe him everything just because I exist, but he does. He thinks because he's my father, something I didn't get a choice in, that I'm to bend and bow to his every whim. He honestly believes I should be grateful for being his daughter. Grateful that he's fed me and housed me, and forever in his debt.

Lifting my chin in defiance, I muscle up every ounce of courage I have, and look him hard in the eye. In the past, my defiance has always been met with painful words or violence, and I've been conditioned to expect it and avoid it all costs.

But in the past, it was only me who suffered for my actions, for my cowardice.

I can't let him hurt Charlie. I can't. Just the thought of my father doing to him what he's done to me fills me with so much anger I start to see red.

"I have a new family now. A family of my choosing. *And I will not abandon my child*," I say, and squeeze Charlie a little harder as I say it. I feel the truth in the words with every fiber of my being. Charlie is *mine*, he's mine.

And so is Johnathan.

I'm owning them right now. From this point on, they're my family, the family I got to pick for myself.

My father's eyes finally drop to Charlie and fill with so much loathing and disgust my hands itch to wrap around his neck. I never thought I was capable of violence. After all I've endured, how could I possibly inflict pain on another person? But the way my father is looking at Charlie makes me feel murderous.

If I had that gun Johnathan said is under the bed, I'd be extremely tempted to use it.

"I can see you are going to refuse to be reasonable," he says through clenched teeth as his eyes lift. He jerks his head towards his goons. "Escort my daughter to the car."

"No!" I cry out, but it doesn't stop the goons as they come for me, their tree trunks for legs easily eating up the distance.

"Beth," Charlie starts crying in earnest, and my heart breaks as I feel his tears soaking my shirt.

I can't protect him and I can't fucking stop this. Just one-on-one with one of these guys would be nearly impossible.

Taking three of them on is beyond futile.

At the last moment, I push Charlie towards Sophia. I don't know what else to do.

"Please take care of him," I beg.

Do what I can't.

Sophia meets my eyes and her face is flushed with anger on my behalf. "I won't let him get away with this," she promises as she hugs Charlie to her chest.

But even though her father is the Chief of Police, I know there's nothing she or her father can do to stop this.

My father is, and has always been, higher up the food

chain. His connections reach all the way to the Oval Office.

The three goons reach me, and two of them grab me by each arm and start dragging me back.

I want to cry out, to tell Charlie I'm sorry, so sorry, but I'm afraid of further traumatizing him.

I'm the worst fucking protector ever.

As I'm dragged past my father, he grins a very self-satisfied smile. I honestly can't comprehend how he can be so smug over this shit. He couldn't even take me on by himself, he had to bring in three goons to do his dirty work for him.

And that's when it hits me. My father is a coward and has always been. He refuses to fight fair because he knows if he does he can't possibly win.

The smug smile dies on his lips as he takes in my angry, non-terrified glare.

For once in my life, I'm honestly not afraid of him. He can drag me away against my will and lock me back in my room, but I'll stop at nothing now to escape him.

The two goons drag me out the door and down the driveway to an awaiting black limousine. The back door is opened and then I'm shoved inside. The door slams shut and I immediately check the handle.

It's locked from the outside.

A moment later, the other door opens and my father slides in. I scoot into my corner and stare out my window, unable to bring myself to look at him.

The front doors open and slam shut, then the car starts moving.

"Elizabeth," my father says, and I stupidly glance over at him.

He backhands me across the face, and it happens so fast, so suddenly, I never saw it coming.

I reel back as pain explodes across my right cheek, and then he backhands me just as quickly across the other cheek.

"That's just a taste of what's to come for all the trouble you've caused me, you little ungrateful bitch," he hisses.

I stare at him in shock at first. I mean I knew what was coming, but usually he waits until we're in the house before he dishes out the violence.

Reaching up, I tentatively touch my cheeks, then my bottom lip. Yeah, he busted it open.

My father reaches down and yanks on the bottom of his suit jacket before leaning back. His eyes meet mine and he grins as tears fill them.

But the joke's on him.

I turn away from him and stare out the window again, unable to stop the tears pouring down my cheeks.

But I'm not crying because my father just bitch-slapped me.

No, I'm crying because at this moment I absolutely hate myself.

I couldn't protect Charlie.

And I just broke my promise to Johnathan.

20

JOHNATHAN

The broken-down girl in my living room sure as fuck isn't who I thought would be here when I got the fuck home.

Charlie is nowhere to be seen, and the seething rage that fills my veins is about to explode.

My Beth is missing.

The front fucking door is wide open, and I think this girl's name is Sophia.

"Where's my wife and son?" I ask gruffly as she stares up at me in shock.

My phone begins to vibrate and chirp in my pocket, but I ignore it as I move closer to her.

"Where are they?" I shout as I grab her by the shoulders.

She's not answering me, only a small blubber comes out of her mouth.

"Johnny?!?" Charlie shouts as he comes racing down

the stairs. His little shoulders are heaving as he slams into me.

"They took Beth!" Charlie wails as he wraps his arms around my waist.

Pulling him up into my arms, I growl.

"It was her father," Sophia finally manages to say to me. "Her father and his goons somehow followed me here."

"What do you mean *followed you here*?" I turn to stare at her.

My rage must show through my eyes because she takes a step back away from me. "How the fuck did you end up here in the first place?"

"Beth... She called me and I came to see her..."

"Beth wasn't supposed to be calling anyone. This was the only safe place she could be!"

Fuck!

My phone begins to vibrate and chirp again. Pulling it from my pocket, I really don't feel like fucking around with anything Simon has to say. Fucking, hell.

Sliding the phone on, I say into it, "Beth's father took her."

"And now another damn complication I have to attend to. Can't you keep your damn woman under control?" Simon sneers into the phone.

"Simon, why the fuck are you calling me right now?"

"Sasha is on the move. We have a team set for grabbing him. We need you to be there..."

"Not happening. I need to get Beth back from her father…"

"Your love life is not my fucking concern."

"No, but it's Lucifer's… If we don't have her, we don't have the Senator."

"Damn you," he mutters quietly, and I can just see the machinations turning over in his mind. "You won't be able to get her. They have security…"

Glaring at Sophia, I pull Charlie with me as I move into the kitchen, away from the damn ears of some stupid girl. "I need James. We'll go in tonight to get her."

"We need James as a backspot with his rifle."

"Not as much as I need him for his cat burglar skills."

"I swear you Neanderthals need to keep your dicks in your pants."

"Let Lucifer know the score; I'll get James ready to go."

"You'll get no backup. If you fuck this up, your ass is out to hang, not ours. We'll probably keep James, but you? No."

"Nice to know you care so much, Simon." I disconnect the call and head out to the living room.

"You put Beth in mortal danger…" I say as I lift Charlie in my arms.

"I swear, I didn't know… How… How could I?"

She's getting up from the chair she's been sitting in, and with one fucking look she sits right back down. "Don't fucking move."

Setting Charlie down, I say, "Buddy, go into the

kitchen and get a coke. I need you to play with some Legos for a bit... I'm going to call a friend and I need to talk to this girl here."

"O...Okay. Are you gonna get Beth back?" he asks and his little eyes are full of tears.

The tears spill over onto his cheeks and I feel all that fucking rage enter my body again.

"Yeah," I say with some anger in my voice. "No one takes what's mine."

"Good... her daddy looked really mean."

I give as much of a reassuring smile as I can. It's not like I won't be bringing her back, but I am way too fucking angry to be much of the nurturing type right now. He takes it though, and gives me a brief hug around my neck. "Thank you. I like her lots, she said I was her child."

"You are, and you're *mine*. Now go get you some of that off limits coke. Sophia gets to watch you while you're all bounced up on caffeine."

"Okay." He's still not sure of everything, but I know he believes what I tell him.

Watching him walk away, I feel an ache in my chest. I'm a man of my word, and I failed them both when I said I would keep them safe.

But I can fix this.

Pulling my phone from my pocket, I dial James.

"What do you want, asshole?"

I laugh at that, because even in this mess, I remember James is on a counting-down-till-doomsday clock.

I cursed his ass, he knows it, and I know he knows that I know it.

"We got a job tonight. You ever hit a senator's house before?"

"No."

"Ain't you the fucking chatty one?"

"Fuck you, take it back."

"Not a chance. Anyways, meet me here at eleven. We'll head out and try to get some good intel ahead of time."

"Fuck you," he says before hanging up on me.

Dialing Simon back, he asks, "What is it, Johnathan?"

"I need all the intel we can get on the good Senator. Full work-up, if possible. Also, I need to know what's the proper amount of leverage Lucifer wants to use on the asshole."

"Is that all?" he asks with a sigh of annoyance. He must have spoken to Lucifer already. He knows I'm going to get my way.

"For now. If I need anything else, I'll let you know."

"One thing, Johnathan, before you go. Lucifer has mandated this is a strictly no-kill operation."

"Got it," I say before disconnecting.

It figures. A dead body at the Senator's home would cause too much of a stir right now. We could probably get away with it, but it wouldn't be good for business. Especially if we want the Senator on board with our future for him.

Turning to Sophia, I say, "Tell me everything you can about Beth's home, her father, and his security."

∼

"What the fuck is she doing here?" James asks as he walks into the house. Sophia is sitting on the couch with a sleeping Charlie by her side.

"What's wrong, James?" I snicker. "Why are you getting anxious around females all of a sudden?"

"Fuck you. What's with the chick?" He doesn't even bother looking at me, he's glaring at Sophia.

By the look on her face, I don't think that's the first thing she expected him to say and do the moment he walked into the house.

"She got traced here by Beth's father."

"Hmph. So now we got to bail your woman's ass out of her daddy's little prison?"

"That about sums it up. Though, while we're there, we get to do some larceny, if you're up for it."

His face lights up with a smile. "Now that's something I'm always up for."

Motioning him towards the kitchen, I tell Sophia, "You can take Charlie up to his room if you need. There's a guest bedroom upstairs."

"But I want—" she stammers.

"What you want right now doesn't mean shit. You got Beth into this mess, now I have to get her out of it."

Her eyes go wide and she has to blink away tears

before she says, "Look, I didn't know he would be following me."

"That doesn't matter. Beth is in danger because you pushed her too hard." It's probably not fair, I'm laying the full guilt trip on this girl, but when push comes to shove, I need this girl here to protect Charlie like she told Beth she would.

"I know..."

"Then do what she asked. Take my boy upstairs, put him to bed, and then settle in for the night."

"I can't stay the night, my dad..."

"Your dad will understand. Tell him this is Lucifer's decision, and that you are safe."

"Who the hell is this Lucifer everyone has been talking about?" she asks as she lifts Charlie up and heads towards the stairs.

"The devil of course," James says.

Shaking her head, she heads up the stairs. I watch James, though, while she's moving, and his eyes are glued to her ass the whole way.

Yep, he's next.

"Alright, asshole. Let's get to the compound. We need to get some shit that won't kill people."

It's the fucking loadout strapped to my body that feels wrong. Non-lethal bullshit darts and shit.

How the fuck am I supposed to do shit like this if I

can't fucking kill someone?

They're going to have guns and orders to kill on sight. Not me, nope.

I'm going to be fucking shooting god damn blanks like a neutered dog.

"Looks pretty easy to get in. They have a rotation window in the southeast corner of the estate that gives us three minutes to waltz right through to the south entrance," James says as he looks over the dark estate.

We could have done this job during the day, when there would be less security around with the Senator at his office, but I figure we need to put the fear of hell into Mr. Norton.

I gotta give it to Simon, I don't know how the fuck he messed up with all the intel we needed to remove the fucking Doctor, but the Senator's home intel is really fucking good.

We've got guard rotation, security system overrides, and he's even worked his way into the Senator's personal computers.

Yeah, this fucker is going to go down. We just need to get in there without killing anyone and get back out.

Fuck, when did life get so fucking complicated that I can't resort to fucking killing someone?

Hopping over the small hedge surrounding the backyard, I count to thirty before I motion for James and start moving. We rush through the grounds, both moving in a straight line.

No bobbing and weaving for us.

We found a very small blind spot on the video feeds and that's our avenue of attack.

Once we get to the house itself, we'll have Simon cut the feed to a loop of the last five minutes. No cars or lights have gone across the grounds in that time, so we should be good as the video shows nothing but the normal outside.

Pressing myself up against the brick wall, I nod to James. "Get the lock on the door."

Kneeling down, he fiddles around with the lock to the kitchen's mudroom before standing back up. "Got it."

Nodding, I gently ease the knob in a circle before pushing it open. Three guards are outside the grounds, two in the guard shack, and one on patrol.

"Move in. The guard should be passing here in one minute."

Walking heel to toe, we quietly move into the mudroom.

Shutting the door behind us, I say, "Alright, should be a guard moving around the first floor. We need to secure him first."

Nodding his head, James walks first out of the small room and into the kitchen. We both studied the house's layouts.

There shouldn't be any issues beyond this guy.

After we get through here, we need to head upstairs to the second floor. First to Beth and the guard we believe that's stationed at her door. Then we'll move around a bend to the master bedroom.

From there, it's a matter of subduing the two goons who are protecting the Senator.

Just because I'm not allowed to kill someone doesn't mean I can't carry a pistol with me. The gun alone gives me the ability to intimidate the goon we find in the living room.

My barrel presses tightly to his temple and my hand clamps over his mouth.

"Move, talk, or try to get help and you die," I murmur in his ear.

He's a professional though, so I highly doubt he's really going to let me take him out of the fight easily.

Nodding to James, I watch as he pulls a hypodermic needle from the pouch on his wrist.

Grinning at the goon, James says in a low voice, "You're going to take a nap now."

That's all the guy needs to start struggling against me. I don't have the best of holds, but with a swift crack to the side of his head with the handle of my gun, he slumps into the chair.

I watch as the needle goes into his neck.

"What kind of cocktail did we just put in him?" I ask James.

Shrugging, he says, "No clue. Simon said it's what dreams are made of, and should make him lose all control of his muscles. So he's probably gonna shit and piss himself."

I wince. "That's mean."

Nodding, he motions me towards the archway leading to the stairs then holds up his hand.

Inside his hand I see a little metal whistle.

What the fuck?

Turning to me, he says with a determined look on his face as he lifts the whistle to his mouth, "Take it back."

"What?!?" I ask, incredulous.

"You know what I mean. Take it back, or you and me are going to have a really bad time."

"Are you fucking kidding me?"

This fucker is crazy.

"I said take it back." Putting the whistle in his mouth, he puffs up his cheeks.

"For fuck's sake," I say as I drop my hands and growl. "I take it back."

He noticeably deflates and slips the whistle into his pocket. "Good, now let's get moving."

Stupid fuck. I had my fingers crossed the whole time.

He's so going to be getting wifed up soon.

I go first. I holster my gun then pull out the tranquilizer pistol. It's a Co2 shooting little thing, and thankfully it's not a noisy bastard.

Making my way slowly up the stairs, I get to the first landing and then take it even slower up to the second landing. It's here I need to be careful. I've got a hall to my left that should be empty, but to the right of the staircase should be another one.

There the goon will be watching Beth's door.

Pulling a thin camera wire from my pocket, I attach it

to my phone. Looking at the screen, I slide the wire around the corner.

There, louder than life, is the guard. He's sitting sprawled out in his chair, watching something on his own phone.

I'm betting it's porn.

Pulling back the wire, I motion to James that I've spotted our guy.

Slowly moving to the corner, I take careful aim with my gun and shoot.

This isn't like the movies though, where some guy gets hit and he instantly falls down. Nope, he's not out yet, but this is one of those extremely powerful, loopy drugs so that helps.

"What the?!" he grunts, before I slam directly into his side, headbutting him with all the force I muster.

James is there an instant later, shoving a piece of cloth into his mouth. Tape comes next, and then a good hard punch with my brass knuckles knocks the guy out of the fight completely.

James wraps his arms around the guy as I move to Beth's door.

Testing the handle, I find it's unlocked.

Opening the door, I move quickly into the dimly lit room. It's not exactly what I pictured her room to look like.

The room is almost sterile in its stark emptiness.

There's a bed with beige blankets and sheets. The walls

are some type of light brown too. Carpet is a boring off white. Dresser is there, but it almost looks utilitarian. The only real piece of personality comes from the nightstand where a picture of Beth and a woman who I think is her mother is.

James pushes past me with the unconscious asshole who he drops to the floor with a heavy thump. "Fucking guy is heavy as shit. Fucker been eating too many twinkies."

At James's voice, Beth's eyes snap open in stark terror before she spots me.

There is a small look of hope there in those hazel eyes as she slowly comes off the bed. Her lip is split and she has a big black eye from where her father must have struck her.

I can't believe a man would do something like this to his own daughter. It makes my skin crawl with disgust for him.

"Johnathan?" she asks as if she can't believe it's me.

Nodding my head, I sweep her into my arms.

She feels absolutely right here in my arms. I don't like the 'love' word, but I sure feel something like it in my chest as I hold her as tight as I can.

Her hands grab my cheeks as she pulls me down to a deep kiss. She shows absolutely no hesitation as she kisses me with all the passion inside of her soul. I'm momentarily stunned before I find myself returning the kiss with everything I have.

Pulling away from her, my cock is semi-hard as I say,

"We need to get moving. Still gotta visit your old man before we get out of here."

Eyes wide, she shakes her head. "He's never going to let me go, Johnathan, not if he can help it... I'm so sorry I made a mess of..."

"Don't start. It is what it is. This just speeds up the process of taking control of your father's life."

"Is Charlie okay?" she asks.

"Yeah, our boy is good. Passed out right before we left the house. I got your friend Sophia there watching him."

"Thank god."

"Time to move, guys. We need to secure the old man so I can get to stealing some shit. You got anything in here you want to take, Beth?" James asks as he looks around the barren room.

She goes to the nightstand and pics up the picture frame. Holding it to her chest, she shakes her head. "Nothing. He's taken anything I ever held dear away from me already. I just want to go home."

Home. She called my house *home*. Fuck that makes my dick swell. She's going to look so good at home with a big, fat pregnant belly.

Pulling her into the hallway, we move slowly towards her father's area.

Reaching the corner, I murmur to Beth, "Tell the men you need to talk to your father."

She nods her head and sets the picture frame down on the floor before straightening herself out.

Turning the corner, she slumps her shoulders and her

head goes into a meek, little submissive posture as she asks, "Can I speak to him please?"

"He's sleeping. Come back in the morning," I hear one of the men say.

"But—"

"Go away, or we'll have to let him know you're misbehaving again."

I see Beth just barely turn the corner before she falls to the floor in an almost believable act. She makes it look like she tripped on something.

"Oh god... my ribs," she gasps as she looks right at me and gives a small wink.

"Fucking hell," I hear the other guy say as they move towards us.

She crawls past me, saying, "Please don't hurt me... Please."

One thug passes around the corner and stops in shock as I lift him up off his feet with a vicious uppercut to his chin.

The second man falls back as he gets slammed into by James. I've seen James tackle people before, and he's not the biggest of Lucifer's men, but when he slams into the second guy it looks like a NFL linebacker is taking out a junior high kid.

The man slams into a wall with his head leaving a sizable dent in the plaster.

Running over to the guy, I lay into him a couple of times with my knuckles before he's out like his buddy.

Panting just slightly, I look over at Beth. She's pulled

herself into a sitting position and she leans against the wall we were just hiding behind.

"You okay, baby?" I ask as I kneel down in front of her.

Wincing, she holds her hand out for me to help her up. "Yeah, but my ribs really do hurt. They like to hit me where it won't show."

Growling, I pull her into my arms. "I swear I'm—"

"Remember the rules, John, no killing," James says as he zip ties both guards before gagging and duct taping their mouths shut.

Begrudgingly, I nod my head. I don't have to like it; I just have to do it.

We walk to the Senator's door, and with hard kick from me, the lock shatters the wood holding it shut and the door flies open.

"Wake the fuck up, asshole," James calls out as he runs into the room.

Sitting up straight, the Senator looks around in bewilderment.

I can only imagine this pile of shit's thoughts as he looks around him. Probably wondering where the men who are supposed to be protecting him are at.

He's there, sitting in bed, the lights from the hall showing him wearing actual fucking sleep pajamas, like he's from the fifties or something.

"Hello, Father," Beth says in a fake, cheery voice. I can hear the sickly sweet tone she's using and it makes even me want to cringe. "Look who I brought home! It's my husband, the dirty, foul-mouthed biker who's going to knock your little darling up!"

Fuck, she even giggled at the end.

Laughing at him as he tries to go for his nightstand, I rush over to kick it away. The lamp goes flying into the wall where it shatters.

"Not a good idea, Dad. We don't need to be bothering people at this time of night," I say with a smirk.

"Whoever the fuck you are... I swear you're going to regret this."

"That's no way to speak to your son-in-law. Anyways, all the phone lines and alarms are currently disabled."

The man looks up at me then orders. "Get out of my house before I have you killed, you little shit."

Raising my hand, I reach back to punch him before he screeches, "Not in the face!"

That gives me pause.

Looking over at Beth, I ask, "The face?"

She shakes her head. "No, because that's his money-maker. You hit him there and it ruins whatever your plans are."

"Ah."

Well, I guess I'll go the other route for now.

Motioning to Beth, I say, "Baby, I need to talk to this pile of shit, and you might not want to hear what's going to be said."

"Trust me, nothing will matter to me. This is the last time he's ever going to see me," she says as she sticks her chin out.

Fuck it, it's her choice.

Sitting down on the edge of the bed, I snap out a fist at the man's stomach.

I don't punch him with my full strength, considering I still have my brass knuckles on, but it's enough to make him start heaving and gasping for air.

Grabbing his messy hair, I throw him off the bed and onto the floor before me.

"Careful, John. Dude likes being on his knees in front of guys," James laughs.

Senator Norton begins to tremble as he lies there in front of me. He looks like he's about to cry, and it makes me feel so damn warm inside.

"Let's get right down to it. We've been watching you for a good long while there, Dick... You like the word *dick*, don't ya?" I say as I kick my foot out at him, catching him in the leg.

He doesn't respond and I look over to James. "You got the video file, buddy?"

"Dude, why did you guys have to put it on my phone? Even I feel dirty watching it."

Shrugging, I point to the Senator. "Show the man his past sins."

"See, things are kinda wonky, Dickie boy. All those votes to stop same-sex marriage, to end civil rights and shit... And you like to get it in the ass from big, black men. You're the classic example of a pile of shit."

The video plays, loud sounds of grunting coming from the speakers.

Beth's eyes widen as she comes around to look at what's on the screen. I feel sorry she looks, but what can I do? She wanted to stay.

"Holy shit. I... He..."

I nod my head. "Yeah, the guy giving it to him is wearing a superman cape... I have no clue what kind of kink shit this is. But your dad is a one hundred percent hypocrite, man-in-the closet type of fuck."

Turning away from the phone, she says, "I think I'm going to wait outside of the room..."

"Don't blame ya."

"See, tiny dick," I say as I lean down to watch his face. A face that is showing the pure horror of a man who's about to lose it all. "We don't mind what you do in your life, but you sure as fuck wanted to control other people."

"What... What do you want?" he asks in a whisper.

"You in the Governor's seat within the next two years," I say. Motioning to James, I order, "Go get his safe and all the electronic shit you can find. I want a copy of anything he wants to hide."

"Got it," he says as he jogs out of the room.

Looking up at me in astonishment, the Senator asks, "What?"

"Well, you see you're in a position ripe for advancement. Where you're at now isn't as valuable to my boss as where you can be. We get you there and you keep your life as it is. Minus your daughter. She's coming with me."

"But... but I..."

"Lucifer wants this for you. I suggest you nod your head right now."

The man goes deathly white at the name. He should. Someone like Lucifer holding your life in the balance tends to make people listen up.

But then he has to go and say, "You can't take her. I refuse to allow—"

Fuck the 'no face' rule. I backhand him so hard his head slams into the carpeted floor. Standing up from the bed, I pull him by his hair and he screeches.

"Stand up like a man, pussy," I growl.

When I have him finally standing up like a man, I say, "That's your only warning. You will never get a second warning from my boss. Do you understand? What we say goes from now on. We will ruin you professionally, then in the dead of night, sometime in the future, I'll take your life."

Tears spill down his cheeks as he begins to whimper like some little bitch. "Okay... Okay... Please don't..."

"We'll be in touch with you real soon, Senator Norton," I say and let go of him. "And for fuck's sake, stand up like a man."

Straightening up slowly, he tries to look like a man, but in his eyes I see the little coward bitch he really is. Fucker hit his daughter like a scumsucking pile of shit.

Turning my back to him, I start to walk away.

Wait I forgot.

Turning around to him, I say, "One more thing."

"What is it?" he asks with a sigh.

Grabbing him by the shoulders, I slam my knee into his balls.

Air rushes out of his lungs as I say, "Tell your fucking guards on the ground to go home for the night. Do it in the next five minutes or I'll come back and remind you how much I hate you."

Walking out of the room, I grab Beth by the hand. "Let's get going, baby. I've got a surprise for you once we get out of here."

21

BETH

I'm free. Truly free. I almost can't believe it. The day started out like a nightmare and now everything feels like a dream.

Johnathan came for me. He fucking rescued me and put my father in his place. Thanks to him, I won't have to spend the rest of my life looking over my shoulder, on the run, or trapped in my father's prison.

"Are you cold, baby?" Johnathan asks me as he, James, and I step out of the car.

I shiver as the cold night breeze hits me and smile at him. "Just a little."

He shrugs out of his leather jacket and drapes it over my shoulders. His warmth envelopes me and I swallow back a contented moan. Fuck, this man.... This man has done nothing but take care of me and protect me.

I owe so much to him... and I all have to give in repayment is *me*.

"Johnathan..." I say and reach out to touch his arm as he and James start to walk across the gravel parking lot.

We haven't had a moment alone, and I still need to apologize and thank him for everything.

"Yeah?" Johnathan stops and arches a bushy brow at me.

"Can we talk for a second?" I ask.

I don't know where we are or why we're here. All I know is that Johnathan has some kind of surprise for me. A surprise that lies in what looks like a dark, abandoned warehouse...

James glances back at us but Johnathan waves him on. James smirks knowingly and nods his head before walking up to the concrete building that lies at the end of the parking lot.

Johnathan turns to me and I step up to him. I don't know how to say this. How do I properly thank him for what he just did? How do I properly thank him for changing my life?

I tip my head back, peering up at his face. In the moonlight he looks so dark and foreboding, but I'm no longer afraid of him.

For whatever reason, this hard, powerful man has a soft spot for me.

"I'm sorry I broke my promise to you," I start and Johnathan scowls. "I fucked up, and I know I shouldn't have—"

He grabs me by the hips and pulls me close, causing my words to cut off with an unladylike grunt.

Even when he's being gentle, landing against his chest feels like landing against a wall of bricks.

"Don't worry about it," he growls.

"But—"

He cuts me off by growling again. "Shit's in the past."

When I open my mouth to argue, he shakes his head. "It's dead and buried, Beth. Leave it."

I want to argue with him. Just letting it go feels too easy. I feel like I should grovel and plead for his forgiveness.

He stares down at my face and he must be able to read my mind or something. "If it will make you feel better, I can always spank you later for it."

I blink up at him, unable to tell if he's being serious or not…

And then he grins.

Rolling my eyes, I shake my head. "Yeah, I think I'll have to take a pass on that."

His grin takes a devious turn and he gives me a light smack on the ass. I squeak in surprise and end up jerking closer to him. "You sure, baby? I think you'd like it."

By the hard bulge in his pants, I can definitely tell he likes it. A warm flush spreads through me and I lock my knees together.

"How can anyone like that? Being hit like a child?" I ask even as the little slap he gave me makes me very aware of my ass.

Something flashes in his eyes and he groans.

"Fucking hell. Sometimes I forget you're so damn innocent."

I'm feeling playful and rather exuberant after tonight's accomplishments so I lower my lashes coyly and say, "Innocent? Who, me?"

"Yes, you," he growls and his mouth comes crashing down on mine.

There's pain at first. My lip is still busted from my father backhanding me, but the ache only seems to add another dynamic to the kiss.

I need this. I need him.

Trapped in my room, I was afraid I had lost him forever, and I regretted every second I held myself back from him.

I regretted all the time I wasted fighting this crazy thing between us.

I'm tired of living in fear. I'm tired of just existing and waiting for a slim chance of freedom.

Life is short, too damn short. Tomorrow I could be dead.

I'm ready to experience everything life has to offer, and I want to experience every crazy moment with Charlie and Johnathan.

I press closer to him and lift up on my tiptoes, molding my breasts to his chest, my hips to his hips. The jacket he draped over me starts to slide off my shoulders as his hands roam over me.

I'll never get enough of this.

The total chaos of his every kiss. Each time is different but no less passionate than the kiss before it.

His mouth devours mine. His teeth nipping at me like he wants to eat me. His tongue diving deep.

And I offer myself up eagerly.

Somehow I've become a willing sacrifice on the altar of Johnathan.

A low rumble begins in the base of his throat, like thunder off in the distance. It grows louder and louder until he's tearing his mouth away from mine.

Breathing harshly, he rasps, "You're going to be the fucking death of me."

He yanks the jacket back up before it meets the gravel, and then grabs me by the back of the head. His fingers lace into my hair as he presses his forehead against mine. I pant and stare into his eyes as I catch my breath.

"Why did you stop?" I finally ask once I have enough oxygen. "You worn out, old man?"

His eyes spark with mischief and then I'm rewarded with another slap to my ass.

I yelp and he laughs. "As much as I want to finish this, we're expected inside."

Now I'm curious. I got completely swept up in the moment and forgot he has a 'surprise' waiting for me.

"What did you get me?" I ask as he draws my arm into his and leads me up the parking lot.

I can't decipher the look on his face when he grins

this time. His eyes go cold but he looks like a kid about to dive into a mountain of chocolate.

"Revenge."

∼

As we step into the warehouse, every little hair on the back of my neck stands on end. Outside, the night is growing darker and colder, but in here the air is thick and full of something I can't place.

Anticipation?

Menace?

Johnathan's grip on me tightens as he leads me across the dusty floor, weaving me through old industrial-sized machines that probably haven't been used in ages.

We finally reach the back of the warehouse and push through a door that leads to what must have once been an office.

Lucifer is the first person I see. He straightens as we step inside and turns towards us in greeting.

His lips stretch into a smile. "Ah, so glad you could join us, Johnathan." His eyes flick towards me and his smile seems to warm a little. "Beth."

I nod my head and offer a polite smile in return. I can't quite thank him for having us here because I'm confused as fuck and don't know what is about to happen.

Johnathan just grunts and his eyes scan the room. He's searching for someone or something.

"He still alive?" Johnathan asks as his searching gaze narrows in on Lucifer.

"Of course," Lucifer says, his bright eyes flashing with humor. "I wouldn't dare dream of depriving your wife of her wedding gift."

My wedding gift? What the fuck? Why would I want some mystery person?

A pain-filled grunt comes from behind Lucifer.

Lucifer grins and steps to the side, revealing the rest of the room. "We've only... tenderized him a bit for you."

I blink at Lucifer, not understanding the hidden meaning, before another grunt draws my attention.

I look to the center of the room and see Andrew bending over someone seated in a chair. At first, all I can see is their hairy legs, and it strikes me as being strange that they seem to be completely bare. Are they not wearing any pants?

Andrew straightens and turns. "'Bout fucking time." He shakes out his right hand as if it's paining him and then he walks up to Johnathan and gives him a friendly slap on the back with his left hand. "He's all yours, buddy."

"Thanks for keeping him warm for us," Johnathan grins and once more tugs me forward, but as soon as I see who is sitting in the chair I freeze in shock.

Sasha, the man who killed Lindsey, groans and slowly, as if he's in a great deal of pain, lifts his head and his eyes lock on mine.

I see my own shock reflected in his eyes before they fill with hatred. "You..." he hisses.

I glance towards Johnathan, my heart fluttering with panic. "Why is he here?"

Johnathan opens his mouth to answer me, but before he can Sasha yells out, "I knew you would be trouble."

Johnathan's face hardens and he releases his grip on my arm.

"I should have killed you and all your worthless friends!"

Johnathan reaches into his pocket and walks up to Sasha in three big steps. Pulling his hand out of his pocket, his knuckles glint in the overhead light before his fist connects with Sasha's mouth.

There's an awful crack and I can't help but wince.

"Shut your mouth, you fucking waste of flesh."

Sasha moans and as Johnathan pulls away, I can see his mouth is now a bloody mess. Johnathan punches him again, this time in the ribs. Sasha doubles over, all the air whooshing out of him.

Johnathan looks over his shoulder, towards Lucifer. "You get everything you need out of him?"

Lucifer nods his head. "Yes, he was surprisingly easy to break. By all means, carry on Johnathan," he grins.

Sasha gasps for air and makes all kinds of horrible wheezing noises.

Lucifer points to a cart covered in a variety of shop tools and medical instruments. "You're welcome to use my personal collection if you wish."

Johnathan glances towards the cart and makes a disgusted face. "I don't need all that shit when I've got my fists."

Lucifer smirks and nods his head. "True, but your wife might find something of interest."

Both men look at me expectantly, and I feel like the floor was just yanked out from beneath me.

Do they expect me to torture Sasha? Have I somehow given them the impression I'm capable of such a thing? I know I expressed my hated for the men who hurt my friends and me, but this...

I don't know what to do. The world around me is spinning out of control. How could Johnathan possibly think I'd want this? That I'd be okay with this?

This is evil and sick.

Johnathan hovers over Sasha as the man tries to breathe.

After a few minutes, Sasha finally draws in a couple of deep breaths and straightens. I cover my mouth with a gasp as I catch sight of his mangled mouth. His teeth are broken and he's bleeding profusely. Steams of saliva and blood drool down his chin.

Sasha mutters something but it's a completely unintelligible, slurred Russian mess.

"What was that?" Johnathan asks.

Sasha spits out a wad of blood and a couple of teeth before sneering at Johnathan. "I said your wife is a dirty whore."

Johnathan punches Sasha again in the stomach.

Again, the air seems to go out of him, but he recovers more quickly this time.

Sucking in a breath, Sasha wheezes out, "So dirty and ugly, even my men wouldn't touch her."

Johnathan takes another swing at Sasha, aiming at his head, but stops at the last second.

Sasha cringes, expecting the hit, as Johnathan looks back at me. "You want a piece of this, baby?"

I shake my head slowly back and forth and take a step back.

No, I don't want a fucking piece of this. What I want to do is run far, far away from here and pretend it never happened.

Sasha starts laughing as if he finds this hilarious. His bloodshot eyes lock on me and there's a manic quality to them. "They wouldn't fuck your disgusting pussy, but they fucked the shit out of your pretty little brunette friend."

Oh my god, is he talking about Amanda?

"Shut the fuck up," Johnathan bellows and punches him in the head.

Sasha's head goes flying back and for a second I think Johnathan might have broken his neck.

I hold my breath, wondering if it's over now.

But then Sasha's chin drops back down and he spits out another thick wad of blood and spit.

Sasha can't seem to look up when he groans, "They fucked her in her mouth."

Johnathan punches him in the gut.

"Stop," I hear myself whisper, but the sound is too small.

Sasha wheezes and it sounds like something inside him is rattling before he chuckles. "They fucked her in her pussy."

Johnathan takes another swing, his fist connecting with Sasha's jaw again. There's a crack, and this time my voice is louder when I cry out, "Stop!"

Sasha's head whips to the side and seems to bounce right back. He groans pitifully and a gush of blood spills from his lips. It takes him several tries before he can successfully spit out more teeth.

I don't know how he survived the punches Johnathan just threw at him.

The man should be dead.

He coughs and hacks, and sounds like an old man when he wheezes out, "They fucked her in the ass."

Johnathan pulls his arm back, prepared to take another swing when I scream out, "Johnathan, stop!"

Johnathan freezes in place and shoots a worried look back at me.

"The more she cried," Sasha coughs out. "The harder they fucked her."

Johnathan's face contorts with rage and I'm afraid he's about to follow through with his swing.

"Johnathan, please," I plead and his face falls.

Slowly, with a look of regret, he lowers his arm and then walks over to me. "You okay, baby?" he asks while pulling me into his arms.

I shake my head and feel the tears I've been crying splashing against my cheeks. How could I possibly be okay after hearing all of that?

"You want to leave while I finish him off?" Johnathan asks as his arms squeeze protectively around me.

Johnathan is big and warm and safe, but I can take no comfort in him.

"Is it true?" I hear myself whimper.

Johnathan goes stiff and I know the answer before he mutters it. "Yeah."

Fuck! I can't believe Amanda had to go through all of that. I don't want to imagine it, but after everything Sasha just said, I can't stop the horrors she must have endured from filling my head.

Amanda cried so much, and she was the most afraid out of the three of us...

"I thought you said she was safe," I sob, a fresh wave of sorrow slamming into me for my friend.

"She was," Johnathan explains reluctantly. "Once we rescued her."

"Oh god," I groan.

I push away from Johnathan and he lets me go. Bending over, I start to dry heave, overcome with sudden and intense nausea.

"I'm sorry, baby," Johnathan apologizes as he pulls my hair back for me. "I was just trying to protect you..."

His big, warm palm comes down on my back, rubbing in soothing circles as my stomach clenches and my body tries in vain to force something up.

Thankfully, or not, I haven't eaten in hours so the nausea passes with no results.

A shadow appears over me and I look up to see Lucifer. He holds out a bottle of water for me.

I wipe my mouth with the back of my hand and straighten.

"Thank you," I croak out as I accept the bottle.

Lucifer nods his head and watches me with keen interest.

I take a moment to gather my composure and drink from the bottle. Johnathan continues to rub my back and lingers by my side. Once I think I can handle it, I look back to Sasha.

Just the sight of him makes me sick, and it's not because of his poor physical condition.

"Come on," Johnathan says, his arm coming to wrap around me. "Let's get you home. This was a bad idea."

I nod my head and can't help but agree with him. This was a very bad idea, and I have no clue what Johnathan was thinking.

I don't belong here. I don't belong in this kind of world, and right now all I want to do is escape it.

The thought of returning home, of curling up in Johnathan's arms and crying my heart out, gives me the energy to put one foot in front of the other.

We make it halfway to the office door before Sasha starts laughing.

And that fucking laugh will haunt my nightmares.

"I let them fuck your friend before I fed her to the pigs!" he yells out with glee.

I stop in midstep and it feels like someone just ripped open my chest and yanked all my insides out.

"What?" I gasp in horrified shock and spin around.

Vaguely, I'm aware of Johnathan murmuring, "Don't listen to him," but it's so hard to focus on him over the roar in my ears.

I take another step towards Sasha and have to shrug off Johnathan's arm. "What did you just say?" I nearly scream at Sasha.

Sasha tries to grin, but it ends up just a horrifying spread of his mangled mouth.

He has the gall to shrug his shoulders. "She was still warm and beautiful, even with her brains leaking all over the place."

Oh god.

Oh god... oh god... oh god...

I know he's not lying, he's too damn smug about it, and I don't know how to process it.

How? How could someone do that?

Only a monster...

The majority of my brain has shut down, overloaded by the information. I'm not even aware of walking up to the cart and facing Sasha until I have the gun in my hand.

I look down the barrel and aim it at his ugly head.

My hand is shaking as I stare at him.

I've never wanted to kill someone so much in my life.

I would be doing the world a favor by putting an end to his evil existence.

How many times did I wish I had a gun when they held me captive?

My finger twitches over the trigger as Sasha stares back at me, and there's a look of such pleased triumph in his eyes that I wish I could kill him twice over.

With the gun in my hand, staring at his forehead, I can't help but remember my last vision of Lindsey.

Her hair spread around her face.

The blood staining it red and leaking into the carpet.

Her empty eyes.

Her life snuffed out like she was nothing.

To them, she was just an inconvenience.

Something to get rid of.

And knowing, even in death, they abused her fills me with such a sad rage my entire body is shaking from it.

Sasha spits out another glob of blood mixed with spit and leans forward in his chair.

His eyes are focused and intense as he says, "She was the best fuck I ever had."

I blink at him, seeing the lie instantly for what it is.

Does the evil fucker actually want me to kill him?

My eyes roam over his body, and it's kind of funny, I was so focused on what was happening to his head I didn't even realize he was naked.

He's been stripped of all his clothes. His ankles are strapped to the legs of the chair and his wrists have been strapped to the arms.

Both his toes and fingers are bleeding.

Someone has pulled every single one of his nails off.

His upper thighs are an angry red and it looks like someone singed all the hair off with something hot.

Bruises are beginning to bloom all over his body. Most notably across his chest and lower stomach.

His private parts may be bleeding as well, but I don't want to look too closely at them.

If I had to guess, I'd say he's been in here awhile.

Good.

Noting my hesitation, Sasha's eyes narrow and he hisses angrily, "Do it."

And I want to, more than anything.

I want to kill him so bad I'm fucking crying, but I just can't seem to do it.

I try and try to pull the trigger, and Sasha goads me on but it's not right. He deserves so much more than a quick death.

He deserves to suffer like my friends and I have. Like Charlie has.

"Beth..." Johnathan's voice comes to me. "Do you want me to do it?"

I shake my head and my sobs intensify. My body is shaking so hard now, the gun in my hand is swaying wildly.

If I'm not careful, I might shoot someone accidentally.

"Give me the gun," Johnathan says gently, and I feel my arm being pushed down before the gun is slid out of my hand.

"Do it, you ugly fucking bitch!" Sasha screams, fighting the bonds of his chair. He's hissing and spitting, and fighting with all his might.

Johnathan pulls me into his arms and turns me away from him.

"It's okay, baby," Johnathan murmurs, stroking my hair back. "We'll take care of him."

"No," I sob out in misery and cling to him. This is the gift Johnathan gave me, and now that I understand what it is, I can fully appreciate it, "I want to be the one to do it."

I owe it to my friends. I owe it to myself to see that this man gets the justice he deserves.

"Baby..." Johnathan says, his coarse voice too gentle for the thoughts I'm thinking.

Grasping his shirt in my fists, I look up at him and say, "I want him to *suffer*, Johnathan."

Johnathan looks down at me and slowly nods his head, but his eyes are full of hesitation. "What do you want to do?"

I take a deep breath and I know the choice I've made is right. After everything I've learned tonight, it *feels* right.

"Do you have any pigs?"

IT'S the dead of night. We drove for three hours to reach a secluded farm after a call was put in to some guy named Harrold.

Above me, there are so many stars in the sky. Stars I can't normally see and they're beautiful.

"Fuck, he's heavier than he looks," Andrew grumbles as Johnathan helps him lift Sasha's body.

"Doesn't help that the fucker won't stop fighting," Johnathan grunts as he struggles with Sasha's bound but still kicking legs. "Stop moving, fucker."

"On three," Andrew says.

Johnathan nods.

"One... two... three..."

They swing Sasha's body in unison and send him flying over the fence, straight into the pigpen.

There's a great deal of squealing and grunting as the pigs are abruptly awoken from their slumber.

Johnathan wipes his hands on his pants and walks over to me. Though this whole sick idea was my idea, I don't think I can actually stomach watching what is about to happen.

I stand about ten feet away from the pigpen, keeping my distance.

"You okay?" Johnathan asks, walking up to me and pulling me into his arms.

He's been asking that a lot. And during the drive here, I've had plenty of time to think about what's about to happen.

I nod my head and look back up at the sky. The stars twinkle and sparkle, and a part of me hopes that Lindsey is up there, watching what I'm doing for her.

For all of us.

The noise coming from the pigpen increases in volume. The pigs are agitated and loudly grunting their displeasure.

"Shit, I don't know how long something like this is going to take. You sure you want to stay?" Johnathan asks.

I nod my head again in answer, afraid to speak less I burst into more tears.

"Come here then so I can keep you warm," Johnathan says pulling me closer.

Muffled cries begin to emanate from within the pen and I can't help but shiver.

Are they eating him now?

I glance towards the pen but I can't see anything except for the pigs swarming around something.

Lucifer stands right up next to the fence with Andrew beside him. There's this strange grin on Lucifer's face as he watches what's happening, and I swear, in the moonlight, it almost seems like he's glowing.

Shaking my head, I turn my head back and bury my face against Johnathan.

Suddenly a piercing scream slices through the quiet and I tremble.

"Shit. The pigs must have gotten the gag off," Johnathan mutters.

The screaming goes on and on. Sasha cries out, begging for someone to help him.

I burst into tears.

Johnathan's arms tighten around me. "You sure you're okay?"

I nod my head up and down and cling to him.

I just can't stop thinking about how many women begged Sasha and his men to stop.

How many children begged him...

Did they cry out for help? Did they plead for mercy like he is?

Did they hope that someone would magically appear and save them? Someone like Johnathan?

I heard at least one child crying for their mother, but I know there were others. Others like my Charlie.

"Help! Please! Somebody please help me!" he cries out in English before switching to Russian.

How many are still out there? Sold to the highest bidder? Trapped in some hellish nightmare?

"Fuck, this shit's messed up even for me," Andrew grumbles. "I'm outta here."

"Have a good night, Andrew," Lucifer snickers at him.

I hear a car door opening then slamming shut. The car starts up and then tires are rolling against the dirt.

The screams go on and on, and I cry and cry, but I feel like something is finally being purged from me. Some horrible sick thing I've been carrying around inside of me ever since I was taken.

By the time Sasha's cries begin to weaken, I'm no longer sobbing. My body is filled with this warm, fuzzy numbness.

"It's almost over, I think," Johnathan says gently.

I nod my head, wipe some of the tears from my eyes,

and look up at him. "But the guy in charge, Alexei, is still out there…"

The man who wasn't willing to get his own hands dirty, but who is truly responsible for all of this.

Johnathan's face hardens and his eyes darken. "We'll get him," he says with such conviction I instantly believe him. "That fucker is number one on my shit list. It's just a matter of time before I find him."

And there he goes again, offering me the things I've never had before. Safety and protection and justice. He's so fucking amazing, I'm not sure I even deserve him, but I'm not giving him up.

No, he's mine now and I'll do anything to keep him.

I stare up at him in amazement. I'm pretty sure I love this man. No, I'm fucking sure I love him.

Johnathan starts to frown and shifts uncomfortably. "What? I got something in my beard?"

I shake my head and laugh a little.

His eyes instantly light up. "I do, don't I?"

I laugh again, and I'm on the verge of telling him what I'm feeling when the headlights of an approaching car draws our attention.

I look over to see a big, black Escalade rolling through the grass. The car stops just before the grass becomes dirt.

The car idles for a couple of minutes before the driver's side opens and Simon steps out.

"Holy shit," Johnathan says with awe. "I can't believe Lucifer got him to a fucking farm."

Simon scowls down at the dirt like it's somehow offended him before slamming the door of his car.

"Simon," Lucifer calls out. "So glad you could join us."

The look Simon shoots Lucifer is pure murder.

Lucifer chuckles and motions him over. Simon walks stiffly towards him, cursing under his breath.

When he finally reaches the fence, after avoiding every little dip and groove in the ground, he stands so tall, so stiff, I just blurt out, "That guy seriously needs to get laid."

Johnathan gives me a surprised look and then bursts out laughing. "He so fucking does."

Lucifer and Simon glance at Johnathan, probably wondering what the hell is so funny.

Lucifer smirks but Simon is glaring daggers.

"Something funny, Johnathan?" Simon asks, obviously not amused.

"Yeah," Johnathan says and then bursts into another fit of laughter. "Fuck it, James is off the hook."

"What the fuck does that mean?" Simon snarls.

"It means you're next, motherfucker!" Johnathan continues to laugh. I don't think he can stop himself at this point. "You're about to get wifed up, Simon!"

22

EPILOGUE

Beth

Christmas

"I want one," Johnathan breathes into my ear, leaning over the back of the couch I'm sitting on with Amy.

His hot breath sends a delicious shiver up my spine as I stare down at the baby in my arms.

Noah, Amy and Andrew's infant son, is wrapped up in a fluffy blue blanket, his eyes full of wonder as he peers up at me. He has his father's dark hair and his mother's warm eyes.

"He's so beautiful," I gush to Amy. "And so small."

Noah's little fingers are wrapped around my index

finger and he keeps trying to pull it into his mouth to suckle on.

For such a small guy, he's surprisingly strong.

"He is," Amy agrees with proud pleasure.

"Can I keep him?" I ask, half teasing and half serious.

Seriously, I've never held a baby before and there's just something extremely satisfying about cradling his warm weight in my arms.

Amy tips her head back and laughs. "Maybe you can babysit him when he's a little older."

"I'd like that." I smile, and then look back down at Noah. "You hear that, big guy? You and I are going to have lots of fun."

Noah smiles up at me and my heart *melts*.

I don't know what it is, but I've been feeling extremely sensitive lately. My emotions are heightened and sometimes out of control. It could be because of all the crazy events that have happened over the past couple of months, but I just seem to feel everything a little more now.

There was a memorial a couple of weeks ago for Lindsey that was hard as fuck to get through, but with Johnathan by my side, I survived it.

Honestly, I don't know how I made it through life up to this point without him by my side. He's become my rock. Always there to offer his support and catch me when I fall.

And I love him so damn much for it. So much, sometimes I think I might burst from the force of it.

Ever since the night at the farm, things seem to have settled down a bit. Johnathan and I were officially married in a small, secret ceremony hidden from the press, and I no longer have to worry about my father coming after me if he decides to ignore Johnathan's warning and gets a wild hair up his ass.

We also legally adopted Charlie. I have no clue how Johnathan managed to pull it off so quick, but he's officially ours now. And every day, we've been growing closer and closer as a family.

I lean my head back and peek up at Johnathan. His eyes are molten and his expression is scorching.

He's made no secret that right now his mission in life is to knock me up. In fact, it's all he tries to do. I think if he could get away with it in Lucifer's house, he'd try to get me to sneak off with him right now and have a go at it.

No doubt the sight of me holding a baby in my arms is making him hot.

"Mommy!" Abigail calls out, skipping over to us. "Look what Charlie made for me!" she exclaims holding out a little blue flower made out of Legos.

Amy smiles warmly at her daughter and it's a little surreal. With her brown hair, and fine, delicate features, Abigail looks like a tiny replica of her mother.

"That's lovely," Amy tells her. "Did you thank him for it?"

Abigail's big brown eyes widen and she turns, calling out, "Thank you for the flower, Charlie!"

Charlie's cheeks pinken as he shuffles over to join us.

He looks at her and then down at his feet. "You're welcome, Abigail."

Johnathan's warm breath hits my ear again. "I think our boy might have developed a crush."

I think he's right, especially because of the way Charlie keeps sneaking little peeks at Abigail but looks down at the floor every time he's noticed.

"Come on, Charlie, let's go play some more," Abigail smiles and skips up to him. She grabs his hand and starts to tug him back towards the gorgeous silver and white Christmas tree when Lucifer and his family finally appear.

"So sorry about that," Lily apologizes as she sweeps into the room. "The FaceTime call with my mother took a little longer than expected."

Amy and I both smile at her and tell her it's no problem at all. With a look of relief, she joins us on the couch and starts cooing over Noah.

Honestly, I can't believe I'm spending Christmas in Lucifer's house of all places. When Johnathan originally explained the compound to me, I envisioned a prison-like setting, not this gorgeous, multimillion-dollar mansion. Granted, the mansion is surrounded by prison-like walls, a couple of guardhouses, and twenty-four hour patrols and surveillance, but it's still gorgeous.

Lily has really outdone herself on the Christmas decorations. The entire room is decorated in white, silver, and gold, and under the ginormous Christmas tree are dozens of beautifully wrapped presents.

Lucifer walks into the room carrying their young son, David, with his two other children, Adam and Evelyn, following behind him. Like Abigail, Evelyn seems to greatly resemble her mother, but her features are softer and more child-like in appearance.

Lucifer walks towards Lily while both Adam and Evelyn breakaway and walk towards Charlie and Abigail.

Adam seems to be glaring daggers at Charlie and it sets me on edge a little.

Adam walks right up to where Charlie and Abigail are standing and glares down at their connected hands. For a moment, he looks so damn angry I'm afraid he's going to do something.

"Adam!" Abigail squeals, a bright smile lighting up her face. She immediately drops Charlie's hand and throws her arms around Adam.

The whole scene is kind of strange, and I'm not entirely sure what I'm witnessing. Adam seems to soften as Abigail hugs him, but I catch him shoot another glare in Charlie's direction.

Is he jealous? Isn't he a little young for that?

"Look what Charlie made for me," Abigail says happily. She steps away from Adam and holds out the little blue flower Charlie built for her.

Adam takes one look at the flower, snatches it out of Abigail's hand, and snaps it in half.

Abigail's eyes widen in shock and her bottom lip trembles. She bursts into tears, drawing the attention of everyone in the room.

I look up at Johnathan and we both share a *'what the fuck'* look.

"What's going on?" Amy asks, rising from the couch. I don't think she witnessed what happened.

"Uh... Adam broke Abigail's flower," I supply.

"Adam," Lily gasps angrily and stands. She marches over to Adam, who doesn't appear at all contrite, and grabs him by the arm.

Leading Adam over towards the fireplace, I politely turn my attention away as she starts to lay into him.

Lucifer glances around the room, and then his gaze narrows in on Simon and Andrew who have been sitting on the other couch.

Andrew stands and heads over to comfort his crying daughter.

"Simon," Lucifer grins, his eyes twinkling with mischief as he approaches him.

Simon stiffens and eyes Lucifer warily. "Yes?"

"Here," Lucifer says, thrusting out David towards Simon. "Hold David for a moment while I have a talk with Adam."

Simon looks at David, who looks to be about a year and a half old, and looks ready to bolt, but Lucifer doesn't give him the chance. He gently drops David into Simon's lap and walks off.

Little David is the spitting image of his father, and like Lucifer he's almost painfully beautiful, even with the little bit of drool dripping down his chin.

Simon stares down at David with wide, horrified eyes

and his face goes deathly pale as David's little hands grab his white shirt and he begins to babble.

Behind me, Johnathan bursts out laughing and even Amy giggles.

"I think he likes you," Johnathan says.

Simon glances up and shoots Johnathan a glare.

Little David, though, appears to be completely oblivious to Simon's discomfort, babbling non-stop before he decides to try and shove one of the little fists gripping Simon's shirt into his mouth.

"Good god," Simon gasps, causing all of us to burst into another fit of laughter.

Simon grabs the little boy by the waist and holds him away from him. The two stare at each other, Simon at a loss of what to do and David drooling and smiling.

"It's okay, Abigail," Charlie says, drawing my attention back to him. He picks up the broken Lego flower and has it put back together in two seconds flat.

This seems to appease Abigail. She sniffles and smiles through her tears at him. "Thank you, Charlie."

Charlie nods his head and blushes. He's so sweet, and I'm so proud of him.

"Can you make me one, too?" Evelyn asks, looking hopefully at him.

"Sure," Charlie smiles at her. "What color do you want?"

"Pink!" Evelyn declares and bounces with excitement.

"Uh... hello?" a soft, feminine voice calls out, drawing everyone's attention.

I turn towards the sound to see a beautiful, dark-haired woman standing in the doorway.

Her eyes widen in surprise as she takes in the room and all the people gathered.

Is she another wife I haven't met yet?

"Who's that?" I whisper to Johnathan.

He frowns, his bushy brows knitting together, and says, "Shit. I think that's Lucifer's sister. What's she doing here?"

I glance towards Amy, but she looks just as confused as I am.

I look towards Simon and see he is no longer staring at David. No, he's staring at the woman and looking like someone just punched him in the gut.

"Meredith," Lucifer says, and slowly approaches her. The woman may be his sister, but he doesn't look particularly happy to see her. "What do we owe the pleasure?"

The woman glances nervously around the room again, at all the surprised faces, before her expression hardens with determination.

She lifts her chin in the air with the regal bearing of a queen, and says, "Matthew, I need your help..."

PLAYLISTS

Beth's Playlist
http://spoti.fi/2jbyfVn

...Ready for it? - Taylor Swift
Immigrant Song - Karen O, Trent Reznor, Atticus Ross
Black Wave - K.Flay
Call the Shots - Louise Dowd, Toni Halliday
River of Fire - In This Moment
Into the Darkness - The Phantoms
You're the One - Charli XCX
Rise Up - J2, Keeley Bumford
No Mercy - Pvris
Another One Bites the Dust (Epic Trailor Version) - Hidden Citizens, Jaxson Gamble
What a Wonderful World - Joseph William Morgan, Shadow Royale

Johnathan's Playlist
http://spoti.fi/2CLH4xz

Stay Vicious - The Gaslight Anthem
Sleeping Dogs - Zakk Wylde, Corey Taylor
Gimme Shelter - Stone Sour, Lzzy Hale
Absolute Zero - Stone Sour
Stillborn - Black Label Society
Lift Me Up - Five Finger Death Punch
Trouble - Five Finger Death Punch
Into the Fire - Asking Alexandria
Where the Wind Blows - Blacktop Mojo
Defy - Of Mice & Men

ABOUT US

Izzy Sweet & Sara Page – The one and the same brain.

Sean Moriarty — The real life alpha bad boy that Izzy tamed.

Residing in Cincinnati, Ohio, Izzy and Sean are high school sweethearts that just celebrated their 11th wedding anniversary, though they've been together since they were teenagers – over fifteen years.

Both avid and voracious readers, they share a great love and appreciation for a great story, and attribute their early role-playing days as the fledgling beginnings of their joint writing career.

You can see more of our works at our website - www.dirtynothings.com

NEWSLETTER

Sign up for our newsletter - no spam- and download an Izzy Sweet book for **free**

http://bookhip.com/CKHPSJ

KEEPING LILY

My husband traded me away to save his own life…

And now I belong to the devil.

One night and everything in my life changed. Two words and my world turned dark.

"Take her."

Owing the most ruthless crime lord in Garden City five million dollars, my husband chose to trade me and my children away to save himself.

I was on the cusp of freedom, so close to divorcing that scumbag I was married to.

Now I'm enslaved to a man who is obsessed with me. A man so wicked and beautiful they call him Lucifer.

So alluring, he makes the angels weep with envy. He's so powerful, I can't stop myself from bending to his will.

He's determined to master me, and he won't rest until I give him all.

He wants my light, and he wants my dark.

He wants my body, and he wants my heart.

But most of all, he wants the one thing I can't give him. The one thing I can't bear to part with...

My soul.

Chapter One

Lucifer

"Motherfucker!" Comes out of my mouth in a growl as I shake my hand. The punch to this piece of shit's jaw sent tingling sensations up my arm.

Mickey Dalton sputters gibberish out of his busted lips. "I... I... Swear I will pay... just gotta..."

I'm tempted to keep this up, but fuck it. I have bigger fish to fry than this small time fucking gambler.

Looking over the man's shoulder, I nod to Andrew. "Ensure he fully understands how much he owes. Remove his pinky."

"Yes, sir." Andrew nods.

"Wha... No!" Mickey shouts as Andrew heads to the table where he keeps a black bag stowed.

Turning around, I look at Simon, my right-hand man. "Where are we at with the other three files?"

"Two have been collected on, the last I was waiting on your judgment."

"Marshall Dawson."

"He has flat out refused to cooperate with any of our attempts to collect. He believes his status is untouchable. He will give us no answer on where he was or what has happened to our money."

"Is he finally home?" I ask.

"Arrived earlier tonight."

A metallic snip rings out into the room followed by a high-pitched scream. I turn to see Andrew wiping the blood on the guy's t-shirt.

Andrew raises his voice only slightly as he grabs the man by the throat. "Stop fucking squealing, asshole. Lucifer doesn't like hearing pigs fucking about."

Walking out through the door and into the hall, I look to Simon. "How are the spreadsheets with Bart coming along?"

"Clean, with everything accounted for..."

"Yet, you still have doubts?" I ask him as we walk.

"I do. I just can't explain why."

"Keep an eye on him then."

SIMON HOLDS an umbrella over my head as we walk out of the abandoned hotel. The shattered glass door slams shut behind us as he ushers me into the sleek black Mercedes SUV.

Getting comfortable in the backseat, I reach over and pull the file left on the other seat for me. The name Marshall Dawson is neatly typed on the tab.

I let out a quiet sigh to myself. I knew this one was going to come back as a thorn in my side.

Marshall Dawson is a waste of breathable air. The man used the connections he had with my father and another city boss to secure a loan from us. Five million in *cash*.

Five fucking million dollars with nothing to show for it.

Five fucking million dollars down the drain.

I took this on as a favor to Sean O'Riley. A favor to a now dead and buried man.

Shit like that doesn't sit well with me. But when I went to the top to seek retribution, I was stonewalled. I was told the man who killed Sean, and all the surrounding issues, have been dealt with.

Fuck that. I want my pound of flesh.

Shaking my head, I open the file. It's no use going down that train of thought right now. I can pursue it another time if I need to.

I slowly flip through the pages we have on Marshall.

It's funny how we can put a file together on a person where he is reduced to twenty or so pages. I can see every payment he has made on his mortgage to how many times he has been in the overdraft with his bank.

I look at his legal outstanding debts, and I look at the five-million-dollar debt he now owes to me personally. Anger is slowly creeping through my veins.

Flipping through the pages, I look at his family life. Since he borrowed the money I have had one of my men keeping close tabs on his family. He is married to Lilith Merriweather, aged twenty-seven, and has two children, a boy and a girl. Both children under the age of seven.

I look at the picture of Marshall for a long time as we drive through the late-night rain. The man is closer to my father's age than mine. How did he marry a woman so young? Money and his slimy charm must have played a large part of it.

I look through the pictures of his family quickly. The children are pretty in a child way. Blonde hair and blue eyes, they must take after their mother. Marshall must have married way out of his league.

My fingers stop as the picture of his wife comes up. Emerald green eyes, sensuous pink lips, high cheekbones, pale flawless skin and long blonde hair. All of those parts on their own would make her remarkable.

Even if her face was overall plain just one of her features would stun a person. But together they make something otherworldly.

She is beauty incarnate.

Fingers tracing the lines of her lips, I frown. How the hell did that man marry a woman like this? I flip further through the pictures of her. There aren't many, but what I do see shows me that she is unlike any other woman I have ever laid eyes on.

She is perfection.

There is a rather candid photo of her putting groceries in the back of her red Volvo station wagon. Her hair is all over the place. Her slender legs are encased in yoga pants, feet in Uggs. Her daughter looks like she is giving her problems as she tries to watch her and still put groceries in the back.

Even this... domesticity calls to me.

There is a glamour shot of some type mixed in and I can see just how haunting those eyes are. They are calling to me, pulling me in to get forever lost. I can feel my hands curling into themselves. She is pulling me from where I sit in the SUV.

"Take me to Marshall's, James," I say to my driver.

Looking back at me from the front seat, Simon says, "Now? You don't want to wait until tomorrow?"

"No. We're going there *now*."

The car makes a few turns as we pull off the freeway and then back on again.

My eyes drift out the window for a moment to look at the rain that has been pelting down on the city all week.

Looking back to the picture, though, I see something I haven't seen before—a light. Inside I feel an ember flaring to life.

My muscles are going taut with expectation.

I need to see this woman; I need to see if what the pictures show me is true.

Lily

MY HUSBAND, MARSHALL, is sleeping beside me, snoring loudly, and I have the strongest urge to smack him.

I want to scream in his pale, pudgy face. I want to tell him to wake the fuck up. I want to ask him why he's back in my bed.

But I just lay beside him and stare up at the ceiling instead.

It's time to accept reality.

Our marriage is done.

Dead.

Today was the final nail in the coffin.

First thing in the morning, after I get the kids off to school, I'm going to meet with a divorce attorney. I can't go on like this. This is no way to live, this is just…existing.

And I'm sick of it.

After growing up dirt poor, I married Marshall thinking I would finally have financial security. I would always have a roof over my head. I would never go hungry again.

Foolishly, I believed his lust for me would turn to love. That like an arranged marriage, our feelings for each other would grow after time. If we had children, we could make a real go of it.

But this, the lack of love, the lack of care, isn't worth it. I rather starve than stay in this loveless marriage.

Marshall has been gone for weeks, *traveling on business*. He's gone more than he's home. Ever since our first child, Adam, was born six years ago, he's been finding more and more reasons to leave us.

There's always some client on the other coast that needs his help. Or some corporation up north that has to have his expertise or they're going to lose millions on... something...

It's funny, even after almost eight years of marriage I still don't know exactly what his job title or true profession is. Whenever I ask him about it he just brushes me off, doesn't have time to explain it, or says I wouldn't understand.

Like I'm some kind of idiot.

If I was an idiot I wouldn't know about all the women he's been hooking up with. I know that's one of the reasons he's always leaving us. He has a girlfriend in every city.

Yet, he won't even touch me when I throw myself at him.

I sigh, looking down at the red nightie I bought from

Victoria's Secret and pull the blanket up to cover my breasts.

He won't even touch me when I've taken great pains to dress up for him.

Suddenly my eyes feel swollen and my nose stings. I have to blink back my tears and take a deep breath. Rolling my eyes back up, I focus on the ceiling.

This shouldn't hurt, dammit. This isn't a bad thing, this is good.

This is... *freedom*.

I no longer have to pretend this is a real marriage. No more keeping up appearances on Facebook. No more making excuses for him with my family and friends.

No more trying to explain to the children that daddy is sorry but he had to miss their birthday—again.

This is a fresh start, a new beginning.

I've been doing everything on my own for years now. Losing him won't make much of a difference.

Marshall suddenly grunts loudly and rolls over.

The air turns sour and I resist the urge to gag.

Gah, he is such a pig.

Chapter Two

Lily

I'm not sure what wakes me up. It could have been the light turning on.

Marshall's loud, "What the fuck?"

Or the soft, menacing voice that says, "Hello, Marshall. I'm not interrupting anything, am I?"

Even under my warm blanket, that voice sends a chill down my spine and I peel my eyes open, shivering.

At first, the light is too harsh on my eyes and I have to blink several times before the strange man standing in our bedroom comes into focus.

This must be a dream, I convince myself and squeeze my eyes shut. I open them again but I still just can't believe it.

There's no way that man is real.

Standing in the center of my bedroom, the man is illuminated by a halo of light coming from the lamp. The light seems to love him, clinging to him. He's glowing and so alluring, he looks almost angelic.

"What the fuck are you doing in my house? You can't just come walking in here..." Marshall sputters. His fat fists grab the blanket, yanking it away from me as he pulls it up his hairy chest.

I gasp as the cool air hits my breasts and the sound draws the attention of the angelic stranger. He turns his icy blue gaze on me and I'm utterly stunned as our eyes meet.

With just a look I feel held by him.

Trapped.

Frozen.

Helpless.

He's so beautiful it *hurts* to look upon him. The kind

of beauty that's so strong, so deeply felt, it's like experiencing a piece of music that *moves* you and staring into the sun at the same time.

Tears prick my eyes and my skin tingles as I break out in gooseflesh.

His face is a composition of features so perfect that now that I've glimpsed them I fear all other men will be forever compared to him.

Chiseled cheeks, full, pink lips. A strong jaw and straight nose. Blonde hair so pale it's nearly snow white and brushed back from his forehead.

It feels like an eternity passes as we stare at each other across my bedroom and then his eyes break away only to slide down, warming as they lock on the pale swells of my breasts.

A flush creeps up my chest. I'm not naked but in this little lacy nightie, I feel like I am.

I grab the blanket and Marshall cries out as I yank it back. He shoots me a dirty look but I give him my coldest glare and practically dare him to try and take it back.

Screw him, no one cares about his hairy man-chest.

The stranger watches our little tug of war, his lips curving with a hint of amusement.

Marshall finally gives up on trying to wrestle the blanket away from me and decides to steal my pillow instead. Covering his chest with my pillow, he hugs it tightly and puffs up as he says, "If you leave now, Lucifer, I'll forget this incident ever happened."

Lucifer? Is that the stranger's name? How strange and

morbid. Yet, I swear I've heard that name before, on the news or in the paper...

The stranger's eyes flash and the amusement disappears from his lips. Two dark shadows shimmer behind him and I swallow back a gasp as I realize those two shadows are two other men.

What the hell is going on? Who are these men and why are they in my bedroom? I turn to Marshall and watch him squirm uneasily.

What did Marshall do?

"You'll forget this ever happened?" Lucifer says coolly and his eyes narrow with menace. "Just like you forgot to pay me back the five million dollars you owe me?"

All the color drains instantly from Marshall's face and his eyes dart from side to side as if he's trying to figure out an escape plan. "I already paid that back. You'll have to talk to Sean if you want your money."

"Sean's dead."

I watch Marshall's mouth open then close, then open again. He sputters and gasps like a fish out of water, his face starting to turn blue from the lack of oxygen.

I can't believe Marshall borrowed five million dollars. What would he need with so much money? I know I haven't seen a penny of it.

"I paid Sean the money," Marshall finally gets out, and then rushes on to say, "I don't have five million to pay you..."

Lucifer takes a step towards our bed. "That's too bad."

"Wait!" Marshall cries out in panic, the grip of his

fingers tearing at the pillow he holds to his chest. "Maybe we can work something out? I could—"

"I've had a look at your assets. You have no means to pay me back," Lucifer says dismissively and takes another step toward the bed.

I look between Lucifer and Marshall and now I'm starting to feel panicked. Lucifer has only taken two steps towards our bed but there's clear menace in the way he's moving.

What is he going to do? Are they going to hurt Marshall?

Are they going to hurt me?

Lucifer takes another step and Marshall whimpers. He *whimpers*.

The sound has my hackles rising and I wonder if there's something I could do. I glance towards my phone on my nightstand. The moment I don't think they're looking at me I'm going to make a grab for it.

But it might be too late for Marshall by then...

I could start screaming, but the only good that will probably do is wake the children.

Marshall is pushing back against the headboard like he believes he could escape through the wall if he tries hard enough. Then he shoots a pleading look towards me.

As if I could help him...

Marshall's eyes widen suddenly as if he's had a revelation.

"You want my life as payment?" he squeaks out.

Lucifer lifts an eyebrow and inclines his head. "Yes. That's how these things usually go, isn't it?"

Marshall licks his lips nervously, looks to me then back to Lucifer. "Would you accept another life as payment?"

He's not about to say what I think he is, is he? No, he wouldn't. No decent human being...

Lucifer's upper lip curls with disdain but his voice sounds interested. "What are you proposing?"

Marshall is too cowardly to stop hugging his pillow so he nods his head to me instead. "Take her. Take my wife in my place."

I'm so shocked, so floored, I suck in a sharp breath that never ends.

"You want me to kill your wife?" Lucifer asks and it feels like all the warmth was just sucked out of the room.

"No, of course not..." Marshall recoils at the murderous look on Lucifer's face. "Just hold her as a deposit, an insurance, while I get you the five million."

"You mean a ransom?" Lucifer clarifies.

Marshall nods his head up and down. "Yes, yes, that's it. A ransom."

My lungs full of air, I expel it all in a loud, "How could you!" and make a lunge for Marshall.

I'm not an object he owns. He can't just trade me away to some creepy, beautiful stranger to save his own neck.

Marshall squeaks and scrambles away from me. I end up chasing him until he falls out of bed, landing on his ass.

I grip the edge of the mattress, panting with anger as I watch him scuttle backward until he bumps into Lucifer's legs.

"As much as I would love to accept your offer," Lucifer says as he pushes Marshall away with the toe of his shoe. "I'm afraid your wife is not worth the five million you owe me."

Damn. I blink up at Lucifer, feeling utterly conflicted. On one hand, I don't want to be given away, but on the other, it stings the ego a bit to hear I'm not worth five million dollars.

I snort though as Marshall goes to his hands and knees, kneeling in front of Lucifer to beg for mercy.

"Please," Marshall begs, reaching out and grabbing Lucifer's leg.

I'd pity him and try to help the poor bastard if he didn't just try to trade me away in his place.

"There has to be something else I can give you…" Marshall sobs.

Lucifer makes a face of disgust and looks down at Marshall like he's a bug he'd like to step on.

"Anything," Marshall wails as Lucifer kicks at him. "Anything."

I sit back on my heels and watch Marshall beg while taking the kick, wondering how all of this happened.

Lucifer's head lifts and his eyes lock on me. His features are still, utterly calm, but there's something dark stirring in the depths of his icy irises.

"Anything?" Lucifer queries.

"Yes, anything!" Marshall nods his head with sudden enthusiasm.

"I'll accept your offer," Lucifer grins at me. "If you give her to me permanently, and throw in your children."

"No, no! You can't!" I scream and I'm off the bed in an instant.

Marshall yelps and scuttles back until he's hiding behind Lucifer's legs.

Lucifer between us, blocking me, my hands clench into fists and I pant, trying to control the rush of rage that has flooded my head. I swear if Marshall offers this... this... inhuman monster my children, I'll strangle him with my bare hands.

Lucifer smirks down at me as if he finds all of this amusing. I bristle under that smirk but suddenly feel self-conscious standing so close to him. He's tall, with at least a foot on me, and I feel puny now standing in front of him.

"Well? Do we have a deal, Marshall?"

Marshall continues to use Lucifer as a shield like the coward he is. He pokes his head out only long enough to peek at me. "Yes!"

"No!" I screech and lunge forward, reaching around Lucifer to grab Marshall.

Marshall squeaks and stumbles backward, just out of my reach.

Lucifer grabs me by the arms, stopping my forward lunge and hauls me back. Chuckling, he pins my arms to my sides and I screech and struggle, trying to escape his grasp.

"We're done here, Marshall. I suggest you leave now before I change my mind..."

"Leave? Why do I have to leave? This is my house!" Marshall protests.

Head tipping back, I glare up at Lucifer and continue to struggle. Damn, he's stronger than he looks, though it is hard to tell just how built he is under that suit he's wearing.

Once again Lucifer looks me directly in the eyes, staring into me as if he can *see* inside me. "Not tonight."

"But... but..." Marshall starts to sputter.

Lucifer's face hardens, his features as cold and harsh as the blizzard swirling in his irises. "Simon, remove him."

"No. No! I'll go!" Marshall says, panicked, and though I can't see what's going on due to the huge body blocking my view, I can hear a great deal of shuffling going on behind Lucifer.

Marshall grunts loudly and then there's a thump. "Hey! I'm going, I'm going!"

The bedroom door opens and then slams shut.

I jerk in Lucifer's arms in surprise but then feel all the fight go out of me. No matter how much I squirm, no matter how much I try to free myself from his grasp, I can't escape him. If anything, I feel like all my struggles have only tightened the grip he has on me.

Head dropping forward, I quiet my panting so I can

listen to Marshall stomping and continue to throw a tantrum about being removed from his own home.

After a minute, Lucifer sighs and I feel his grip loosen a little. "James, assist Simon. If Marshall wakes the children, feel free to make him regret it."

"Yes, boss," the second shadow answers and I don't even hear him as he walks out. I only know he's gone by the sound of the closing door.

A moment later there's some muffled arguing coming from the hallway then all goes quiet.

The seconds tick by. My panting slows as I catch my breath.

All at once I am suddenly aware that I'm alone with this strange man.

The air thickens.

Slowly, I lift my head and peer up at him. He's looking down at me so intensely I gasp.

My gasp seems to amuse him, and a slow smile spreads across his lips.

I stare at him in disbelief, my mind racing a mile a minute, trying to process everything that just happened. My mouth feels dry and my stomach is twisted. I want to believe this is a nightmare, that I'm still sleeping in my bed.

My husband didn't just trade me and our children away to save his own neck. He couldn't... He wouldn't...

Yet the fingers tightening around my arms remind me that he did.

I can't let this happen. I can't accept this. I have to

protect my children. He cannot have them! I won't let him hurt them.

Gathering up every ounce of courage I have inside me, I lift my chin and say, "You can't have us. We're not objects you can own or trade away at whim. I am a *person*, a person with rights, and I will not stand for this!"

Lucifer's eyes twinkle at me and it's so condescending I just want to spit in his face.

My anger only seems to amuse him even more. Head tipping back, he chuckles with mirth and just as I start to struggle again, he lifts me up.

It only takes him two long strides and then he throws me.

I go flying through the air and land on my bed with a grunt.

He's not far behind me, and quickly I get to my hands and knees, scooting back as he approaches.

Long, strong fingers going to the bottom of his suit jacket, he begins to unbutton it as he asks me, "Who's going to stop me?"